THE RANGER

J.G.TEE

Ordering Information:

Prime Seven Media
518 Landmann St.
Tomah City, WI 54660

Printed in the United States of America

TABLE OF CONTENTS

CHAPTER ONE

GO GET THEM

Lying in the long grass on the brow of the hill a young man laid on his stomach propped on his elbows with a pair of glasses (binoculars) in his hands peering through the slightly parted long grass, his black Stetson has a pleated black leather band around it as it hung down his back on its storm strap, so it could not be seen, this give the lying man as much cover as possible.

This gave him a good view of the wide valley, and a chance to be able to survey it, putting him in such a position that would make him invisible from anyone looking up from the valley below, lying so still it gave him the chance to view every inch of the terrain below, being so still the birds had resumed their singing, as he melted into the landscape, the long grass also shaded the lens of his glasses (binoculars) meaning there was no reflection making him become part of the surroundings.

This in a way is good as the birds would stop singing if anyone approached his position giving him a warning, he was relaxed as his horse would alert him if anyone moved or a unusual problem occurred. With patients and alertness, the young man kept searching the valley below, searching the land inch by inch taking his time and moving his head so slow to avoid detection.

Looking to the right of the valley the waiting man could see at the far side a line of posts about three foot high painted white, these posts are marker posts that indicate the boundary of a ranch, also just past the posts there could be seen a small herd of cattle chomping on some tall lush green grass, looking intensely at these animals he could see by their actions the animals had not been disturbed.

Scanning the valley from right to left he followed the contours of a wide winding stream as it flowed it, periodically forming pools of water, also toppling into small waterfalls, as it crossed it would be occasionally hidden from view by some small wooded areas and large rock formations, the stream also twisted and turned as it navigated itself across the large valley floor, until it reached the left side of the valley where it disappeared into a very large rock formation at a passage between two hills.

The young man with the glasses followed the streams contours right up to the hills where it disappeared from view, from his position it would be best to go down to the valley floor though a narrow path near the hills to the left as it would give him a lot more cover.

Crawling back from the edge the young man went straight to the big black horse took a pair of moccasins from his saddle bag and changed his footwear, he knew the men he hunted were down there, but it was not possible to detect them from his present position, (where are they) he thought, knowing they were down there somewhere meant hunting them, he knew they could not have gone through the valley without him seeing them the valley being so big and wide.

On reaching the valley floor his plan could now be put into action after making a quick but through scout to the left between the hills and not finding his quarry his intention now is to follow the stream through the valley, after satisfying himself no human sign could be detected in the hills to the left.

Starting from where he stood he decided to follow the banks of the stream in the other direction across the valley to the right, so began hunting his prey, the three hunted men could not know how close this man was to them, if they saw him first there is the chance they could kill him, the young man needed to use all his knowledge and skill as the men he hunted were killers, the young man became suspicious of every turn so moved slow and carefully using any cover possible, after moving forward for about a mile the big horse stopped his head went up sniffing the air, the young man patted the horses neck slipped from the saddle and drew his rifle from its scabbard as he then slowly moved forward silently levering a shell into the chamber of his Winchester, crouching low the young man approached the small wooded area on the bend of the stream, by his movements you could tell by his actions this routine had been carried out before, his eyes moved continued to survey every inch of the land around him, his ears strain to pick up any sound, when moving along a stand of thick fir tree's his ears strained and detected the sound of voices on the other side of this stand of trees, the man crept along silently until reaching a break in the tree's adjusting his rifle to a waist high position his finger on the trigger he jumped into view and yelled out loud.

"Raise your hands in the air in the name of the law". His eyes opened wide his speech came to a halt and realized there had been a fatal mistake, so once again yelled.

"Take cover now" then dived to his right towards a large tree to take cover his warning came too late, as diving back through the tree's the sound of two rifles being fired was heard as the sight that came into view slowed him down his grasp of the situation was all wrong as he felt a bullet hit his right shoulder and heard a woman scream.

Five days earlier in the town of Wheeler a quiet little town in north Texas, on this quiet evening after dark Senator Stevens with his family started their evening meal, his family consisted of his wife, his fourteen year old daughter, his eleven year old son and a year old baby son, it was Thursday the day before payday the stillness of the town plus the fact the house sat a little back from the town made it a peacefully serrean star lit evening.

The Senator and his family were as usual having a normal pleasant evening like they always did when suddenly. Three men broke into the house with guns in their hands levelled at the family, the man who looked like there leader happened to be around thirty years old and gave the orders, his two companions who were both young men in their late teens, this job could be there first job outside the law as they looked like they did not know what to do without their leader the older man who told them what to do.

"You two tie those three up leave the Senator free" the leader ordered.

"Yeh! OK" the two young men replied.

After they had completed the task, there leader did not seem to trust his men because, telling one of them to hold a gun on the Senator while he checked the families bounds.

"Right you two go through the house, check all drawers, cupboards, trunks and boxes pick up anything of value, silver, gold or cash bring it all back here do you understand" there leader told them

"Yes, I understand" the first man sullenly said.

"I understand also" the other young man replied.

"You Senator open the safe and pass over the payroll you have in it" the leader ordered.

"What safe" the Senator replied.

"Senator I am not stupid, I made it my business to enquire about the payroll and found out you keep your business payroll overnight to pay your staff the following day, so open the safe "the leader ordered.

"What safe" the Senator asked.

The elder man became angry and using the back of his hand smacked the Senator.

"Don't lie to me, I know you own the haulage company in town and you drew the money from the bank today, which you do every week and as usual you take it home to pay your staff the next day, I know you do this, now where is the payroll" the man yelled.

"What safe" the Senator replied calmly.

"I have had enough of you, I know you have a safe, now you will open it, or I will shoot your family one at a time" the man said.

"You would not dare, that will be murder, you would be hunted down like dogs" the Senators naive wife told him.

"Lady, I would, so shut up" the man told her.

One of the younger men came back into the room with a bag full of items he had picked up.

"There is a safe in the cupboard in the den (room) down stairs, but it is locked so could not get into it" the young man informed them.

"Well Senator open the safe or I start shooting" the elder man said.

"No" the Senator told him.

The man picked up a cushion from the settee and threw it into the cot on top of the baby pressed the mussel of the gun into the cushion and pulled the trigger shooting the baby in cold blood.

The Senators wife and daughter screamed, the Senators son struggled to try to get free from his bounds, the Senator rushed forward to attack the murderer of the helpless baby, the murderer stepped to his left as the Senator reached him, then pistol whipped him to the floor, after about fifteen minutes the Senator regained conscious a bloody gash on his head.

"Now you know I mean what I say, open the safe or I will shoot your brat of a son" the murderer informed the Senator.

"From your action killing a one-year old baby a child that could not recognize you, tells me you intend to kill us all anyway because you do not want any witnesses to your crime, the murderer of a child you will hang, I am sorry darling" looking at his wife.

"I understand darling, I love you" she replied.

"No, I will not open the safe, if you kill us you will have no one to open the safe and you will not get what you came for I WILL NOT OPEN THE SAFE" the Senator shouted.

"Are you sure" the man asked.

"Yes, I am" the Senator returned.

The murdering thief once more picked up the cushion using it to deaden the noise from his gun, raising the gun he shot the young boy through the head, the two women turned their heads away at the sight of the blood and brains being splattered over a wall behind the boy. holding each other the mother and sister to the boy cried uncontrollably.

"Senator this is your last chance open the safe now" the killer ordered.

"No" came the defiant reply.

The killer was now getting angry and not thinking straight and started cursing and swearing at the brave man standing in front of him, you could see the anger building up inside him, as the anger built up inside him it made him so mad all reasoning was lost, therefore automatically rashly raising the gun and cushion he shot the Senator three times.

"NOW YOU open the safe" yelling angerly

"Ha! Ha! Ha! Ha! Ha! Ha!" the Senators wife laughed out loud.

The killer back handed her to stop her taunting laughter.

"Open the safe NOW" the murderer ordered.

"Ha! Ha! Ha! You stupid man you have just killed the only man who knew the combination" the lady informed him.

The Senators wife looked at him with no hidden disgust in her eyes, the killer became more angry when seeing the look of scorn on the woman's face, also because of stupidly getting angry, walking through to the next room the three men looked at the safe, just one look told the killer it would be impossible to open the safe now, meanwhile back in the lounge the two ladies tried to get free but found they were tied very tight and it was not possible to escape.

"Darling we are bound to tight there is no chance of getting free you heard what your father said, these men now have to kill us as we have seen their faces" the Senators wife tried to prepare her daughter.

"Yes mam" she replied a tear in her eyes.

After having a good look at the safe their leader became more angry as on inspection, they found the safe was cemented into the wall to get the safe out of the wall would be to blast it out apart from having no blasting powder or dynamite the safe would be too heavy to carry away, with this deduction realization came to him, in his anger picking up and throwing anything at hand he could find, being so mad he just wanted to destroy.

The killers name is Paul Grant and all his life was known as a bad man now knowing there was no way of being able to get the payroll, grabbing the cushion and gun he pointed them at the two ladies about to fire then stopped, because the fault was all his and was angry, he wanted to take his anger out on someone else unfortunately the two women came into view.

"You two strip them" Grant ordered.

"OK Boss" the young men replied.

"Right you two fuck her this one is mine" Grant said as he took a handful of the young girl's hair and dragged her into the next room.

The first young man had just started raping the mother as they heard the terrible cry as Grant brutally raped the young girl as being raped herself the lady closed her eyes as tears ran from them.

The Senators wife and daughter were subjected to a vicious attack they were raped repeatedly, tortured by these beasts who were enjoying inflicting pain on the ladies and laughed louder the more the ladies cried out.

Grant and his two crones Max and Billy had the intension in the beginning to break in steal the payroll and anything else worth taking, kill the Senator and his family and get out of there and build up some distance before the town woke up.

But due to the Senator and his family, Grants stupid mistakes and his anger had made him lose all reason, the three animals got carried away with their murder, rape and torture they have made another mistake they have forgotten the time, Grant was the first to realize that it was only a couple of hours until dawn, jumping up hurriedly putting on his clothes, yelling at the two young men to get dressed, picking up the cushion and gun Grant coldly put a bullet through the heads of the two women.

"Quickly get dressed and let's get out of here" Grant urged them on.

"OK we are coming" Billy said. Max only grunted as he dressed.

"Come on let's go and don't forget the bags" Grant said.

"OK, OK, keep your shirt on" a Young man said.

"Hurry, we must get out of here before dawn" Grant called moving fast for the door.

The three killers quickly dressed, picked up their horses from the rear of the house where they left them, loading the booty over there saddle horns they mounted there mounts and rode out, keeping the horses at a walking pace just as a ribbon of light came on the horizon heralded the coming dawn, Grant gave out a long sigh of relief as the three men crossed the town boundary heading out on the waiting countryside, Grant relaxed a little believing they had not been seen and increased the speed to a cantor.

Unknown to him two persons did see them depart.

At 0700 the following morning two men walked towards the Senators house, these two men were employees of Senator Stevens, every week on a Friday morning they go to the house to escort the Senator and the payroll, it is a normal routine, there job was to meet the Senator at about 0700 and walk with him to the haulage company office, the first man was a large burly man, this man is the Senators foreman and friend John finely, who has been working for the Senator for twenty seven years, the other man is called Lenny one of the Senators drivers and has worked with the company for the last three years.

John the foreman knocked loudly on the door of the Senators house and found it unusual that the door was not already open, (the Senator was a man of habit an early riser) normally the door would be open, he was puzzled not receiving an answer to his knock, John knew it was out of character the Senator would be expecting then to call, John knocked on the door two more times and still received no answer.

"Lenny have your gun ready we will have to investigate," John pulled his .38 police special slowly pushed open the unlocked door, slowly the two men advanced into the house, the first horrible sight that came into his vision made him jump there lying in front of him was the baby in the cot lying in a pool of blood.

"Lenny run and get the sheriff, and I said run" John shouted his orders. John assessed the situation but did not touch anything, the only action he took was out of common decency was to cover the two ladies with sheets.

The sheriff arrived fast and carried out a thorough search of the scene, being a trained lawman, in his mind he was able to picture what had taken place, looking at the bodies it took him seconds to build up a picture of what happened, the baby in the cot, the boy with most of his head missing, the three bullets in the Senator, the sight of disgust as he realized the torture the two women went through one of them being a fourteen year old girl. This all told him there was some very bad men out there who must be brought to justice, disgusted at the scene in front of him made him angry, but because of his training and experience as a lawman his training clicked in immediately he started organizing things.

Sheriff Ken Cooper started giving orders straight away.

"John, I want you to get the undertaker and help move the body discreetly, " Lenny go find Sam ask him to come here, after that go down to the haulage yard and get some hands for a posse, I need a dozen men now go" Ken ordered.

"Ken, I want to go with you" John said.

"Sorry John you are a well-known member of the community I want to deputize you, I want you to look after the town for me and answer any questions the people of the town ask, spread the word discreetly" Ken explained.

"You know this is a nice house, I did tell the boss it was to isolated but you know him and his preference for peace and quiet" John told the sheriff.

"Isolated, quiet, this should not happen, to a man who only wants a bit of peace and quiet," he paused then continued with venom in his voice "Monsters, Animals or creatures as vile as these should not be born, as a sheriff I can understand robbery and murder but not this, John we have to get these evil men" the sheriff told John.

"Yes, Ken I agree" John agreed.

"I hereby promise I will do everything I can to get justice for the Senator and his family" the Sheriff swore.

"Hi! Sheriff how can I help" Sam asked as he arrived at the scene.

"Sam you are our best tracker we have, three men left here after murdering the Senator and his family, I want you to pick up the tracks of these animals and follow them, the posse will be here in a moment or two we will be right behind you OK" the sheriff explained.

"OK sheriff" Sam replied.

The sheriff was spot on with his assumptions no sooner had Sam took his first turn, the posse arrived outside the house.

"Right men the Senator and his whole family including a baby has been murdered, we must do all we can to get these evil men let's move out" the sheriff rode out, and the posse followed.

Sam the scout is the man the sheriff gets to do any scouting that needs to be done, Sam has Indian blood and is the best man they have to do tracking, after reaching the river Sam lost the sign they had been following, searching the river bank both up and down the posse looked everywhere for two hours had to admit defeat, a demoralized posse rode back to town.

They may have lost the tracks, but no way was the sheriff going to leave it at that, his first step was to accumulate as much information as possible.

The sheriff decided to start knocking on doors starting with the houses nearest to the Senators house, after a few doors without any success, Ken knocked on the first door of a house just south of the crime scene.

"Hello sheriff how can I help you" the young lady asked.

"Howdy Mrs. Kane I am asking around in the hope I can find someone who maybe saw three men leave town early this morning" the sheriff asked.

"I'm sorry sheriff I was fast asleep, I slept until well after dawn I rose late this morning in fact I had to rush to get my son to school, wait a minute my son said he saw three riders early this morning, I told him it was a dream and it would be best to forget about it, I took him to school".

The sheriff walked briskly to the school, asking if it would be possible to see young Tommy Kane, the sheriff took Tommy down to the headmaster's office and showed him some dodgers (wanted notices) the boy picked out the picture of Paul Grant.

"Yeh! Ttthaatss ttthhe mann" the towns hobo's slurred voice could be heard.

"You know this man" the sheriff asked.

"ssure hhimm annd ttwwoo friends rrrrodde oout ooff towwnn thisss mourning" the man told the sheriff.

The sheriff now unfortunately had two unreliable witnesses a young boy and a drunken hobo, on top of these there is, the doctors report, a report from the undertaker, and written reports from both Lenny and John after collecting all the information possible.

"John, I want you to remain my deputy for the rest of the day and look after things for me" the sheriff said then left the office.

"OK sheriff" John replied.

The sheriff proceeded straight to the livery stable, seeing the holster he borrowed a spare mount with the borrowed horse and his own horse, he left town with the second horse and by doing frequent changes, it was possible for him to cover a lot of miles faster, because time was short, he needed to get things done as fast as possible, to do this the sheriff rode the two horses hard for four hours only stopping at his destination pulling up outside the circle star ranch approaching the door, on the front of it there was a sign a circle with a star in it.

The Circle Star ranch is a working ranch, but it is also the headquarters of the Texas Rangers, the sheriff walked straight through the door, when doing so a large man rose from a desk and walked over to him a smile on his face and hand out stretched.

Sheriff Ken Cooper and Texas Ranger inspector Nobby Strong have known each other for many years in the past they rode together, they have a strong bond and have been friends for a long time.

"Jenny" Nobby yelled, a young lady put her head around the door.

"Yes sir" she asked.

"Two coffees' please" Nobby told her.

"Yes sir" came the reply.

"Now Ken how can I help you, by the look in your eyes and the dust on your clothes I would say you rode hard to get here, and you don't do that for a social visit" Nobby enquired. Ken smiled.

"Nobby, Senator Stevens and his whole family including a baby was wiped out this morning" Ken continued giving his friend all the gory details and all the information collected.

"Nobby I can go no further, I have done all I can, these three men must be stopped, I hope you can help" Ken asked his friend.

The young lady called Jenny came to the desk with the coffees.

"Jenny could you ask someone to get Ben Brookes for me please" Nobby asked.

"Right away sir" she said leaving the room briskly.

Five minutes later a young man walked through the door, Ben Brookes entered the room, being only twenty-four years old but with his association and experience with the Rangers had learnt a lot.

Ben had applied to join the Rangers when seventeen his application was excepted on his eighteenth birthday as a trainee, and for the last six years had rode with many of the Rangers gaining experience, by doing a large assortment of jobs and never stopped learning, After his twenty first birthday, Nobby The Texas Ranger Inspector thought because of his eagerness to learn and the good reports from other senior Rangers. the inspector decided Ben could be a fully trained ranger therefore give him jobs on his own.

Ben Brookes even though still fairly young looked mature due to jobs that had to be done but never lets it get him down and most of the time has a smile on his face, Ben stood five foot ten inches in his stocking feet with a slim wirery figure, Dressed in a normal style of a man of the west, on his head was a black low crowned Stetson, with a black leather band with a buckle on the right hand side his shirt was a maroon colour (dark red) everything else he wore is black, trousers, leather vest, boots, belt, gunbelt and bandana. His gunbelt crossed from his left hip to his right leg to his holster lying on the right leg the butt of the colt .45 police special which has a shorter barrel than the normal .45 revolver, the butt facing to the rear meant the wearer used the straight draw with this type of draw the hanging hand hung so the user could just grip the gun and draw by just lifting cocking then pull the trigger. the holster was tied to the leg to prevent snagging looking at the butt of the gun you could see it was discolored with being frequently used.

Ben at a young age had decided to be a dedicated lawman and wanted to do a good job, this made him consider the various aspect of the job including reading law books, looking into the ways of drawing and shooting, seriously he studied the different methods used to handle a weapon and found the straight draw was best for him.

Trying the cross-draw Ben thought you lose vital seconds because you had to reach across your body grip the weapon then line the gun, to Ben it did not feel right so discarded this method.

When looking into the cavalry twist, even though the gun hung in a comfortable position it did not feel right drawing the gun, the cavalry twist was normally used by soldiers or ex-soldiers, a soldier has his gun butt forward in the holster, to grip the gun the user had to twist his wrist to grip the gun twist it back to be in a firing position, Ben never felt comfortable with this method.

The other main method of drawing was the swivel holster, they call it a draw but you did not draw, you grip the butt of the gun swivel the holster and pull the trigger, this is a modern way of trying to give the user an edge, the problem with it is it reduces the range of fire to realign the target you must move the body and this is where you lose the edge it may have given you in the first place.

"Ben this is a friend of mine, say hi to sheriff Ken Cotton of the town of Wheeler" Nobby introduced them.

"Hi! Ken" Ben greeted.

"Howdy Ben" the sheriff returned.

"Ben do you know Senator Bill Stevens" Nobby asked.

"I know of him, but we have never met, I did vote for him I like his policy's" Ben explained.

"Ben the Senator and his family were wiped out last night" Nobby informed Ben.

"How" Ben asked.

Nobby explained to Ben exactly how Ken explained the incident to him, first mentioning the baby shot in its cot, the relaxed stance left Ben and the smile disappeared, as the story unfolded his face had a grimmer and grimmer look, when being told about the rape of a fourteen-year-old girl, the look of anger on his face said it all.

The sheriff and the Inspector of the rangers had observed the change in this normally pleasant smiling young man, changing into a determent grim faced fighting machine, Nobby paused and with a grim face gave Ben his orders.

"Ben, I want you to track these animals down if you can capture them do so, but if they do decide to fight you may have to kill them, how soon can you start son" Nobby inquired.

"About an hour sir" Ben informed them.

"Good, that gives Ken and I time to catch up while having some lunch, I'll see you back here in an hour" Nobby told him.

"Yes sir" Ben answered.

During the next hour Ben fed and watered (SHAD) his horse shadow before saddling up, making sure his bedroll and spare set of clothes were tied behind his saddle, his saddle bags were filled with a pan, coffee pot, food and coffee, spare revolver, glasses (binoculars), Cleaning kit and first aid kit, with everything ready to ride Ben made time to eat before reporting back to the Inspector.

"Now Ben sit down for a moment as Ken informs you of their progress plus you can read the paperwork Ken has managed to put together" Nobby told Ben.

Ben read all the relevant information browsing through the statements then asked a couple of questions about the people who made them, finding two of them from the boy and drunk would not hold up in court but he did not dispute them.

"Right sir shads out front I'm ready to ride" Ben announced.

"Ken will show you what and where they have progressed to, it's up to you son, good luck" Nobby said.

Ben and Ken rode most of the way back at a canter stopping a couple of times to let the horses blow they made good time, but it was almost dark as they arrived back in town, Ben expressed his desire to check the scene of the crime first, picking up John from the jailhouse the three men visited the Senators home.

"John, Ken is there anyone who might know this house better than you two" Ben asked.

"Well there is the house keeper, it was her day of yesterday she might be some help" John said.

"Could you please ask if she could come here" Ben asked.

John left the house, while waiting Ben covered the baby's cot and the two beds that had blood all over them, around half an hour later John returned with a lady looking about thirty years old, her eyes were dark as she cried.

"This is Mrs. Tanner" John introduced her.

"How do you do Mrs. Tanner, this is a bad business and I know you are upset but I need your help to catch these animals" Ben held her hand and smiled.

"Glad to meet you sir anything I can do I will" she said as she composed herself.

"Now Marm I have been told you know this house better than anyone else, I want you to go through the house let me know if you notice anything unusual, and with Johns help make a list of anything you know is missing, specially any items marked or engraved" Ben instructed her.

As Mrs. Tanner carried out his instruction Ben looked for sign, under where the baby had laid on the floor, found the bullet that passed through the little body, Ben estimated the spent bullet to be a .44 by the look of it, the sheriff praised the next one out of the wall where the young boy had stood, it looked the same as the first one, the same applied to the two bullets taken out of the mattresses of the beds, meanwhile Mrs. Tanner went through every draw and cupboard she knew the family well so knew where the ladies hid their jewelry and other things of interest like money on their completion of the search John asked Mrs. Tanner if she would be up to coming into the house tomorrow to clean it, she said yes.

"Thank you for your help Mrs. Tanner" Ben said to her.

"Ranger I found this pocket knife on the floor in the next room it has the word Max scratched on it, I showed it to Mrs. Tanner she said she had never seen it before" John explained.

"Forget the Ranger part my name is Ben, I'll take the knife along with me it might be of some use" Ben admitted.

"Are we finished here Ben" Ken asked.

"Yes, at the moment I'd like to have a quick look in the morning before we pull out its now to dark to go any further, if you could Ken will you get the bullets from the undertaker after he removes them from the Senators body" Ben requested.

"OK Ben will do" Ken assured him. They returned to the office.

"Ben why did you want that list" Ken asked

"After doing the crime, the men who done it must know they have committed a major crime, also they know it is a hanging offence, so they will move fast to get as much distance from the town as possible, we know the boy saw them around 0700, they have had all day to travel and will stop for the night, they will check the booty (items stolen) I know at that time the trio will sort out what items not wanted and throw them away, at the first chance, at the first town the items that can be hocked (sold) will be exchanged for money, knowing about these items could give me a lead, if I did not know about the item they are likely to throw away the items would not mean anything to me but if I do know about them and find them, I will then know I am on the right trail, knowing about the stolen items could help me catch them" Ben explained.

Ken and John looked at Ben and at each other, neither of them had thought of things in that way it showed them that Ben was thinking well ahead of them, they looked at him with admiration, Ken seeing Ben as a young man, did not think the young man would have the experience to be able to do the job, now seeing how though a job Ben was doing and of the details he found Ken started to change his mind about Ben.

By this time the man sent to the undertakers had now returned, placing all the bullets found on a flat surface, looking at them through a magnifying glass.

"Well that confirms it, all the occupants in the house were shot by one man, it looks like Paul Grant killed them all the two younger men robbed and raped which still makes them guilty" Ben told them.

"Ben, we still have time to look over the Senators office" Ken said.

"OK Ken let's go but after that its supper for me then I'm of to bed we need to get going at first light I'll be outside your office at dawn" Ben informed them.

Ben, Ken and John walked into the Senators office.

"OK start searching" Ken told them.

Stopping at the door Ben surveyed the room thinking (Grant and his two assistants already searched the place) if you wanted to conceal something where would you put it, not cupboards or drawers because they would have already searched them, now wait a minute think, if I wanted to leave something in case of an emergency what would I do. Where would I hide something, (think, think,) Ben was saying in his mind, I would leave it in plain view, yes, I know walking across to the big polished wood desk

Looking at the desk top he could see it had not been disturbed, there was an in and out tray and a box named pending his eyes lit up, looking in the box at the bottom under three other letters there was two envelopes addressed to John and Ken with the words, (TO BE OPENED IN CASE OF MY DEATH) signed by the Senator.

"Ken, John could you come here please" Ben called them.

"What's up Ben" John asked.

"The Senator was prepared for his death by leaving you both a letter" Ben informed them.

Giving them the letters, there was a pause as the two men opened them and read the letter, both letters contents were the same, each one had a key and combination for the safe.

The letter.

Ken my friend if you are reading this letter, I will be dead I hope you and John can help me to help the people I leave behind.

1.   The first page will inform you of my next of kin.
2.   Next you will find details of my lawyer.
3.   John could you take temporary charge of the business.
4.   Wages will either be in the safe or the bank, you will find in the letter I Have left you a note to the bank giving you authorization to draw money if you need it.

Thank you

Bill.

"Ken, I guess we will have to carry out Bill's wishes" John said.

"Yes, we will, first thing in the morning we will show Ben where we lost their tracks we will sit down together and talk, one thing we can do is pay the crew" Ken replied.

"Ben how did you know these letters were there" Ken asked.

"I didn't all I did was ask myself where I would leave the information if I was the Senator" Ben told them.

"I think we cannot do anymore here let's go to the café in town and have a meal on the town" Ken said.

"After eating I will make sure Shad is OK then its bed for me, I will meet you here just after dawn as I have breakfast before we move out" Ben told Ken and John.

Just as Ben had said the night before the three men had breakfast together in the café, after breakfast with shad walking behind him Ben looked at the ground outside the Senators house it was a good job the weather was good the night before, the ground was soft outside the late Senators house, because everyone including himself had walked to the house the recent horse tracks must belong to the murders.

A little after dawn as they left town and as there had been no rain the night before the tracks were still visible and with a sharp trained eye was able to follow the faint tracks. About a mile down the trail narrowed Ben pulled up and dismounted looking at the trail and checking the bushes for a couple of hundred yards remounted.

"Ben what was that all about we will take you to where we lost the tracks" Ken said a puzzled look on his face.

"These tracks are the ones left by the three men because they are the same tracks I saw outside the Senators house, but I now know that one of the men I think is Grant is riding a gray with a loose shoe and is medium build, the second man is light in the saddle so is most likely slim or skinny and rides a brown horse one of its shoes had a bar on it, the third man rides a black and is either fat, heavy or is carrying something heavy also this man has just finished eating an apple the core is over there by the bushes. I now know what to follow" Ben rode on.

Ken and John looked at Ben in amazement John even had his mouth open, Ben smiled and rode on following the tracks, a few miles up the trail Ben once again dismounted and disappeared into the brush then remerged fifteen minutes later, Ben remounted and waved for the other two to follow, Ken the sheriff seemed reluctant to follow him, it looks like they still doubted his abilities to do the job.

"What's wrong Ken" Ben asked.

"You say for us to follow you but the tracks we can plainly see goes' in that direction" Ken pointed out.

"That is what they want you to see" Ben replied.

"Who" John asked.

"Grant and his friends of course" Ben said.

"What do you mean Ben" Ken asked.

"Ken, John dismount and come here" Ben said.

Ben with the aid of a stick explained his findings.

"This is what happened" Ben said.

Pointing down the trail and showed them a fast-moving stream.

"Now look at the tracks you would be right to say there is three sets , if you look at them you will see they are made by the same horse, look hard and you will see they are made with the horse with the loose shoe Grant has rode his horse down to the stream walked it backwards forward into the stream again, turned his horse up stream after half a mile, will come out and join up with the other two and head in a completely different direction.

"Come with me" Ben said and walked through the brush the other two followed, now the other two men went through the bushes with a branch from a nearby tree but the person who did it did not do it properly and left patches which I did not miss.

"Let's ride" Ben said after a mile , Ben pointed out where the three men met up again, the other two waited for Grant to join them under that tree, tethering the horses they stood here one of them had a smoke (cigarette), this man has worn boots the other man has pattern boot you can tell by the print of the boots sole, over here you can now see where grant met up with the other two and how they rode of in that direction.

"No wonder we lost the trail" John said.

"Right this is where we part, I have to get after these killers" Ben told them.

Ken stuck out his hand.

"I am impressed son go get them" Ken told him.

"Go get them" John repeated.

Ben rode off leaving behind a couple of confident men who had faith in him as Ben disappeared from view into a stand of trees, Ken turned to John.

"I almost feel sorry for those killers with Ben on their tails"

CHAPTER TWO

I WANT TO GO WITH YOU

During the last six years Ben has learnt to do his job properly but also knew you never stopped learning, even though still young due to his experience in the field it had taught him to be wise enough to be able to assess people and put himself into their place.

The information gathered already about the men who killed the Senator has already started to show lapses in their intelligence they are getting complacent, Ben expects them to push on hard for the first day, and as they think they rode out undetected and did not know of Ben following them they will get slower, like taking their time, rising later in the morning, also camp early in the evening, taking frequent breaks they will carry on in a southerly direction in no hurry.

Their action ultimately gave Ben an advantage as on the other hand Ben will keep up a steady pace not tiring the horse but taking less breaks, he will rise before dawn and camping as near to sundown as possible, also eating and drinking in the saddle gives him vital bits of time and will only have hot food and coffee when camping, this type of travel can cut down time considerably.

Tracking is not just looking at the ground all the time you must sometimes use common sense because not all signs are on the ground, on the third day it was obvious the killers were not far ahead the horse droppings had steam coming from it and the embers of their fire were still warm.

Ben dismounted took the glasses (binoculars) from his saddlebags and crawled on his belly up the slope to the brow of the hill, enabling him to be able to survey the valley below.

Ben knew for certain that the men who committed the murders by the sign were somewhere in the valley below, but where the valley is large with various places of concealment, they must be found, knowing the trio is getting complacent does not make them fool's known how dangerous these men are it makes sense that the killers would keep into cover as much as possible.

Surveying the valley Ben could see by the movement of the animals and birds an area where animal movement stops it is a sign that human activity is present, Ben looked at such an area so keeping into cover advanced slowly but had not taken into consideration that other people or other activity might be taking place,

When Ben jumped around into view with rifle raised and yelled.

"Raise your hands in the air"

There was no way in the world that Ben could imagine seeing a naked man and woman bathing in a pool of water, this caused him to lose vital seconds and realized his mistake, so yelled again at the naked couple.

"Take cover NOW" diving for cover himself.

Ben happened to be right about the three killers, the murders had entered the valley just ahead of himself, there first concern was water to drink and fill their canteens as they were short, therefore made their way to the stream, seeing horses there meant someone had already beaten them to it.

Dismounting the three killers drew their guns started to sneak forward until the naked couple came into view and watched as the two-occupied couple walked into the pool to bathe. The trio was on the verge of shooting the man when Ben made his move, the killers changed their target.

Shots were fired and by the pain Ben knew a bullet had hit him in the shoulder, but also knew he must retaliate or die, the three men rushed from there concealment and charged at Ben, the rifle still in Ben's hand barked as the trigger was pulled Billy the young looking killer was a head of the other two, his face changed from white to red and his body flew backwards as the heavy bullet hit him, changing his aim Ben snapped of a shot and knew his bullet had hit Grant by his movement and the cry as the missile hit him, Grand turned one hundred and eighty degrees and ran for the horses, this left only one man the one called Max, grabbing the naked lady around the throat and levelled his pistol at her pushing the barrel into her side.

Ben could tell the young man did not know much about guns the gun in his hand was a .44 and needed cocking but Ben could see the whole gun and it was not cocked lifting the barrel of his rifle pulled the trigger at such short range the bullet shattered the man's arm the broken bone protruded the young man screamed fainted as blood flowed from the wound, getting to his feet Ben checked all the men and found them all dead including the young ladies companion after ripping the sleeve from the young man's shirt and wrapped the wound to stem the flow of blood, looking for Grant but nowhere could he be found, taking advantage of the situation Grant had made his escape.

"Sorry Marm, could you please go into the water and wash the blood of your body, dry yourself and get dressed" Ben told her.

"Thank you" she said in a low voice as she dressed, she thought with a sigh of relief (Thank god, he is a good man).

There was a lot to do before moving of and with the hole in his shoulder, his decision was to get the lady to help him if she can after her ordeal. While the lady dressed Ben collected all the horses together including the horses belonging to the two bad men.

When the lady returned she was dressed in a blue shirt and jeans and black Stetson and boots, Ben looked at her and under his breath said (wow) she looked good as she came into view, Ben omitted a shrill whistle, the answer was a loud neigh as shad ran to him and nuzzled his shirt.

"That is a good horse you have there" the lady said.

"Yes, he is my pal" Ben replied.

"I understand" she acknowledged.

"Marm how do you feel" Ben asked.

"I am a bit shaken, but I am all right why" she asked him.

"If you are up to it, I need your help" Ben stated.

"How can I be of assistance" she enquired

"First, we must find something to bandage my wound, if you can I would be in your dept. if you could clean and bandage the wound to stop the bleeding if possible" Ben instructed.

She took from her saddle bag a bottle of ointment she always carried, after washing his wound she applied the antiseptic ointment taking his spare shirt and ripped it into strips bandaged his shoulder.

"I'm not sure I have stopped the bleeding, but I have definitely slowed it down" she reported.

"Thank you, your next job is to dress your naked friend before rigamortis sets in we cannot take him to town the way he is people will talk" Ben told her and winked.

"Thank you" she said.

"OK Marm my name is Ben".

"Mine is Jane"

"Jane, you are the only able-bodied person here, so I need you to assist me" Ben explained.

"OK yes I'll do my best" Jane replied.

As Jane set about dressing her dead friend, meanwhile Ben checked the unconscious man, made a fire, put a pot of water on the fire to boil for coffee.

"Jane have you finished that job" Ben asked.

"Yes Ben"

"Jane the next thing that has to be done is the biggest job that is necessary but before we do that, we will rest have a cup of coffee and there is some jerky meat in my saddle bags" Ben told her.

"You make the coffee, I will supply the food we did come out here for a picnic and swim it would be a pity to waste the food wouldn't it now" she said.

After having a much-needed break, some sandwiches and coffee plus a little chit chat which helped them to get to know each other, a short time later they were refreshed enough to get on with the jobof loading the horses, lashing the dead bodies on their saddles and getting the prisoner onto his horse, then breaking camp they started for town.

"Jane how far is it to town" Ben enquired.

"About five miles south of here" Jane replied.

"OK let's ride" he said.

As they rode towards town there was very little talk, as they both had lots to think about, Jane worried most of all of walking into town with her dead lover's body over a horse, she knew if that happens, she will be in a lot of trouble, Ben's worry was his injury and the perusal of Grant was very important.

"Jane how far is it to town now" Ben asked.

"Just over a mile maybe a mile and a half" came her answer.

"Jane, I like you, it would not look good if you ride into town with your friends' body so get going, disappear" Ben told her.

"Thank you Ben I owe you, call me if I can help you in any way" she replied and rode on.

Ben stopped, dismounted tethered the horses letting them blow for a while checking the horses with the bodies on to make sure the lashings were still secured, next checked the prisoner who complained about the pain from his shattered arm now awake, Ben ignored him let him cry there was no sympathy for rapists in the west, women were so short of, most decent men protected them, stopping in this way also gave Jane a head start after a few moments Ben mounted up and rode slowly towards town.

Entering town on the main street north of the town, Ben saw the sign for the sheriff's office so headed for it, the sheriff on seeing the cavalcade came out of his office to meet it, as they came near the sheriff spotted Ben's badge.

"Hi! Ranger could I be of assistance" the sheriff called out.

"Sure, sheriff could you arrange for the two bodies to be taken to the undertakers, one of them could be a local man, could you put this man in one of your cells I'll send the doctor over after I have seen him myself" he explained.

"OK Ranger see you soon" the sheriff said

"The name is Ben I will come back after I have seen the doctor, I will let you know the situation" Ben told him.

"OK Ben" he acknowledges.

The doctor found that the bullet had passed straight through the shoulder no bones were broken, (you have done a good job dressing your wound) the doctor rewashed his wound put on a fresh bandage,

"I advise you to get some rest" the doctor informed him.

"Doctor has there been anyone to see you with a bullet wound in the last few hours" Ben asked.

"No! no one" came the reply.

"Good I definitely hit him hopefully it will slow him down, his horse has a loose shoe if not fixed it will definitely slow him down, I'll have a nap then get after him" Ben said.

"You can't ride with your shoulder like that apart from the pain it will get sliffer and you could open the wound" the doc reported.

"Doc I must get after this man, I will try to slow down but it is imperative I get this killer, give me a list of what you think I should do and I will try to do it, this has to be my decision, now doc I brought a prisoner in that needs your attention" Ben told the doc.

Ben and the Doc walked over to the sheriff's office the doc went to the cells, Ben sat at the desk in front of the sheriff, where he explained to the sheriff, a) Senator and his family. b) his job of bringing the three men to justice. c) catching Grant as he is the leader and killer.

"Now sheriff I must contact H.Q. let them know the situation, I must get some sleep, so if you can hold the prisoner for me until I have word from H.Q." Ben informed him.

"OK Ben get some sleep, I'll look after the prisoner until you return" the sheriff assured him.

"Thanks sheriff" Ben said.

Entering the hotel Ben approached the desk ordered a room, picked up the key signed the register climbed the stairs, tired as he was he still took time to check his weapons before going to bed, putting his pistol under his pillow then slept.

Sleeping deeper and longer than intended Ben cursed himself for doing so, another thing that made him a bit angry was that his shoulder throbbed and started to get stiff, being a ranger he did what had to be done, washed, shaved and dressed, because of the stiffness there was a bit of difficulty putting on his gunbelt but with tenacity he succeeded.

Being hungry a visit to the hotel restaurant was on, finding a table he ordered a meal of stew and dumplings, half way through the meal Ben felt the presence of someone standing at his side looking up as his hand moved towards his gun then relaxed on seeing Jane standing there.

"Howdy Marm" Ben said.

"Hello, could I speak with you" she asked.

"Sure, pull up a chair would you like something" Ben invited her.

"Thank you" she replied.

"No just a cup of coffee please" she said.

"Now Marm what can I do for you" Ben asked.

"I would like to make you an offer, which would help us both we could be a help to each other" Jane told him.

"Sounds interesting" looking at her.

"Let's go to your room" she said.

"OK" looking puzzled.

Ben was getting more and more intrigued and wondered what Jane could be up to, (wanting to know why she wants to go to his room, it was not normal for a lady to ask to go to a man's room.)

"Your muscles have become stiff and you are in pain because of your wound, take your shirt off" Jane ordered.

"OK your right" came his reply.

"Sit down here" she said holding a chair.

Jane opened her bag and extracted a bottle, avoiding his wound she massaged his arm and shoulder rubbing the oil into it, she massaged for fifteen minutes, replaced the bandage.

"OK Ben lift your arm, now lower it, draw your gun" Jane instructed.

"Jane that feels great, now what can I do for you" asking her.

"I know you are leaving town today I want to go with you, hold it before you open your mouth please listen to me, I know you are going after Grant, I want you to listen to my reasons for wanting to go with you, the man I loved has just died, I need to get out of town desperately, I want to learn about what you do so I can write a book about lawmen and how they carry out their duties, maybe the best reason for going I could tend to your muscles therefore keeping the stiffness away so you can carry out your duties" Jane informed him.

"Jane your reasons are good, the man I am after is a monster and does not care about life, I'm after him because this man murdered a whole family, a one year only baby in a cot, a ten-year-old boy, plus rape and torture of a fourteen year old girl," Ben paused as Jane cried

"Carry on Ben" she told him

"OK Jane, if you fell into his hands it would not be pleasant for you, I know you would be killed, in his eyes you would be a witness and unnecessary baggage, it would be dangerous for you, so I must say no" Ben concluded.

"Look I know it could be dangerous, but I must leave town it is also bad for me to stay if you cannot help me, I will have to do the best I can myself, I could do with your help and guidance" Jane said.

"You have put me in a bad position I would hate myself if you died or worse because of me" Ben stated.

"It will take you a couple of days at least to catch Grant wont it, during that time you could teach me the way to survive out in the open on my own, you could teach me how to shoot also show me how to live of the land, if there is the possibility of danger you can tell me, and I will hide please Ben take me with you" Jane ended.

"I don't know Jane I have never travelled with a female before it's a wild country there is no facilities available for a woman, you cannot wear dresses or carry a lot of luggage a long" Ben pointed out.

"Please give me some credit I am not stupid I did a lot of thinking before I approached you, I know what to expect, take me treat me as a trainee agent, we all have to learn, I expect no special treatment you will not get any complaints from me, as for what I have to wear and what I can carry tell me what I would need, and I'll do it" Jane explained.

She was excited because she could see by his attitude that she could win, she thinks Ben might be coming around to her way of thinking or it looks that way.

"I need to think about this I have to go to the telegraph office and report to the sheriff before I can leave, I will see you back here in an hour" Ben told her.

Ben now had a lot to think of, on purpose his stroll to the telegraph office was slow as the situation went around and round in his head, deep in thought about the reasons for or against taking Jane with him she had already given him the reasons for her to go with him, the only other advantage in taking her along would be the sharing of the chaws (work in camp) therefore making it easier for him.

The obvious reason against her coming a long is the fact she is a female, even though she covered that successfully at the hotel, she said treat her as one of the boys, but it would disturb his usual routine, and could not strip of and go for a swim when he felt like it, and could also do without the distractions, thinking of things for and against they were all things possible to live with.

Changing his thoughts to the lady herself, what is she like, she has already had a bad experience apart from her initial scream she handled the situation well in fact acknowledged she had done better that most other females, by the time of his arrival at the telegraph office, Ben had almost decided to say yes, she could come with him.

Arriving at telegraph office there was a message waiting for him, telling him to carry on after Grant if he could, leave the prisoner with the sheriff, Ranger already dispatched to collect him, Ben headed to the sheriff's office.

"Hi! Sheriff" Ben greeted.

"Howdy Ben you look a lot better" the sheriff said.

"I feel better thanks" came his reply.

"Well, what you going to do with this killer" the sheriff asked

"Don't get any ideas about this man the evidence shows that Grant did all the Killings, Grant murdered the Stevens family, but this man will still hang because of raping the women and rape is a capital offence," Ben explained.

"What now Ben" the sheriff asked.

"I have just been to the telegraph office, read this I have to get after Grant, a ranger will be here tomorrow, I would like you to look after him, and also give the ranger this envelope for me" Ben asked him.

"OK Ben it feels a bit heavy" the sheriff said.

"Yes, it is my report a bag of spent bullets from the Senators house and a penknife which puts the prisoner at the scene of the crime" Ben informed the sheriff.

"I'll see to it Ben" the sheriff assured him.

"Maybe you can give me some advice, I met an attractive young lady called Jane this morning I am curious about her do you have any information on her" Ben enquired. The sheriff smiled.

"Ben, Jane is a nice lady, unfortually she is in trouble and could cause you trouble, In a way it is not her fault, a married man took a liking for her and asked her to go out with him, she agreed and fell in love with him, this man is a local prominent wealth man and his family is not happy about the situation, to cut the story short the family has put a death sentence on her and a bounty on her head, they have already said she is going to die and if she leaves town they will hunt her down, I'm afraid she has stepped on some toe's, being a rich family the killing will not be done by them it is certain someone will be hired to do their dirty work" the sheriff ended.

"Thanks for the info" Ben replied.

"When do you intend to leave Ben" the sheriff enquired.

"Around an hour or so" Ben stated.

"Good luck son" the sheriff said.

Once again there was a lot to think of, if Jane did not come with him she will die so technically this means there is no way that Jane can be left behind, Ben admired her with all the problems she has she remained calm, she did not tell him which could of made him take her she even had the guts to try and get away herself and must have known without some experience she has little chance of making it she would be tracked and almost certain to be dead before getting a short distance maybe a couple of miles if she is lucky.

Entering the hotel Ben spotted Jane sitting at a corner table in the dining room she looked up at him as he approached the table and sat opposite her, she tried to read his poker face without success.

"Do you have a room in the hotel" Ben asked.

"Yes"

"What room, front or back of the hotel"

"Two doors down from your room at the front of the hotel"

Ben put a finger across his lips as the waiter arrived at the table.

"Two specials, apple pie and cream, coffee to follow please" Ben ordered.

The waiter hesitated as he saw Ben's badge before carrying on.

"Yes sir" the waiter replied.

"Jane if you look out of your hotel window what is the building directly facing you" Ben asked.

"The General store" came the reply.

"Just sit tight I will be back" Ben slipped out of the back door which leads to the backhouse(toilet) once through the door turning right and walking down the alley, at the end of the alley keeping out of sight Ben sneaked a look up, down, high and low, returned inside and took his chair at the table.

"Jane, I made some enquiries about you, I know your problem, I would have been happier if you had confided in me" Ben said.

Looking at Ben's straight face she sat quietly, her heart stopped, and she had a desperate look a small sigh left her lips.

The meals arrived as they sat eating in silent not saying a word, Ben seemed to be concentrating on his food, but really waited for Jane to break the ice and start talking.

"I'm sorry I should have told you, I meant to but thought if I told you the answer would be a definite no, I am sorry I didn't tell you" Jane told him.

"Jane, I would have hated you and dropped you of at the next town if I found snipers shooting at me maybe even killing me, did you not think of these things when you asked me" Ben told her bluntly.

"No, I didn't" she answered.

"Jane if you want help and there is the chance that person would be in danger don't you think it was only fair to tell him"

"Sorry" she said in a low voice.

"Listen I want you to hear my words and do everything I say I will explain later, after our meal I want you to go to your room, when in your room I want you to walk back and fro in front of your window try to look like you are thinking or reading, put your bonnet, parasol and bag in plain view of the window, look out of your door check the hall is clear if it is slip out of your room, I will leave my door unlocked enter my room and lock the door behind you do you understand" Ben told her.

Jane looked puzzled, she looked at Ben's straight face, and stared into his cool blue eyes, she could not read anything but knew it is something important, she nodded her head and whispered (Yes) the meal ended Ben stood up his hand out.

"Thank you Marm for the information, I'm sure it will help me in my investigation" Ben said loudly

Ben had on purpose told Jane out loud, loud enough to enable the waiter standing not far away to hear, half an hour later Jane slipped into Ben's room, fifteen minutes later Ben tapped on the door she let him in.

"What is this all about" Jane asked.

"Jane, I have given a lot of thought about this problem both mine and yours, it has not been easy, but I have finally come to a decision I have decided to take you with me" was his answer.

Janes face lit up she jumped to her feet, opened her mouth to celebrate, Ben quickly clamped his hand over her mouth, at the same time put a finger over his lips, Jane kissed Ben (Thank you, thank you) she said excitedly.

"Jane you are constantly being watched by a man from the upstairs room of the building across the street from the hotel, that is why I told you to do the routine I said for you to do before coming here, this man over the street is in a good position to look into your room, now Jane let's get organized you must pack a bag without him seeing you do it what you need to pack is;-

Two pairs of jeans, two dark coloured shirts, two sets of underwear, two pairs of socks, a pair of boots, a bandana and Stetson and a warm coat. you can take a small amount of jewelry but no cosmetic's, we must keep things to a minimum we cannot take a lot of baggage, now go back to you room and pack when you have everything together drop them into my room, I will tell you what to do next.

As it happens the set of drawers Jane kept her clothes in stood in a blind spot for the man looking into her room, on the other hand the bag she required was on a chair on the opposite side of the room which meant she would have to walk passed the window to get it, Jane walked across the room a couple of times pretending to read a book in her hand, like most women in town she wore a long dress the second time she crossed the room she dropped the bag on the floor and hid it by putting her dress over it with the book still in her hand she walked slowly across the room pushing the bag as she walked until out of sight of the window, Jane looked lovely in the pale blue dress with dark blue trim, Jane new what to buy Ben had not seen her a lot but had to admit she is very catching because of the close fitting clothes she wears that emphasizes her lovely shapely figure.

Meanwhile Ben proceeded to carry out the task that had been decided on, the first place to visit was the sheriff's office.

"Sheriff when the Ranger gets here tell him I have taken one of the criminals horse so I can ride relay, (riding relay meant having two horses, you can alternate between horses) this method meant the horses would not get tired quickly and you could go further without stopping, In this case Ben was lying as it was necessary to have a horse for Jane, the same story was told at the livery stable as the holster arrived and saw him saddling the two horses, tying the horses to the hitch rail outside the hotel now everything was now ready to put his plan for there departure, Jane entered the room carrying her bag.

"Jane unpack your bag and put your stuff into those saddlebags putting female items and jewelry in the bottom of the bag" Ben told her.

"OK Ben what's next "she asked.

"Do you know the recreation area (Park) south of town" he asked.

"Yes, I often go there to walk and read its quiet and I can be by myself it's a place I go to for peace and quiet where I can think" she answered.

"Right Jane listen because I want you to carry out my instructions to the letter, I want you to walk through the area slowly reading your book also carry things you would normally carry with you wear a bonnet, carry your parasol and purse, now Jane as you walk do not look around someone might see you do it and become suspicious, walk all the way through the area out the south gate, keep walking in a straight line until you meet me" Ben instructed her.

"I understand" she replied.

"Let's go" Ben waited until Jane had entered her room before making his move.

CHAPTER THREE

THE ESCAPE FROM TOWN

Jane entered the park and carried out the instructions Ben gave her she walked slowly reading as she walked along, she paused a couple of times to admire the trees and flowers but did not look round, just carried on walking, about a hundred feet behind her a man strolled ideally along stopping when she stopped, Ben unknown to Jane had raced ahead of her and had spotted the man trailing Jane, crouching behind a patch of thick brush watching the man's actions.

Walking into the wooded area she did not see or hear Ben as she walked past his place of concealment, just carried on walking slow as instructed, the man following Jane did not know of Ben's presence keeping pace slowly walked behind Jane as the man passed the hiding place Ben stepped out behind the man and with a club made from the branch of a nearby tree striking the man unconscious dragging him into cover, dragging the body around thirty feet from the path so no one will hear him, tied the body of the man to the tree trunk, tied his hands behind the tree trunk, tied his feet together and gagged him.

Moving fast through the wooded area to the trail climbing into the saddle directed Shad to the park exit, Jane smiled as she saw Ben waiting for her which quickly changed to shock and surprise as Ben gripped the flimsy dress and ripped it of her, before she could say anything.

"Jane put this on and climb onto the brown horse" throwing her a coat.

"OK" she said, still surprised climbed into the saddle.

Tearing a small piece of the dress, Ben hung it on a nearby bush as the horse moved slowly forward as directed Ben tore a few threads of the dress and periodically put them on a bush, separating more threads which once placed where they could be seen gave a false trail for anyone following, with patience and because the man who was trailing Jane is now indisposed this gave him time.

"Right Jane I have taken care of the man who followed you, because I tied and gagged him with a bit of luck it will give us a couple of hours start and as you can see, I have left a trail for them to follow." Ben explained.

Ben knew what to do because a few days earlier he had been in this area and it had been possible to explore, he is now putting his knowledge to use, after a few miles on Ben's order they came to a halt.

"Jane go through that break in the brush on the right you will find yourself on rocky, stony ground follow the rocky track for a couple of hundred yards you come to a small forest area, if you have any garments like corset or belts take them off in your saddle bags you have a change of clothes put on , jeans, shirt boots bandana and Stetson, now give me your bonnet and parasol, once you have changed wait for me I will be there soon." Ben instructed her.

Moving forward a further hundred yards Ben threw the parasol into the surrounding trees, riding forward still depositing strands of thread from the dress until reaching a stream where by the side of the stream the bonnet was left getting Shad to walk backwards until they reached the break in the bushes that Jane passed through, after going through himself Ben dismounted and with a branch he wiped away his and Jane's tracks then rode to where Jane waited.

"Now if you don't mind could you tell me what you have been up to" Jane demanded.

Telling Jane of his ruse to confuse anyone following them, Jane now new she had picked the best person to help her to escape from the past and could not help admiring him.

"Why did you make the remark about my clothing" Jane asked.

"We have a lot of riding to do, you must be comfortable, so you must wear looser clothes whenever you can otherwise you will get irritated."

"I see"

"Are you more comfortable" looking at her raising his eyebrows.

"Yes except for the flies and bugs" she returned.

"When we stop Ill sort that out for you"

"And when do you plan to stop" she asked

"In approximately two hours" came the reply.

"If you can tell me, where are we heading" she asked.

"We are going back to the pool of water in the valley, we will follow this stream to the hills over there, go over the hill into the valley, we will once again follow the stream along the valley to the pool using the stream as much as possible, when we arrive at the pool we will have a break" Ben explained.

"Why go there" she asked

"The pool is the last place I saw and shot Grant the man I am after now the weather has been good during our period in town, so there is still the chance of some sign, a man who has been shot would normally head for the nearest doctor we know that the doctor has not seen him I will guess on leaving this pool Grant headed out in one direction to get away changed to another direction in an attempt to fool anyone behind him"

"OK Ben you know what you are doing" she nodded her head.

Side by side they walked their horses talking as they moved a long Ben pointed out to Jane different items she could find as you travel, like things you can eat and things that are poisoness as they approached the pool of water.

"Listen, what do you hear" Ben said.

She strained her ears, shrugged her shoulders resignedly.

"I can't hear a thing"

"Good that's right"

"What do you mean" she queried.

"You can't hear anything because there is nothing to hear, stop your horse sit perfectly still do not say a word" a finger over his lips.

The birds started to sing, and rabbits scurried around.

"What do you hear now" he whispered looking at Jane, she smiled back at him.

"Jane when anything moved or makes a noise the birds and animals stop singing and moving until they know they are safe" Ben explained.

Once again it went silent, Jane said nothing but noted all things Ben had told her as she intended to make notes. They arrived at the pool.

"Jane strip" then had a long pause, a shocked look came to Jane's face she looked at him, seeing a smile on his face.

"In my saddlebags, you will find a bar of soap give yourself a though bath wash of all make up powder and oils, also beside the soap there is a small bottle before putting your shirt on rub the oil onto all exposed parts of your body including face and arms, I'm going hunting for sign" a broad grin on his face.

The shocked look was replaced by anger she laughed and swung a slap at him, mounting laughing out loud moved off.

Jane smiled, happily stripped naked walked into the inviting pool of water, realizing Ben did this on purpose because knowing that she felt dirty and irritated being in the saddle for hours, she said to herself.

"Thank you, Ben,"

When Ben came back Jane had almost completely dressed she had only her shirt to put on.

"Before putting your shirt on put the oil on your shoulders and on your chest down to your bra then your arms and face" she followed his instructions but looked a little puzzled.

"Thanks Ben"

"Mount up Jane lets ride"

"When do we stop to eat and stop for the night, I have noticed you are favoring your shoulder it needs attention" she told him.

"An hour before sundown, that's in about an hour and a half time we are not going to catch up with Grant tonight, so the shoulder can wait until then."

As they moved in a easterly direction, Ben showed Jane the sign left by Grant, the marks left by the broken shoe, how the grass had been flattened, broken twigs on the brush indicating someone had rode by, the change in the hoof prints as the horse gathered speed and slowed down again, by the time Ben had finished Jane's head was full with all the information, that it was hard to remember it all, finally after finding a place to make camp, Ben called a halt.

"Right, let's make camp"

"Here! Why here"

"it's a natural dip in the land surrounded by low brush which gives us protection and a warning as someone approaches it has a slow running stream this place is not perfect, but it will do, now we need to make camp, make a fire for food and coffee, but dowse the fire before turning in for the night."

"What can I do" Jane asked

"Clear a patch of grass down to earth to make a fire"

"Show me how Ben"

"Take this knife and clear a patch right here" pointing to the ground.

"OK Ben"

Tethering the horses and relieving them of the burdens allowing them to graze on the lush green grass and drink from the nearby stream so left them to get on with it, foraging around there was plenty dry twigs to be collect for building a fire, looking at Jane he smiled as was still trying to clear a patch of grass away for a place to build their fire, walking over to her taking the knife from her hand Ben made four deep cuts then peeled the turf back therefore completing the task in minutes, she poked her tongue out at him, while making the fire as instructed Jane.

"When you make the fire put dry soft grass (not green) build the fire up with dry twigs never use wet or green twigs or branches as they give of smoke, two reasons why you don't want to sit around the camp area coughing all the time and two smoke gives your position away and we do not want anybody bothering us" looking at her and winked.

"I understand thank you" "Jane, you will learn in time"

She watched with interest as Ben took a branch from a small tree then used it as a stirrup to hang a Billie (pot) over the fire to warm food up, with water in the coffee pot it was placed on the fire. While the water heated up with Jane watching as he dug a hole in the ground behind a bush told her it was the toilet and rubbish dump, laying out the bedrolls in the best positions together but leaving a discreet distance between them.

"In my saddlebags, you will see a bag of coffee, bag of beans and some cooked meat could you get them, tonight we will have a simple meal tomorrow as we travel, I will try to get a prairie chicken and maybe some eggs"

"That sounds great to me" Jane replied.

"After we eat, could you see to my shoulder please Jane"

"Yes, Ben I will, what then" Jane asked.

"It's near sundown, we will dowse the fire, turn in for the night, I want to be up before dawn and on our way as soon as possible.

Jane massaged Ben's shoulder as she proceeded, they talked small talk, needless to say Jane being a woman, she had lots of questions about things she was dying to know one being security.

"What about security as we sleep" she asked.

"First I am a light sleeper, second anyone moving around will have to make some noise due to the brush around the camp, third and most of all Shad will let me know even before I hear anything" Came the explanation.

"Shad"

"Shadow my horse"

"Your horse"

"Sure, anyone approaches Shad will warn me, I'll introduce you to him in the morning being as he is a one-man horse and does not like strangers, at this moment don't try to pat him, not until I properly introduce you" Ben explained.

They both slept well during the night, as it had been a tiring day the day before, while it was still dark even before the first light of dawn Ben's eyes opened but his body remained still his ears working overtime lying perfectly still the first sound that came to his ears was the horses moving, as a ribbon of light showed the horizon the dawn chorus started as birds began to sing.

Rising, picking up his gun, getting the fire started pouring water from the canteen in to the pot, putting the pot on the fire to make coffee, taking the canteens with him to the stream emptying the canteens filled them with lovely cool morning water splashing water on his face, going back to camp poured a cup of coffee and woke Jane.

With a drop of water from the pot, shaved, Jane watched him as he moved about and had a shave as she drank the coffee, after the coffee she went to the stream and freshened up, it took the sleep out of her eyes and made her feel good.

"Jane after breakfast get your clean clothes from your saddle bags and put them into your bedroll, we will then tidy up the site and move out"

"What do you mean tidy up there is nothing to tidy up" Jane said.

"Jane if you need to go to the loo do so, because tidy up means filling in the hole, extinguishing the fire and putting the turf back then we ride"

"How is your shoulder this morning" Jane asked.

"A little stiff that's all" came the reply.

"Before you put that shirt on, I will massage your shoulder it won't take long, you won't lose much time"

"OK"

"This man Grant, you said that the man is bad, how bad" Jane asked.

Ben related to her the events with all the gory details about what happened at Senator Stevens house, telling her in detail what had happened to the baby and the rape of the young girl.

"Now you know, as a Ranger I have been given the job of bringing these men to face justice, I have taken two of the men out, but their leader Grant managed to escape, it's my job to get him".

Realizing the enormity of Ben's job, Jane just rode on in silence, Ben expected Jane to slow him down but she did the opposite, she kept quiet, she kept up with Ben, so they made a reasonable distance, over the years doing the job as a Ranger Ben had acquired the ability to think and put himself into the criminals place, once in a while there would be sign to follow this confirmed his thoughts, Grant tried a few times to deceive him by using rocky area's and water, Grant did not know a lot about tracking so only caused Ben a slight delay.

Ben did manage to get a prairie chicken and also found the nest and found it contained eggs, this means they will eat well tonight and the next few days, as they rode along Ben explained what had to be done also what needed to be done and this kept her interested, by the end of the day Ben knew they had done well and made up a lot of lost time, if they could make the same progress tomorrow, they would not be far behind Grant, all day Ben and Jane had chewed on jerky meat and drank water so when Ben called a halt Jane in particular could not be happier.

"Jane, we are stopping a little earlier to give us time to cook the chicken so could you clear a patch for the fire, I'll find some dry twigs once the bird is cooking we will make camp"

"OK Ben" she replied smiled weakly Ben saw she was tired.

"Once the chicken is on there will be little for you to do go down to the stream and have a swim, take your dry clothes with you wash the clothes you have on then wash the dust of you".

"Thank you, Ben, we did do well today".

"Yes, we did, and I would like to thank you"

"Me" she said.

"Yes, you, I know you are tired, after dinner I want you to have a good sleep as I want to push on tomorrow, I know it will be hard for you but another day like today and we will be right behind Grant, now have the swim, eat your dinner, sleep".

"Yes boss" she said and laughed mockingly.

The temperature of the water at this time of the evening was perfect as the naked Jane sank under the water, it made her feel vigerating, alive and more awake, getting back in the camp she spread her clothes on the nearby bushes to dry noticing the camp had been made up.

Cradling a cup of coffee she looked at the stripped chicken on the spit over the fire sitting on her bedroll, Ben checked the chicken with a folk took out his knifecut of a leg and passed it to her, on the completion of their meal they started to talk, Ben smiled when watching Jane drift off to sleep it had been a very busy day, therefore understood why Jane was tired, Ben laid Jane on her bedroll and put a blanket over her, looking at the sky, realizing it would still be light for a while the stream called him, a swim what a great idea and smiled sinking into the water.

Taking the bandage of his shoulder, there was no blood, but the wound was red so decided to leave it uncovered over night the fresh air will help with Jane's help put the bandage back on in the morning.

As normal Ben woke up in his normal way, lying still until the dawn chorus could be heard, listening and establishing everything was as it should be climbing to his feet retrieving his colt went to the fire and relit it, put a pot of water on the fire, going to the stream Ben refreshed himself by sticking his head into the cool water when the water boiled, he poured some of it into the coffee pot putting a little water aside to shave then threw a handful of beans into the pot.

After shaving Ben poured a cup of coffee as the sound of a sleepy voice came to his ears.

"Good morning Ben"

"Morning Jane" was his reply as he handed her the coffee.

Putting the skillet on the fire to cook the eggs.

"Egg and beans for breakfast Jane"

"Sounds good"

On completion of breakfast Ben reached over to his saddlebags and extracted a bandage, Jane saw his intension and said.

"Ben leave that to me I'll see to your shoulder"

"OK"

She fixed his shoulder they cleared up the camp saddled up and rode out.

"Ben when you can would you teach me to shoot, I need to know about firearms, I will not be with you forever, I'd like to know for my own protection"

"I would be happy to teach you to shoot I think it is better to have the knowledge of firearms it is safer and prevents many accidents from happening."

"Good I look forward to it" Jane replied.

Once again they moved at a reasonable pace, not pushing the horses if they stay at a slow pace with frequent breaks this will enable them to get good distance without tiring the horses, from experience Ben had learnt that criminals after a day or two of running will get complacent and slow down Paul Grant is a bad man but still has a brain, Ben was hit and Grant knows about it, therefore it is logical for him to think there is no pursuit, It would be right for him to think Ben had been taken out and will feel safe.

Jane and Ben did there best to get as far as they could as it gives Ben a better chance of catching him, there is various ways this can be done, they must set up camp as late as they can, rise as early as possible and get under way, take frequent but shorter stops only to rest the horses, eat in the saddle, or when they stop to allow the horses to blow, as for eating there is the chicken left from the night before plus each of them have jerky meat and there canteens are topped up with fresh water, It means they spend longer in the saddle it also means there is a better chance of catching Grant.

"How do you know you are on the right trail and that it is Grant ahead of you" Jane asked.

"At first when trailing a person you start with the easy things, like getting to know the sign (prints) left by the horse of the man you are tracking, we know the horse is large, it has a loose shoe on the front left hoof, the horse is grey in colour by the presence of grey hair left as the horse touches the brush, by the depth of the print you can tell if the horse is carrying a heavy or light load or it could mean the size of the rider, the distance between the front and rear hoofs can tell if the horse is walking, cantering, running or galloping" Ben explained.

"You mean you can tell all that just by looking at horse sign" She said amazed,

"Of course this is just the start because these things are constant, you learn more about the man as you track him, I Know I shot him I wounded him at the top of the leg maybe the hip, most men I know would go straight to the nearest doctor, the doc in town has not seen him, that means Grant has medical knowledge and tending the wound himself or it is not to serious, the next piece of information is important Grant is staying of the main trail"

"What main trail, we are in the middle of the country I cannot see a trail" she asked.

"The main trail usually means the easiest route, most people travelling would take this route, Grant has so far avoided this route and picked his way over hills, through brush and used water when possible keeping the main route in site, there is only a couple of reasons for this, first if suspicious thinking of being followed by keeping the main trail in sight, it would therefore enabling him to spot the person following him, secondly it is a chance he is looking for easy pickings remember Grant is a robber and a killer, this bit of information helps me because if I come to a junction I know which way is most likely for him to go making it easier to find sign" Ben stopped talking and dismounted.

Bending down Ben picked up the discarded horse shoe.

"Grants horse has finally lost the loose shoe, this will slow him down"

"Good" Jane acknowledged.

"Don't be too happy, it makes it better for me as this makes him slow down, but it depends on what sort of a lead the man had in the first place" Ben informed her.

After a couple of miles Ben once more pulled Shad to a halt and jumped from the saddle, scooping a bit of horse manure from the ground rubbed it between his fingers and smelt it, returned to the horses.

"Jane could you get the canteen and pour some water over my hands"

"What did you do that for" she enquired.

"By checking the temperature and texture, and smelling to see how new it was after taking in the weather conditions tells me roughly how long ago it was dropped it will give us an indication how far ahead of us he is, the result being not good for us at this moment" came the explanation

"Why" Jane asked.

"Grant still has quite a lead on me"

"The texture is dry, now you could put that down to the heat of the sun, but it is also cool, the sun would normally keep it warm and the texture soft, but it is cold and dry this indicates Grant is about six hours away, we will not catch him tonight" Ben proclaimed.

"I see" Jane muttered.

Travelling along slowly side by side, they rode along chatting as if there was not a care in the world and were taken by surprise as Shad suddenly stopped and pointed to the bushes ahead to the right, Jane for the first time saw an instant change in Ben.

Jane saw Ben change from a pleasant happy cheerful young man into a serious man of action, leaping from the saddle his pistol appearing in his hand like magic, creeping to the brush Shad pointed to, as there was little cover Ben moved fast in a zig zag pattern , braking through the bushes, there lying in front of him was the body of a young man the body had no gunbelt, which was unusual very few men did not wear a gun, his pockets were empty, stepping back Ben signaled to Jane it was OK to come forward.

"We have no horse for him so cannot take him along, we will cover him with stones put a cross up inform the sheriff of the next town we come across" Ben told her.

Jane climbed back into the saddle, Ben told Jane and Shad to stay back, Ben moved forward on foot surveying every inch of the ground for a hundred yards, stopping and turning Ben whistled, Shad snorted moving forward Jane's horse followed.

"The man was killed by Grant to steal his horse, the tracks of the horse with the missing shoe is prominent the stolen horse is a brown with special shoes, that is good as I now know what to look for, one thing that is good Grant is still travelling in the same direction leading the grey horse" Ben explained.

Leading the way constantly focusing on the trail, checking to make sure Grant had not decided to change his course, sitting in the saddle Jane watched Ben in silence about half an hour later they came to the edge of a deep slope in the terrain (hill) below them stood a log cabin nestling in a grove of trees it had a lovely flower garden surrounded by a white picket fence it was a beautiful setting.

"Ben what a lovely cabin" Jane reflected.

"Damn"

"Ben what's wrong"

"Grant has been here that is his grey in the corral let's go"

Nudging Shad they moved forward calling them to a halt just outside the picket fence, called out the usual greeting.

"Hello, the house" no answer, so he called again,

"Hello, the house" once again no reply after a pause gave it another try.

"Hello, the house" Jane looked a little puzzled, Ben explained.

"Jane whenever you approach or come upon a homestead or a camp site it is only right and polite to ask permission to enter so you call a greeting and wait for their permission to go ahead, as there is no answer I will have to investigate wait here" Ben knew Grant had been here, with his pistol in hand he moved forward, the cabin door was a jar, pushing the door Ben slowly advanced into the room, there was nothing in the main room looking into the bedroom an almost naked young lady lay, Ben called for Jane who looked appalled at the sight of the woman's body and started to cover it up.

"Hold it Jane get your note pad out"

"I'm ready Ben"

"OK write this down;- 1) She has a split skull possibly pistol whipped, 2) her face is badly beaten, 3) Marks on her shoulders indicating being forced to lie down, 4) This lady has been tortured by the burns on her breasts, 5) her belly button has been used as an ashtray by the looks of the remains of the cigarette bud still there, 6) lots of blood from between her legs (crotch area) 7) her right leg is broken, Jane this young lady put up quite a fight but Grant was too strong for her because she fought him that is why he tortured her, cover her up, I will go back get her husband and I'll bury them together." Ben concluded.

"What now Ben"

"We will stay a short while to eat, the info we have just taken down I will put into a report and hand to the sheriff of the next town we come across" Ben told her.

Jane covered the body with a sheet, when they both heard a low unusual noise, Ben's hand went straight to his colt, where did the sound come from, they both wondered it was a minute or so later that the sound was repeated, Jane still standing near the body suddenly understood.

"Ben she's alive" as she rolled the sheet down to her shoulders.

"WHAT" Ben exclaimed filled a cup with water and put a few drops on her lips.

"Jane make her comfortable, just wet her lips, I'll get the first aid kit we will see what we can do for her, can you check and see if anything can be done about the blood from her private parts, in case she becomes conscious it would be better you have a look If you need my assistance call"

"I'll do that as you get the first aid kit" she said

"Right" Ben said running out of the door.

Picking up the first aid kit, hurried back into the cabin, Jane looked at him as he came through the door and shook her head.

"What's wrong Jane"

"She was bleeding internally but I could not see why, I have managed to stop the bleeding, I don't know if it was during a fight or what but her back is broken and her stomach is damaged, we cannot move her and Ben we cannot save her all we can do is make her comfortable until she dies." Jane explained tears in her eyes.

"Damn, I wish I had Grant in my sights right now, damn, damn."

"Give me the first aid kit, I will do what I can for her, I'll wash and clean her wounds make her as comfortable as possible, you go down the trail, pick up her husband see you when you get back"

"OK Jane"

Ben retrieved the body of the unfortunate man, after checking with Jane, the next job to be done was to dig two graves out the back of the cabin, after that chore the grey horse had to be shoe'd or it would go lame, it took five hours for the lady to die, Jane and Ben buried the unfortunate couple under a tree in a shady area out back.

"We have done all we can for these folk Jane, let's have a look in the pantry we can eat before moving out of here, if there is any food left it will come in handy can take it with us"

"Sure Ben" she replied solemnly, Ben put his arm around her, she put her head on his shoulder and cried.

Jane had nursed the lady for the five hours, the time it took for her to die, she has done a great job, Jane's strength broke as they buried the couple, all the time Ben had spent with her she has never cried, as she cried his instincts came out talking to her softly to calm her down after a while she lifted her head automatically they kissed, Ben admitted his enjoyment of the closeness they had due to the sad set of this affair.

Giving Jane time to settle down Ben cut two crosses put them on the graves meanwhile Jane took a selection of flowers from the garden placed them on the graves, Ben once more put his arm around her shoulders and steered her towards the cabin.

"We had better eat, get underway, we have lost some time, and after seeing his handy work I'm now more determined to get this man"

"Yes, let's kill this man, this animal does not deserve to live, kill him Ben".

Sitting with a cup of coffee in his hands, Ben was deep in thought as Jane came to the table and sat beside him.

"How far can we get if we leave now, it's been a long day and it is not long till sunset" Jane said.

"Your right I have just been thinking the same, if we leave here we will have to find a camp spot make up camp, as you have correctly observed it's not long to sundown, we have everything we need here so I hope you don't mind if I say we will stay here overnight carry on in the morning Jane"

"I agree it's a good idea," she replied.

Returning to the stove Jane continued cooking the dinner consisting of, Beef stew, potatoes and beans she also found some tins of peaches which she opened for a sweet following up with coffee.

"You know these last few days I have rode with you has opened my eyes to many things, like most people we do not know the job you do and the skills you have to do it. From now on I will look at lawmen with a completely different view, I know you had to go after killers and thieves but not monsters like this man Grant, the torture and death of this woman has shown me why we have a need for people who do your job and how we desperately need you and your colleagues" Jane told him.

"Thanks Jane"

"There is one thing that puzzles me"

"What would that be" Ben asked.

"We have been together for a few days and nights now, you have not made any advances to me is there any reason for that, most men make advances or comments or something like that" Jane asked.

"In my job, I have very little contact with females but I am no different than other men, during our times together I have seen you in the nude amongst other things being human and a man I could not help being slightly aroused because you are beautiful, there are three reasons why I have not attempted to go further, one, I do not want to offend you. Two, I can't say I love you and want to marry you because I don't know if I do, three, you have seen the job I do it would be obvious I thought, not to make advances to you when I have a job with such a short life expectancy so therefore no prospects for you" Ben told her.

"Oh! Ben, you have it all wrong, I am a woman who likes compliments from men If I don't like a person I say so" she explained

"I thought you might be a burden to me, but I have learnt to admire you, you said you have learnt a lot, well I have also learnt a lot since you have been with me, Jane you are beautiful and I would like to make love to you"

"Don't say it do it" Jane replied. She smiled.

"Have you made love before Ben"

"Only once a long time ago, as I have said before I don't know many women" Ben explained.

"I'll tell you what let's finish our dinner, do the cleaning up wash the dishes, you go check the horses, the unfortunate man has some beers in the cooler when you get back, we will have a drink and sit down and talk" Jane suggested.

"OK Jane"

Between them they tidied up and washed the dishes, Ben went out to check on the horses making sure there was food and water also checking the hay in the stalls in the barn, meanwhile Jane quickly moved into the bedroom, she stripped the Bed felt the mattress and found it to be dry looking into the drawers she found clean bedding so made up the bed, Ben wanted to make love to her, with the day she has just had she wanted someone to hold her, to be honest Jane had grown to like Ben so looked forward to tonight.

When Ben returned to the cabin, Jane sat on the divan two beers on the table in front of her, she still had her shirt on but had removed her jeans, Ben removed his gunbelt, Stetson, boots and vest sat beside Jane.

They sat talking for a short while the warmth from the fire the beer and small talk made them mellow Ben put his arm around her she snuggled into him, Ben kissed her but not properly his lips were closed plus pushed against her so hard it hurt her, at the same time the arm over her shoulder his hand roughly grabbed her breast she winced that was when Jane knew that Ben had not made love before and was a virgin.

"Ben, Ben, not so hard you are hurting me, put your lips to mine gently, your lips partly open then mould them to mine" Jane instructed.

"Ahhrr Ben that was better"

Taking his hand Jane placed it on her breast.

"Ben feel it, stroke it, flick the nipple with your thumb, Ahrr Arrr yes that's lovely" she uttered.

"That feels lovely Jane"

"Ben, I want you to make love to me, but I want to enjoy it, I know you want to enjoy it also, would you mind if I show you what I want you to do" Jane said.

"OK Jane"

In the west many men were like Ben a virgin at twenty five years old, men out numbered women by three to one, lots of men at this time never married, lots of men used saloon girls or visited cat houses (brothel) for sex these houses with the red light outside the door, these places were necessary a house in a town with a dozen girls, ran an organized business that would keep the men in a whole town busy, by providing this service it is believed it kept the other women in the town safe from rape.

"The way to make love, is slow you must love your lady with foreplay we all have to learn, a moment ago you grabbed my tit so hard you hurt me, I know that was not your intension when you are too rough I will not enjoy you making love to me, if we make love properly we will both enjoy doing it, OK"

"OK Jane I understand" came his reply.

"Now hold me, caress me as you do so kiss my lips, my neck gently nibble my ears, Oh! Yes Ben that feels great yes yes, put your hand on my shirt feel my tit caress it love it gently squeeze it Ohh! lovely keep kissing me."

Jane undid his shirt running her fingers though the hair on his chest, Ben took the hint opening her shirt pushing her Bra aside his hand cupped her breast the feeling of the silky flesh caused feelings in his pants it did not take long for the beginner to relieve Jane of her shirt, letting the shirt and bra drop to the floor so did his shirt.

"Kiss my tits tease the nipples Oohhh! nice more yes your learning more Ah! Lovely" she murmured.

Ben whispered word of love in her ears Jane smiled, her sounds of enjoyment made him enjoy their sensation as his erection expanded, as two pairs of jeans fell to the floor Jane took his hand and led him to the bedroom, they kissed as the remaining clothes ended in a pile on the floor, with no restrictions his erected cock sprung up as it was free

Lying on the bed Ben pulled her body to him their lips met as his hand ran across the beautiful smooth lovely rounded arse pulled her body to him letting his fingers run up and down her spine she sighed, giggled as her body pushed into him, bending his head his mouth covered her right breast, his hand felt the left tit his thumb rubbing the nipples of her now swollen breasts teasing the hard protruding nipples and now sensitive breasts Ohhhh! Arr! Ahrr! The sounds of love came loudly from her lips.

Jane's hand held his cock, (Ohh! Yes) she uttered, his hand moved over her tummy going between the now open legs his hand rubbed the lips of the entrance of her crotch (Arrr! Eeeeee, Arr eeee), pushing his finger into the private entrance to Jane's body, a gasp came from her lips as his finger probed into her, words came from her lips, (Ben rub the clit, the clit, Ben the clit) she realized Ben did not know what she meant, putting her hand on his hand her finger guided his finger onto the Clitoris, (rub there Ben) she omitted brokenly between gasps, (yes yes more Aahhrrr ! Ohhhhh) the sounds of ultimate pleasure coming from her lips drove him on his erection throbbed as Jane's arse left the bed her body pushing her crotch wet from the juices of love.

"Now please now Ohh! Ohh" please"

Inserting the throbbing erected rampant tool into her eagerly waiting body caused her to gasp loudly, the sensations of there love caused the world to disappear as the passion took over, there bodies vibrated with the action of unsuppressed love making which sent them into a world of their own Ben's body shook as his seed passed into Jane's body, (Ohhhh! Ohhh! Yes Oh! Yes) she cried their passion satisfied, there bodies relaxed.

"Thank you, Jane," getting his breath back.

"Why are you thanking me, thank you I loved every second"

"I think you know or realized I had not made love before and I could not of had a better teacher I loved it" he explained.

Lying together they embraced and kissed passionately for a moment until Ben put his hand between her legs.

"I think you should test me to make sure I have learnt what you taught me" whispering in her ear.

"Yes, I'd love to do it again, but when you enter me do it slow and wiggle it about build up the speed it has a better effect"

"You see I still have lots to learn"

They made love again only this time Ben did not need instructions.

Lying in each other's arms they slowly began to get their breath back once again they kissed.

"Thank you, Jane it was fantastic, and you are wonderful"

"Ben, I loved it also, you are a quick learner" she smiled.

"Only because I had a good teacher" kissed her passionately.

"What a pupil"

"I want to make love to you all night Jane, but I have a job to do so I must rest as I want us to leave as soon as possible in the morning."

They spent the night together, Ben has been so used to waking early each morning, this morning there was no difference except to look at the sleeping beauty beside him, leaning over his lips touched hers, Jane sleepy eyes opened.

"Morning sleepy head" Ben greeted her, she took him by surprise as her arm swung around his neck and a pair of hungry eager lips searched for his, Ben new they shouldn't but the kiss plus the beautiful body pushing against him made him loose control and gave in as they made love again.

"Hey! Trouble maker we must get up and get going" Ben whispered.

"Why didn't you like it"

"Jane, it was fantastic, I would love to stay here, making love to you all day and night, but we must get going we must wash, have breakfast, see to the horses before we move, I must continue with the job, if you agree we will when we can find time for my teacher to give me more instructions" she looked and saw a wonderful face with a cheeky smile on it, she laughed as she jumped out of bed.

"OK Ben I'll get breakfast, you see to the horses" she told him. "I agree"

Because the dead couple had amounted a good larder, they were able to have a substantial breakfast which means they do not have to stop for a while, also they could replenish their supplies giving them food for a few days meaning Ben did not have to waste time hunting.

As the weather was OK last night Ben could still pick up enough sign for him to follow, after riding for around one and a half hours, Ben suddenly brought them to a halt, cocking his leg over the saddle horn, sliding from the saddle slipping his rifle from the scabbard, with the rifle at the ready position, he moved slowly forward disappeared into the bushes it was about fifteen minutes before reappearing into view again his whistle told Shad to advance forward Jane followed.

"What you found Ben" Jane asked.

"Looks like Grant did stop at the cabin where we stopped as he stole some items from the cabin, one of the items was bottles of whisky, after stopping at the cabin, he must have smelt smoke, he crept through the brush, creeping up on a man who had made camp in the woods, it seems he knew the man as he lowered the rifle, (I think he snuck up on the man to steal from him but they recognized each other) I can tell by the mark left by the butt of the rifle, they talked, Grant retrieved his horse, the other man's horse is a piebald, the man is light on his feet, also chain smokes, the type of tobacco is Mexican weed, and also wears narrow shoes with large rowel spurs this man could be a Mexican, after a coffee they mounted up and rode out, the Mexican has had a new shoe fitted to his horse so that fact will help with the tracking" Ben explained.

"Ben, I find it fascinating how you can assess things the way you do"

"Jane climb down we will let the horses blow, we will have a sandwich before moving again"

"OK" she replied.

After a small break they mounted and rode on, Ben and Jane rode side by side but all the time Ben kept his eyes open for sign about two hours later they came across where Grant had stopped for the night, after a brief look around Ben became puzzled, things did not look right, Ben estimated the time it did not make sense it did not seem right (Why did they stop), Ben thought it was not Grants MO (method of) in fact Ben expected Grant to be miles away, why did they set up camp so early, also by feeling the remains of the ash of the fire he found the ash was still warm, meaning the two of them moved of late, this is out of character doing a though search of the area Ben found the reason for the change in Grants normal routine.

When Ben and Jane left the cabin of the dead couple they took food and a couple of bottles of beer, but Grant had taken half a dozen bottles of whisky Ben has just now found the whisky bottles that were thrown into the bushes, Grant and his friend were drunk last night that explains it, calculating as best as possible Ben came to the conclusion Grant was still ahead but there had been little distance made which meant there was no difference from the day before, Ben estimated Grant could only be about six hours ahead.

"Jane making love last night was fantastic and I did think Grant would put some distance between us but because Grant and his friend decided to party last night and they were drunk, there has been little distance made in fact it is possible we may have closed on them, you know what Jane I could have taken another lesson from you"

"That's good because last night turned out to be something special to me, (in her head she thought I love you) I would have loved having the chance to teach you more, but I am happy it has turned out OK for you" Jane said.

Coming together they kissed, after a short break, climbing into the saddle the pair moved out, not wanting to push his luck so told Jane.

"Jane, we must carry on I do not want to push my luck even though I would love to make love to you I must get Grant.

"I understand you have a job to do" Jane returned.

INSTEAD OF CHOCOLATES

Following the sign left by Grant and his pal they came across a well-worn trail in front of them they spotted a sign post informing them of the town ahead, KITTYBURG 3 MILES POPULATION 228 Ben knows a little time has been lost due to Grants pal who knows a few tricks that made it harder to track them Ben thinks they have made another hour on them, It being only an hour away from sundown there is no chance of catching them tonight, they will have to stay in town overnight.

"We will have to stay in town tonight could you go to the hotel and book a double room for the night"

"Yes, yes, yes." Jane cried excitedly.

"Could you also book a table for dinner, Jane pay for the room and tell them we will be leaving early in the morning after breakfast" Ben instructed her and gave her a ten-dollar bill.

"Where are you off to"

"I must report to the sheriff, first to let him know I am here, second I must inform the sheriff of the fate of that couple in the cabin"

"OK Ben I'll see you soon" she replied.

Riding down to the sheriff's office took only a few seconds, approaching the office there was a bunch of around ten men outside the office as the sheriff addressed them.

"Right men be here at the office at sunup at first light we ride." The sheriff informed the posse, as the men walked away, looking at Ben.

"Howdy ranger how can I help you" the sheriff inquired.

"First of sheriff I need some information as you have rightly seen by my badge I'm a ranger, I have been trailing a man called Grant I understand there is another man with him possibly a Mexican, I'd like to know if you know him or anything that will help in my pursuit" Ben explained.

"KNOW HIM, KNOW HIM," the sheriff exploded.

"You have seen him"

"Seen them they robbed the general store shot the owner and rode off with his daughter she is his hostage" the sheriff told him.

"Is this the Man" Ben showed the sheriff Grants picture.

"Yer! that's him"

"Sheriff pray we find her alive"

"You had better explain that statement" the sheriff asked.

"Did you hear about the Massacre of Senator Sevens and his family"

"Yes, that incident flew through Texas faster than a tornado"

"Well that happened just over a week ago, I was sent after them there was three of them, I caught up with them, I killed one, captured the second man, and wounded Grant but unfortunately I was hit in the shoulder this gave Grant the chance to escape as you can see I am still on his tail and I will stay there until I get him, now do you know a young couple who live in a cabin a day's ride south of here" Ben enquired.

"That would be the Mathews only see them once a week they are a nice couple" the sheriff stated.

"Were! We came across the man who had been shot for his horse Grants horse had lost a shoe, we came across the cabin, Grant had been there we found Mrs. Mathews after being raped and tortured she was just alive when we found her, but she had gone through hell and died on us" Ben explained.

"You keep saying us"

"Me and my partner Jane"

"Are you saying the girl Grant took as hostage is dead"

"No sheriff she may not be dead but I know this man Grant and his Mexican friend have whisky stolen from the cabin, the girl will be raped from experience the girl will be left unconscious or tied just dumped as they ride off "

"Damn I wish we could track in the dark"

"At dawn, I will be on his trail again, I don't want the lady to be hurt but it might slow him down enough for me to catch up to him, but just when I think I have caught up to him, something happens to slow me down" Ben said.

"OK I might see you in the morning Ben as the posse musters outside the office at that time"

"I might see you in the morning, but I doubt it by the time you get your posse together we will more than likely be on our way".

Leaving the sheriff Ben took care of the horses, on his way back to the hotel, needing some shells for his gun called into the gunsmiths arriving back at the hotel Jane waited for him.

"Let's go eat"

"By the serious look on your face something is wrong"

Jane and Ben sat in the restaurant having dinner after eating they sat drinking a cool beer each when sitting comfortable Jane enquired again.

"Ben what's wrong "

"Before we arrived in town Grant raided the general store shot the owner then took his daughter hostage"

"That poor girl" Jane said a tear in her eyes.

"Jane we must start early, before the sheriff's posse wipes out all the sign it will make it harder for me to track him"

"Let's finish dinner get to bed" Jane whispered.

"I like that idea" whispering back.

After dinner Ben and Jane happily held hands as they proceeded to their room together, the room Jane had previously booked on the way they talked about the fact that they must rise early to get after Grant in the room it did not take long getting to bed, they made love because of the early rise they merely satisfied their desire for each other before sleeping the night away.

Ben woke up well before dawn as intended it was still dark outside after a bit of kiss and cuddle, rising Ben washed and shaved and dressed, feeling two arms go around him turning the naked Jane came into his arms, Ben kissed her picked up his Stetson and left the room and smiled as her laughter could be heard behind him.

After saddling the horses, Ben tied them to the hitch rail outside the hotel going up to the room on entering found Jane dressed, packing their saddle bags, leaving the room they loaded the horses, walked over to the café which had just opened and had breakfast, Ben had timed things just right as they left the café a ribbon of light broke the horizon.

The sheriff had told Ben the night before the direction Grant had taken Ben and Jane climbed into the saddle, rode slowly out of town until it was light enough to see tracks, as Grant never stayed on the main trail, keeping his eyes open picking up the tracks of the two running horses was easy but Ben soon realized the Mexican knew some tricks which really tested his skills, keeping his wits about him caused him to persevere diligently to keep behind Grant and his partner, the Mexican actually was the one who made it a bit easier to track them because of his habit of chain smoking, the occasional discarded fag end helped Ben at first thought it might be a Mexican ploy. After a short time, Ben knew it was not a ploy the man is so addicted to the Mexican weed a strong tobacco this man could not help himself, so smoked almost all of the time.

Following the sign as it became clearer because of the soft ground, this therefore enabling them to go a little faster, suddenly the sign stopped it had disappeared, bringing the horses to a halt Ben dismounted so it was possible for him to get a better look at the ground, after standing thinking with his jaw in his hand it came to him what the Mexican had done. (this man is good) Ben said to himself as he started understanding what the man had done, they were around one hundred yards from the start of a sandy expanse like a (mini desert) by looking at it the distance across Ben thought it would be about two miles to the other side, getting out his glasses (binoculars) looking at the other side there was no movement, the Mexican had wrapped both his and Grants horses hoofs they leaving no tracks, to confuse Ben more they had dragged branches along behind them to mix up there sign.

"Jane stay here, the sheriff will be along in a moment, keep your rifle handy but remember the sheriff, I will leave the glasses with you, I am going to ride straight across, look for their sign when I find it I will wave, I want you to survey the far side until you see me waving" Ben informed her.

Checking the sand for prints, indents or fagg butts, as he found no sign, Ben knew they had not rode straight across but at an angle left or right, reaching the other side spinning a coin caused him to ride left along the bank which was lucky and saved him a lot of time, finding a cigarette butt, stopping, picking up the butt and smelt it, (yes, yes,)it was Mexican weed. Meanwhile the sheriff and a couple of men with him had met up with Jane.

"Howdy Marm" the sheriff greeted.

"The name is Jane sheriff"

"Where is Ben" the sheriff asked.

"Over the other side looking for sign" she told him, then picking up the glasses she scanned the other side.

On the other side Ben tied a shirt to his rifle barrel and started waving it took Jane about five or six minutes before she saw him.

"Let's ride sheriff" she mounted and started ride the sheriff followed.

On their arrival.

"Hi Jane darling, Howdy sheriff" Ben greeted them

"Sheriff you have a big posse I see" Ben observed.

"My deputy and a dozen men have gone down the Main trail".

"They did not go that way"

"How do you know that" the sheriff looked puzzled.

"I have been trailing Grant for almost a week I know this man, I can tell you there is no way Grant would use the main trail unless his victim is there " Ben explained.

"Well my deputy plus the men with him have the main trail covered, I'll just tag along with you if you don't mind" the sheriff said.

"OK then let's ride"

Leading the way, the rest followed, when checking the sign Ben explained each move to the sheriff who was impressed suddenly pulling his horse to a stop, dismounted and observed the sign closely.

"This way through the brush" Ben said.

"Hold it Ben the sign goes that way" the sheriff announced.

"Sheriff dismount and come here"

With the aid of a stick Ben showed him why the men had left the trail at this point

"Sheriff look close at the tracks yes you can see two sets but if you look closer you can see they are made by the same horse, this man I assume is the Mexican he has walked his horse forward a bit then walked the horse backwards therefore leaving two sets of prints".

"I'll be damned" the sheriff looked at the smug look on Jane's face.

"Now the only place around here to leave the trail is through this brush on the right".

Ben mounted then rode through the bushes after riding about two hundred yards, stopping Shad again waved the sheriff to come alongside him, pointed out the tracks belonging to Grant and his pal.

Following the sign, Ben moved of taking the lead and the sheriff did not query him again, after riding for about half an hour Ben suddenly kicked Shad and yelled

"Yeah" as the horse changed his pace from a walk to a gallop leaving the others behind Ben lifted his Winchester rifle to his shoulder and fired in one continues movement the nearest vulture fell to the ground the other birds flew away Ben left the saddle at a run before Shad stopped and ran to the still figure of the naked girl putting his hand on her chest and finding a small movement Ben sighed with relieve as Jane arrived she heard him call for the first aid kit.

"Right Ben" she called.

"She is alive sheriff but only just"

"Jane after I untie her could you put the blanket over her sheriff could you put a couple of drops of water on her lips and place a damp cloth on her forehead" Ben instructed.

"Is there any way we can help" Jack and Bert asked.

"Sure, could you get some wood together and make a fire fill a pot with water and put it on the fire thank you boys"

"What now Ben" the sheriff asked.

"We will see to the horses, Jane while we are gone check the young lady for me"

"Sure, Ben I understand"

"Sheriff we will stay a while at least until the girl regains consciousness, please could you take the girl back to town, Jane and I must keep after Grant we need to stop this animal"

"Is there any way I can help you".

"After you have taken the girl home could you go to the telegraph office send a wire to Texas ranger HQ let them know I'm still on Grants tail"

"Will do"

"How is she Jane" Ben enquired.

"Grant and his partner has raped her a lot like animals possibly all night, but she has not been brutalized like the last woman, apart from that she has scratched and small mouse bites, she is not seriously injured the only problem is how did it affect her mind, we won't find that out until she comes to" Jane reported.

"That's why we have to stay until she comes to"

"How do you mean Ben" the sheriff asked.

"When she comes to, if she sees a bunch of men here as she has been treated so bad, she could end up screaming in hysterics but with Jane here to talk to her and help her she will be OK" Ben said walked away. The sheriff left standing beside Jane.

"You know for a man so young Ben thinks of everything"

"Yes, he does, I love him "Jane stated softly.

Using half the water when it was warm to clean up the young ladies wounds, they boiled the remaining water and made coffee, Ben poured a cup and took it to Jane, they stayed with the girl who came round about two hours later, the young lady screamed Jane calmed her as she spoke to her, the girl cried uncontrollably for a while.

"Ben could you get my bedroll for me"

"Sure"

Taking her spare set of clothes she gave them to the girl held the blanket up so the young lady could put them on, Jane put her arm around the girl and took her for a short walk, after the walk the girl looked happy as she rode off with the sheriff, Jane waited until the others had disappeared started crying Ben put his arms around her as Jane let out her held up emotions.

"Ben, we must catch this man" she said through gritted teeth.

"Yes, Grant is evil"

"I did not think that one man could cause so much misery, we must get this man"

"Jane, we will have something to eat with our coffee, then we will get after him" Ben said in a low voice turned her head and kissed her.

It was now late afternoon, the sun did not set until nine in the evening, Ben started following sign again at about six in the evening on finding a camping space they stopped, Ben looked at Jane seeing a pair of sleepy eyes.

"We will camp for the night"

"Why are we camping so early" Jane asked.

"It's been a long day, so let's rest a while".

"Thank you, Ben, but know it's still light we can carry on for two more hours, so we are going to" she went to Ben and kissed him.

"Jane, you are tired"

"I'm great really Ben I am a little tired as you said it's been a long day, but we must do all we can to get this man" Jane told him.

"Jane I will make it up to you, this morning I left you with a rifle because I know you do not know about the hand gun well I thought I would get you a present I hope it is OK, I bought you a present and bought this instead of chocolates hope you like it"

Jane's eyes opened the sleep left them as she looked at the rolled-up belt and holster with a gun in it.

"I am giving this so you can protect yourself, as we go along, I will teach you how to use it"

"Oh! Ben it's wonderful, I love you and I prefer this (instead of chocolates) thank you" she omitted excitedly. "I'm happy you like it"

"Like it! I love it much better than chocolates, show me how to wear it please, please" she said excitedly.

"Put the belt around your body fasten the belt buckle at the third hole put the gun in the holster let it hang down your right leg, OK stand up straight let your arm hang loosely by your side, Ben stood back, now take the belt up another hole, put the loop on the hammer, now fasten the thong around your leg tie it with a bow for easy release" Ben instructed.

"Thank you, Ben,"

"Now Jane is that comfortable"

"It is comfortable but a bit heavy on my right leg" Jane replied.

"That is OK you will get used to that in time, the belt is fastened in the fourth hole, every time you put the belt on you must put it on in exactly the way it is now"

"OK Ben I'll do that" Jane assured him.

"Jane this is important you must wear the belt at all times even if you decide to walk around naked all day you wear it, I want you to put the belt on automatically, subconsciously until it becomes second nature, if you decide to have a bath take the belt of after you dry yourself put it straight back on do you understand" Ben asked.

"Do I have to wear it when we make love" she smiled a cheeky look on her face.

"Don't worry about that I will soon have it off" he replied they both laughed out loud.

They were both happy and automatically came into together and kissed passionately, knowing the situation they mounted and rode on.

"Jane, I am teaching you the easiest and best way to draw"

"You mean there are other ways to draw" Jane asked.

"Well, yes of course there is four main ways to draw but, in each case, you would need a different holster, there is the straight draw, cavalry twist, cross draw and swivel holster".

"If you say the straight draw is the best way of drawing a gun I will go along with your choice, because knowing you as I now do I will take your word for it, as I bet you have tried the other ways to find out what is best" Jane looked at him and smiled.

"You are getting to know me to well" he said in mock horror.

Jane stuck her tongue out at him.

"Now what" she asked.

"The straight draw goes' like this, the gun butt is level with your hand so you can draw easier you just grab and lift the gun, the routine is to, flip the thong of the hammer, grab the butt, draw the gun pulling back the hammer as you do, line the gun squeeze the trigger, it sounds easy but to get it correct you need practice" Ben explained.

"When will you teach me that"

"I'll show you when we next stop" Ben declared.

The next couple of hours went by smoothly no real incidents they followed the same sign the tracks, cigarette ends, the only difference for the last few miles, Ben had noticed by the sign of the tracks left by his quarry indicated they have slowed down the two men were not hurrying maybe there is the chance they are getting complacent.

With this in mind it could be possible to catch up to Grant sooner Ben told Jane if they could carry on at the speed they were travelling at it is probably a chance of catching up to the men in two days, Ben looked at the sky knew it was time to camp and a further mile on they came across the perfect spot.

"We will camp here, let's get set up while the water boils for coffee, we will see how you draw and handle your gun" Ben smiled when observing Jane's face loose the tiredness, coming alive.

"Yes, let's get at it" she answered eagerly.

As the pair of them were getting used to making camp between them the task was completed in a short time, before starting with the gun Ben once more went through his instructions again.

"Jane stand here on this spot facing the horses, put your feet slightly apart to give you balance, let your hand hang down by your side, take the thong of the hammer, (now you are in the position to draw and shoot) now follow my instructions slowly, grip the gun butt do not draw, so far that is OK except you have put your finger straight on the trigger don't, lay your finger along the side of the barrel this prevents you from shooting yourself, now slowly raise the gun, OK stop right there, you have just cleared leather start to line the gun at the same time with your thumb pull back the hammer at the same time slide your finger onto the trigger, straighten your arm pull the trigger. (good now put the gun in the holster, now try it again but by yourself)"

Jane gave it a go.

"You are trying too hard, take it easy slowly and smoothly, speed will come later" Ben advised her.

For the next hour Jane practiced and practiced, she only stopped when Ben told her to stop.

"The last three draws were good now come here" walked across to a large tree about twenty feet away.

"This tree trunk is thick enough to be a human trunk, (putting a line on the trunk) this is the approximately height of a man, your gun is empty so the hammer is on a empty chamber now give me your gun, I am putting one live round in the next cylinder, I want you to draw your pistol, line your gun on the tree pull the trigger" Ben instructed the observed, after her shot.

"Oh! I missed"

"You missed because you jerked on the trigger, now try again this time squeeze the trigger slowly, take your time, do not jerk"

Jane did as Ben instructed. After repeating his instruction about four times she squeezed the trigger the bullet grazed the tree trunk, Jane jumped and down excitedly.

"I hit it, I hit it" she yelled threw her arms around Ben and kissed him.

"Jane, you can have two more shots then it will be time to eat, after eating I will show you the next step in your training the important part of owning a gun, I will show you"

They walked back to the camp to eat arm in arm, you could tell by the excited look on her face that Jane had enjoyed herself.

"Thank you, Ben, for my present, I love it, I am also very happy to have you to show me how to use it, now I need lots of practice.

"We will do that as we go along, I don't want you to draw while riding, but if you get the routine of in your head it will help you when you next practice" Ben explained.

After eating, Ben sat down with Jane getting her pistol took it apart, explaining his actions also telling about each bit of the gun, taking a small bag from his saddle bags this contained a small container of light oil, a clean cloth plus an assortment of small brushes Ben showed Jane how to clean the gun, put a few drops of oil on the holster so the gun can be drawn more easerly.

"OK Jane stand up and put on the belt, now try drawing your gun tell me does It feel better"

"Yes, I can definitely feel the difference the draw is smoother, Ben it feels great, Thank you Ben"

"Come with me Jane" she followed Ben. Stopping by the side of the stream, removing his gunbelt told Jane to remove hers.

"Right Jane last one in is a ninny" started taking his clothes of, Jane smiled as she started to quickly undress, both of them held hands and jumped into the water together.

After a very warm day plus pushing themselves to travel as far as they could the beautiful warm water was intoxicating as the water washed over their bodies it made them feel alive plus it took the tiredness from their bodies. The two of them were happy they played games splashing each other, ducking each other, Jane squealed with delight as Ben tossed her in the air to come down with a splash.

Swimming under water Ben surfaced right in front of Jane their lips immediately coming together his hand brushed the lips of her crotch, Jane put her arm around Bens waist pulling her body into Ben, she whispered in his ear (Oh Ben) giggled as Ben kissed her lips, neck, throat, shoulder and tits flicking the nipples caused Jane to moan obviously enjoying every moment as her breasts swelled, nipple becoming prouder, her breathing became heavier and she sighed with a sign of excitement as the fingers probed into her body.

Jane put her hand around the rampant erection her legs opened inviting the penis to probe deeply into her private entrance to her body she gasped, with the probing and thrusting plus speeding up made the actions cause the water to look like it was boiling, a sigh from both their lips as they satisfied there lust.

"Jane" Ben whispered in a low voice, "It will be dark in a few minutes let's get to bed and do it again"

"Yes" she replied in a husky voice.

Picking up their clothes and gunbelts holding hands they returned to camp, extinguishing the fire the only light left came from the moon as they lay in together in the one sleeping bag their arms around each other as they kissed passionately, kissing her neck and shoulders his hand slowly moved down her back from the base of her neck to the cheeks of her arse, Jane sighed and giggled, the kissing continued as his hand zipped up her back, she called out sharply her body pushing into Ben.

Once again his fingers teased her back again bringing sounds as she sighed and giggled, grabbing the cheeks of her arse again pulling her into him the sounds from her lips changed to an (Ohhhhh!) as she felt the growing erection, kissing her lips, neck, throat and shoulders as his hand transferred to her tits. The tits swelled the nipples became prouder, sounds of enjoyment omitted from her mouth, (Ohh! Arr! Ohhhh!) as his right hand felt her right breast his thumb flicked the nipple his mouth kissed her left breast his vibrating tongue caused sweet sensations when causing the nipple to vibrate also, (Ahhrrr! Ohhh! Ohhh!) alternating between her tits (Ohhh! Yes, Ben more, more) she whispered in a deep husky voice.

Jane sucked in her breath as she felt the hand moving slowly down her body starting from the valley between her breasts going over her pushed out chest round her belly button over her smooth tummy to stroke the lips of her crotch, his mouth and tongue played magic on her sensitive breasts, the finger rubbing lips of the crotch which drove her to the next level of arousal she gasped and sighed making more noises of love (Ohhhhhhh! Ahrrr! Arrrr!) she gasped louder as the finger invaded her private space.

"You are beautiful my darling" Ben whispered.

The probing finger drove Jane wild as it moved around her inner sanctum brushing her clitoris, raising her to another state of excitement, grabbing his erection which throbbed with anticipation exploring fingers rubbing her clitoris caused Jane to lift her arse of the bedroll as if wanting more (Arrrrrr!as Yes, Yes) Jane cried.

The juices began to flow Jane being fully aroused cried (Now, Now, Ben, Now) her body tensed in anticipation, gasped as the throbbing rampant erection push between the wet lips, penetrating deeply into her body thrusting in and out slowly at first building up the speed and penetration causing them both to leave the present world, as they entered a different world, as the world around them disappeared into a world of their own, crying with pleasure as Ben's seed entered her waiting body, the fulfilment of the climax gave them an organism, Jane felt as if her body had been taken lovingly apart and lovingly put back together again, the two sweat covered bodies slowly relaxed Ben kissed her.

"That was fantastic, thank you" Ben whispered breathlessly.

"Are you sure you only made love for the first time a week ago.

"Yes, but I had a good teacher" a big smile on his face.

"I must admit you are the only pupil I have had, and I couldn't be more pleased with the outcome".

"I am teaching you how to use a gun and I could not be happier with the progress you have made, it's only right I should show you my progress also I'm looking forward to the next lesson"

"That sounds wonderful" she laughed out loud.

Taking Jane into his arms their lips met in a long lingering passionate kiss.

"Darling I am sorry I have to be the one to spoil things, we must sleep as in the morning we may need to go faster to catch Grant before the animal kills again.

"I understand Ben but we do make a good team, you haven't spoilt anything, the time we have just spent together, has made up for everything, I know we have to move, but you must promise me you will make love to me again like you just have" she smiled.

"I promise", they kissed.

With all the excitement they had both found it hard to get to sleep but the pair of lovers finally went over, Ben as usual woke up in his usual way.

Ben stood up his naked body taking in the warmth of the morning sun looking at the naked Jane started arousal, bending down, taking Jane into his arms their lips came together.

"That was lovely" she whispered then screamed as Ben picked her up then ran and jumped into the cool water, Jane surfaced spluttering an angry look on her face as she dived to grab him but that soon changed as an arm went round her waist drew her to him lips meeting and the free hand going between her legs, reaching down she felt the erected penis,

"Oh Ben" they made love.

Collecting a bar of soap from his saddle bag Ben washed Jane's back, really, they washed each other Jane saw Ben's shoulder.

"The wound has almost completely gone you will be left with a scar"

"Thanks Jane you are great, but we will have to get a move on, or Grant will make more distance".

"Ha! Ha! Ha! You cannot blame me this time, Ben it was a nice surprise I loved it" she replied a large smile covered her face.

"Come on let's ride"

Ben knew they were leaving later than anticipated, but smiled known it was his fault because it was impossible to ignore the sight of Jane lying naked, but Ben had the biggest surprise when dismounting and looked at the remains of a fire, then looked up a smile on his face.

"What are you happy about Ben"

"Grant and his pal is only a couple of hours ahead"

"How" Jane enquired.

"I don't know what held them up, but these coals are still hot"

Riding casually along side by side talking, Ben now knew if they keep on going it is possible the job could be completed today.

All of a sudden Ben moved grabbing his rifle from the scabbard, Jane was on Ben's left, putting his arm around her waist he dived to the right taking Jane out of the saddle as they landed with a jar on the trail, the sound of a bullet passed over their heads, picking up the dazed Jane Ben ran into a rock formation nearby.

"Keep your head down Jane"

"Ben"

"Shh! Jane"

Slowly Ben lifted his head over the rock his rifle at the ready, looking at a cluster of rocks where he saw the tell-tale sign from the suns reflection on the chamber of a rifle, after a brief look Ben was certain by noise and shadows there is two men out there, lining his rifle taking a deep breath and holding it for a few seconds, he squeezed the trigger, the bullet ricochet of the rocks there was a yelp and movement of two sets of feet.

"Jane, I am sorry please forgive me" Ben said.

"Sorry for what"

"I have been concentrating so much on the job of getting Grant I forgot about the bounty on your head, if these men had caught up with us last night while we swam and made love, we would be dead"

"You mean these men were after me" Jane exclaimed.

"Yes! this is not the MO (Method of) of Grant, the only other problem we have is the people paid to kill you, Grant is in front of us we are following his tracks these people have followed us" Ben explained.

"How many are there"

"I make it out to be two"

"What do we do next" Jane asked, lifting her pistol from the holster she loaded it.

"Let's put ourselves in their position, if they could take you alive they would be happy, but I think they have been told to prove you are dead.

As there are two of us and they knew it, we now know there are two of them, I guess one of them would stay behind the rocks to keep our heads down while the second man would sneak around to get a shot at you"

Looking at their position, trying to see which way they would do it.

"If I was the man I would come in on the left" Jane said

A smile came to Ben's face, (she is starting to think just like) me Ben thought

"So, would I

"I take it we will play their game".

"Yes, I think that would be the best idea, because we must try to get them both, Jane you cannot draw and shoot, so you must be ready for them, get behind this rock now sit on that smaller rock with your back against the large smooth boulder behind you, bring your knee's up, rest your arms on them, now hold your pistol in both hands and look along the barrel, Jane anyone comes into your sights shoot him do not pause remember they are here to kill you they no your name so if I get back I Will call you Betty, have you got that"

"Yes" she replied.

"OK get behind the rock"

Jane did what Ben told her, Ben watched until she had climbed into the desired position, Ben left Jane using as much cover as possible moving from one piece of cover to another heading in the direction of the suspected cluster of rocked where the shot had come from when they were shot at, as Ben arrived at the base of the rock formation, the sound of a double bark of Jane's colt could be heard echoing in the clear air, Ben jumped into view, (rifle ready) pointing at the position where the gunman should have been to his surprise there was no one there.

It took a split second to realize ,that he had made a mistake, Ben turned and started rushing back towards the last position where Jane was, half way back once again there came the sound of two shots, by the sound of them they came from two different guns also there was two yells one male one female, looking in the direction of the sounds, Ben saw a man's head come into view his rifle came up to his shoulder, taking a snap shot there was a spray of red where the head had been indicating his snap shot had hit the target, Ben raced to Jane's side she was still sitting in the same position only her head was down, her gun lay on the floor in front of her and her shirt was covered in blood, putting his hand on her chest , sighed her heart was beating, quickly checking the two assassins they were both dead.

The first assassin had been hit twice by Jane's gun the first bullet had hit the man in the chest this bullet could have killed him as it look like Jane's accuracy was spot on the bullet went through the heart, her second shot definatly finished the job this bullet hit the man in the face just below his eye which caused his eye ball to drop out as the bullet had passed behind the eye up through the brain, blew his hat off as it burst though the head scattering blood and brains all over the place obviously his head looked a mess.

The second man was also dead from Ben's gun, It looks like Jane and the second assassin had spotted each other at the same time and both shot instinctively hitting each other, Jane's bullet had hit the man in the stomach the pain of being hit in the stomach caused him to cry out then jump back and raise his head, the heavy bullet from Ben's rifle hit him above the ear taking half his head off.

Holstering his rifle he quickly moved to Jane's side, ripping open her shirt he saw the bullet had entered above her left breast just missing the heart, taking her shirt of and rolling her over, looking at her back there was no exit wound working out where the assassin stood told him the trajectory of the bullet and feeling Jane's back where the bullet should have come out there was a telltale bump on her back that told him were the bullet had stopped just under the skin. Making sure Jane was as comfortable as possible rolling his spare shirt, placing it under her head turning her head so it could be possible to see her face, then building a fire added a pot of water on it, getting a stone (sharpening stone) from his saddle bag,s until the water boiled Ben honed (sharpened) his bowie type knife, Ben worked as fast as possible because if the bullet was removed while she was unconscious it would cause her less stress, putting the blade of the knife into the boiling water for a moment, with the now sterilized knife Ben cut two neat cuts crossing each other and squeezed the bullet out cleaned the wounds after that using pads out of clothing completing the job by using Jane's brassiere straps to hold the pads in place.

At the base of the rocks there was a carpet of green grass where Ben decided to make camp, spreading out Jane's bedroll Ben laid her body gently on the bedroll tucking her in making her comfortable, he then made up the remainder of the camp i.e. :- unsaddled the horses and let them roam, built a fire, made a pot of coffee, putting his bedroll next to Jane's so he can keep an eye on her continuously, the only other job that had to be done was to bury the two assassins. Ben managed to complete all the tasks a short time before Jane moaned, Ben put a couple of drops of water on her lips and smiled as she licked her lips, her eyes flickered after giving Ben a weak smile she closed her eyes and fell asleep, when the fever started Ben watched over her putting damp clothes on her forehead and nursed her all night Ben killed a prairie chicken and made a weak chicken broth, during the night Jane opened her eyes and the fever broke feeding her a little of the weak broth giving her a few drops of water she was weak so fell asleep again.

The next morning Ben broke camp, loaded the horses, then cutting down two twelve foot saplings and a few six foot branches to build a trellis and attach it to Jane's horse, after laying Jane and her bedroll on the trellis Ben mounted rode out slowly proceeding for around about an hour Ben came across a sign saying (Huntersburg) 2 miles population 288.

HUNTERBURG'S LAW

Ben reached the town of HUNTERBURG around 1300 that afternoon as it was lunch time there was quite a few people on the street going down the main street the sign on a shingle hung outside the premises advertising the doctors, next to the sheriff's office an Ideal place to be the sheriff and the doctor came out and helped Ben to carry Jane into the doctors.

The doctor checked the wounds, cleaned them put salve on them, redressed them.

"You did a good job there ranger" doc said spotting his badge.

"Thank you, doc,"

"I'll look after her for you" Doc said.

"Good I'll be back to see her later" Ben told the doc.

"What happened" the sheriff asked.

"Let's go to your office and I will explain"

"OK"

For the next hour Ben explained to the sheriff over a cup of coffee, specially about Grant, the sheriff gave Ben some good news.

"The two men you have been tracking are in town, they have taken a room for five days at the hotel"

"That is good news" Ben said enthusiastically.

"I would say it gives you the chance to have a good night's sleep plus it gives you some breathing space" "Yes, you are right thanks" Ben said. "That's OK"

After leaving the sheriff's office, first the horses had to be looked after, next he booked a room at the hotel, then after freshening up Ben proceeded to the dining room, the meal was great and substantial, while sitting at the table an elderly lady walking by staggered against the table she on purposely dropped a piece of paper into his lap, as this was unusual Ben decided to take the note back to his room where it was possible to read it in safety.

PLEASE MEET ME IN AN HOUR AT THE BED AND BREAKFAST NORTH END OF TOWN ON THE HIGH STREET.

Sitting on the edge of the bed Ben did his best to analyze the situation, it was a strange set of circumstances when people, who do not know you drops messages into people's lap, Ben found it intriguing therefore decided to follow this request before seeing how Jane is keeping.

Folding the note he then slipped it into his trouser pocket under his holster and gun, checking the time Ben saw there was time for him to send a telegram to HQ letting them know of his progress, as luck would have it the telegraph office was on the High street, after sending of his report to Ranger HQ while browsing the shops on the main street. Ben felt as if someone is watching him, it was just a feeling but it was not possible for him to shake it, stepping casually into the gunsmiths who displayed in the window a new brass plated Winchester rifle, standing by the window , Ben removed the weapon from its stand and casually looked as if his attention was on the gun in his hand but his eyes surveyed the street, there was quite a few people around but the man following him stood out like a sore thumb.

The man was not very good at concealing himself, this man stood outside the millinery store pretending to look in the window but there is very few men who would look at lady's underwear, even an amateur could see the man's eyes were not on the shop. Ben knew from experience this is the man who is following him.

The lady who dropped the note on his lap would not like it if her position was given away Ben thought, he must be certain this man is following him and get rid of him, proceeding a short way up the street stopping outside the café which had a angled window which made it possible to see in its reflection what was behind him, the man stopped when Ben stopped, carrying out this routine a couple of times convinced him about the man.

Now he was certain this man was following him, it was imperative to lose him, at the next break in the buildings turning right he hurried along the alley, turned right again, once more turning right brought him back to the high street coming out behind the man in question, the man stood undecided what to do after a moment the man turned down the alley looking up and down the street Ben saw nothing unusual so quickly walked across the high street and down the alley opposite then turned right, walking along the rear of the buildings until the lady from the dining room waved from the rear of a building, looking quickly around making sure no one followed Ben slipped into the back door of the house going to the window closed the blind.

"Come this way mister" the lady instructed.

Walking through into the next room, there were three more people sitting there one an elderly man looked at Ben sizing him up.

"Are you a lawman, we spotted you walking into town with the injured lady" the old man enquired.

"Yes, I am a Texas Ranger" Ben admitted showing his badge.

"Oh! Good, fantastic" the old lady said excitedly.

"We have been unable to get a message out of town, we have asked you here to warn you, your young lady and maybe you could die tonight if you do not take care" the old man stated.

"Since you have me here, with your last statement you have my attention so someone had better explain"

"Alright you are a ranger and are known to be good lawmen, we need to have someone we can trust, we hope you will be able to help us, to start with there is something you must understand, the sheriff his deputies the telegraph staff are all crooked, the sheriff allows lawbreakers to remain in the town for a fee, anyone who enters town who could be a problem to them disappears, every message sent or received are taken to the sheriff first, at this time you see just four of us here we used to be six but two of our group stood up to the sheriff and have mysteriously died, if some honest people come to town with money they somehow die and the money disappears we have tried to get word out about what goes on in this town but mail is searched, messages go to the sheriff" the man concluded.

"Are you people the only ones trying to do this" Ben asked

"As far as we know, we don't know who to trust, a word to the wrong person could mean our death" the lady but in.

"Where does the doctor stand"

"We don't know" came the answer.

"Mind I have never known anyone to be arrested at the doctor's office, in fact as I remember only one person that has

been to the doctors was arrested, was after they left the doctors"
the old man said.

"That is interesting, I must look into the doctor"

"If his goals are the same as ours, we would like to know"

"I will see, how many deputies does the sheriff have"

"Three, two kids who have not been long out of school and a
man who would kill you for a dollar, the main problem is all the
bums and hangers on, the sheriff buy's all the bums a drink when
meeting them he gets +them to keep their eyes open and report
anything of interest to him" the old man told him.

"How many hardened criminals are there under the sheriff's
protection at this time, I do know of two at the moment" Ben
asked.

"From what I can see, most of them are miner criminals the
worst any of them have done has robbed banks so has money,
I think a lot of them are first time offenders who have nowhere
else to run"

"So, there is only six men to worry about"

"There are quite a few bums also a certain saloon keeper who
goes along with the sheriff" the lady said.

"Not Sam" the younger man said.

"Sam who" Ben asked.

"The owner of the Gold Nugget Saloon" the old man said.

"I am not worried about bums, if you get rid of the leaders,
the sheriff, the deputies, you will find the criminals will make a
departure from the town." Ben told them.

"I think you could be right"

"I know I'm right from experience, your next problem will be
to hire a new sheriff"

"What now" the lady asked.

"Well you have given me a lot to think about, it all depends on the doctor" Ben stated.

"The doctor" they all said together.

"Yes" Ben said and smiled as they looked puzzled.

"What now" the lady said.

"I lost a shadow to get here, now I need to get out of here without being spotted, Marm I see out back you have a blue dress on the line, please go out there, look around if it is clear take the dress of the line OK" Ben asked.

"I understand" she said.

Ben managed to get away undetected by going through the back streets and made his way to the livery stable where his job was to look after the horses in particular (Shad) who is a one-man horse, after giving them food and water then picking up the brushes he started to briskly brush shad's black glossy coat, when the man who tailed him finally found him there was a look of relief on his face.

Leaving the two contented horses, while walking to the doctors with his badge on his vest, Ben stopped a few times hoping someone had the desire to talk of the present situation. On his arrival at the doctors the doctor grabbed his arm.

"Your lady has a price on her head get her out of here" the doctor whispered.

"Thank you".

Ben now knew that the doctor could be trusted, looking at the doctor and Jane and winked, put his finger up to his lips, took out a note pad and wrote a message.

The sheriff and his deputies are crooked

Then Ben said.

"Oh, doctor I'm sorry to hear Jane has an infection in her shoulder, how long do you think she will be ready to travel" showing another note.

Two to three days at least.

"I would say about two to three days at least" the doctor said.

We are being listened to

Ben's note said as his finger pointed to the open window, the doctor and Jane nodded, Jane took the pad from Ben's hand.

What are you up to

Jane looked at him as she handed him the note book a big smile on her face.

I have heard the sheriff does not bother the doctor's patients, so this is the best place for you, or the sheriff will kill you for the bounty.

The doctor nodded

This town needs help

The doctor nodded again.

"Jane, I cannot arrest Grant and his sidekick to take back and have a sick woman on my hands, so I will have to give it a day or two until your fit to travel" Ben said,

"I understand I do feel a little faint and feel warm I think I have a temperature" Jane said as she caught on.

"It won't do us any harm to have a rest before we move on, in fact it would be good for both of us" Ben told her.

"Would you like a cup of coffee mister" the doc asked.

"That would be great doc, the name is Ben not mister"

The doctor left the room, Ben walked over to the bed and kissed Jane in a low voice explained to her.

"This town has a lot of trouble, crooked law, hideaway for criminal's sensors of mail and the telegraph system, there are spies all over, the doc does not like it either, Jane watch what you say they listen at windows, if you leave the doctors you will be dead darling because of the bounty on your head" Ben explained.

"Thanks Ben"

"Jane, it is great to see you, now you're going to have to get better or I will not be able to keep my promise" she hit him, Ben kissed her, they both kissed cuddled and laughed.

The doctor returned with the coffee, they sat together and had a whispered conversation as Ben explained what their talk had been about.

"So, Jane is in more danger if she leaves here, doctor would you be in favour of a change of lawmen and the eviction of criminals"

"Yes"

"Good"

"Jane I'm going now but I will be back later" kissed her then left.

Ben had to think about how to get rid of the lawmen, the day before Ben had seen one of the young deputies with a girl and the other young deputy who was very jealous, what would happen if he made a move on her himself, to do that Ben had to get the two young men looking at him chatting up the lovely young blonde they were interested in, looking around to his surprise, this could be the moment, the two deputies sat outside the sheriff's office, a little way up the street you could see the young blonde they were looking at walked towards him, Ben touched his Stetson.

"Hello miss could you tell me where Mrs. Wilson's boarding house could be found" Ben asked.

"Oh! Yes, that is up the street"

"Are you going that way" Ben asked.

"Yes, I'm going past there"

"Could I walk with you then you could point it out to me" Ben said.

"Yes of course"

"Thank you" Ben said.

Ben walked alongside the street close to the the young lady, as they walked together Ben joked and laughed out loud, when touching the girls arm she did not complain she nodded in the direction of the boarding house, taking of his Stetson with a flourish kissed her hand.

"Thank you miss" laughs out loud.

Turning down the alley, the lady carried on up the street, contact has been made so will carry on later again when the two boys could see them together hoping the boys will get jealous causing them to fight and hopefully putting them out of the picture.

As the sheriff does not know what Ben knows, Ben thought it was best to keep in with the sheriff, since the sheriff knows about him, so Ben decided that a occasionally call into the sheriff's office would dispel any reasons for the sheriff to be suspicious, Ben strolled down to the sheriff's office to have a chat with the sheriff.

"Howdy sheriff" Ben said cheerfully walking into the office.

"Hi" the sheriff grunted.

"How's things sheriff"

"How can I help you" the sheriff asked.

"Sorry sheriff you have it all wrong, I thought I might be able to help you, my lady friend has caught an infection in her wound and doc said it will be a couple of days before she can travel, being a lawman, I thought it would be a good idea to offer you my services, I am of course not intending to do your job, but you might have something you wish me to look into" Ben explained.

"Well I" the sheriff began angrily, pulled himself together, calmed down "Thank you for your offer, but I do not require any help at this time" the sheriff answered.

"OK sheriff I'll go see to my horse, have a meal, visit the patient at the doctors, maybe a couple of beers then have an early night, if you do need my help let me know"

"Why not leave your horse to the holster at the stable" the deputy enquired.

"Shad is a one-man horse and does not like strangers, so I look after him myself, the stable hand has been told not to touch him, I don't want anyone to get hurt".

"I bet I could handle him" the deputy said.

"Mister don't even try, anyone who touches him will be a horse thief and horse stealing is a hanging offence, there is no reason for anyone to touch him anyhow" Ben explained.

As the conversation about another man's horse is not normal Ben made a mental note, of the deputies' comments, Ben decided to make some discrete enquires.

Ben left the sheriff's office deep in thought, there is a few things to consider, carrying on to the livery stable, shad was happy to see Ben so greeted him.

After feeding Shad, giving him a bag of oats, poured fresh water into the trough, all the time talking to him and patting him, walked over to the livery stable hand.

"Howdy I'm Ben how are you"

"I'm well thank you, my name is will, you have a good horse there" the holster said.

"Will don't go near him, Shad is a one-man horse and does not like strangers" Ben told him.

"Yes, I know the boss told me"

"Anyone who tries to take Shad will have his hands full, they will be in trouble" Ben explained.

"We have had a couple of good horses stolen before" Will said.

"That's interesting, who's horse were they"

"One of them belonged to the boss of the haulage company it was a beauty"

"Well Shad will be OK"

"Yes, your horse will be alright" will said.

"Well I must go now, but I will be in to check on him in the morning see you Will".

Stopping of at the hotel for a moment, Ben proceeded to the doctor's house, the doctor's wife let him in as doc was checking Jane.

"Would you like a coffee ranger" the doc's wife asked.

"Yes, thank you, the name is Ben" walking over to Jane and the doctor.

"Put this under your pillow" handing Jane her colt.

"Oh! Thank you, I don't think I will need it, but It does make me feel a lot more secure"

"She won't need that" doc said.

"Doc we know she shouldn't need a weapon, but I know with it, she will feel more secure, doc I have thought about Jane, it came to me the sheriff would not have to break in here to get at Jane, If the information was passed to the people who want her dead they will send someone to do the job, a killer with no Qualms" Ben told the doc.

"I never thought of that" Jane omitted.

"I'll keep my gun ready in case" the doc told him.

At that time, the doctor's wife arrived with the coffee's, they sat down with their coffee's close together, so they could talk in a low voice.

"Didn't I see you earlier today with that lovely blonde girl Sally Hill" the doctor's wife said.

"Sure"

"What have you been up to" Jane asked.

"Now you're not jealous are you"

"Me no, why should I" Jane said a little hurriedly then said, "But knowing you, you're up to something, you are crafty and have a reason for everything"

"Jane don't worry, I will tell you later" indicating the open window.

They nodded as they understood, Ben scribbled a note.

THE GIRL IS PART OF A PLAN, WILL TELL YOU ABOUT IT LATER.

Ben passed the note around, so everyone could read it, after talking for about an hour, the doctor and his wife left to go to the kitchen, which left them together for a short while, giving them a little time to kiss and cuddle.

Even though the sky looked light the sun had sank behind the horizon indicating it was not long before it gets dark, walking towards the hotel Ben spotted the sign saying (Paula's Place), feeling a little hungry, the café inside was nice and clean with red and white checked table clothes on each table, taking a seat at the table by the wall his back against the wall so it was possible to survey the whole café a young lady came over to Ben.

"What would you like sir" the waitress asked.

"Miss, I haven't eaten all day could I have, (a large rump steak medium to well done, roast potatoes, beans and gravy and a mug of coffee) please thank you" Ben ordered.

"It will be ready around ten minutes sir"

"Thanks" Ben replied.

On the table lay a copy of the local rag, the editor obviously did not like the sheriff, as the headline proved; –

THE SHERIFF'S PAL CRIMINAL MURDERER.

This headline was prominent and caught his eye, and the story was good, the one thing it did do was to help the departure of the sheriff after reading the story the sheriff new his time was almost up, but a smaller story at the bottom of the page caught his eye, it was of more interest to Ben, the story was about the death of the wife of a member of the town council reading the gory details of the way she died according to the paper sounded just like how Grant would attack a woman, of course there was no way this could be proved it was his dirty work, at this time Bens meal arrived on a large plate with so much on, it almost overflowed.

Ben tucked into the perfectly cooked meal the steak had been cooked exactly right, the coffee was strong and black which washed down the wonderful meal, after eating his own cooking for the past week this meal was fantastic.

When nearing the end of his meal three young men entered the café, they took the table across the room from him, the three young men were boisterous and looked like they were having a good time but as usual with young men they sometimes get out of hand and often take things too far, the young Waitrose who had served him went to the table to serve the young men, one of the men made some rude remarks which everyone ignored, nothing would of happened if one of the young men had not grabbed the Waitrose around the waist and pulled her to him, Ben was about to intervene when an elderly man stood up walked towards the three men.

"Leave that young lady alone you criminals" he told the man holding the young lady.

"Push of you old bugger" the man returned.

The young man holding the Waitrose grabbed the young ladies breast squeezing it very hard causing her to scream the old man moved towards them to pull the girl away from them, one of the young men tripped the old man pulled a gun and pointed it at the old man, a spurt of flame and the loud noise sounded as they were in a confined space the shot came from Ben's gun, the young man screamed dropped his gun as a bullet ripped through his arm.

"You let that girl go now, or my next bullet goes' through your head" Ben told the man who pointed his gun at the old man.

The man holding the girl let her go she helped the old man to his feet looking a bit shaken but otherwise OK.

"Now the question is what do I do with you three, you grabbed that young lady, so you could be accused of attacking her, if I shoot you in defense of the lady it would be alright, you on the other hand was going to kill a defenseless old man so I could shoot you for attempted murder, now you as his interest focused on the third man.

"I didn't do anything, you have nothing on me" the young man said

"You are just as bad as your cronies, you saw them attack a young lady and an old man, you laughed and did nothing to stop these two, so you are an accessory to the fact to these crimes, well I suppose I could shoot you also, Mmmmm it's a tricky problem".

Looking at the young men, the look on their faces gave them away their faces changed from bravado to a sickly pallor as they understood that men had killed to protect women, the young men became hesitant and uncertain.

"Now let's see, do you do this everywhere you go, has your Mam and Dad taught you to act this way, you act like animals" Ben explained.

The young men were sullen with bowed heads shuffling their feet one of them mumbled.

"Stop muttering talk speak up"

"I'm sorry mister my folks were good people I also know my mother would be appalled at my actions" the first young man admitted.

The other two young men followed the first young man.

"As you are young, I am not going to shoot you as I always think a man should have a second chance, if you do anything like this again and I am there I promise I will shoot you understand" Ben told them.

They turned to the door to leave, when the first young man turned around, took a couple of steps to the waitress and old man with his hat in hand.

"I am sorry" the girl nodded the old man grunted.

The three young men left the café quietly.

"Now miss could I have my coffee and the bill thank you"

The waitress put the coffee in front of him an admiring look in her eyes as she moved of a middle-aged woman approached the table.

"I am Paula, this is my place, there is no bill for you now or any other time you frequent my café your meals are on the house"

"Thank you that's good of you"

"No thank you, I like the way you handled the situation and helped my daughter"

"Right Marm"

"The name is Paula"

"Mine is Ben"

"Thanks again Ben" Paula said then moved off.

Ben left the café with a smile on his face, seeing the look on Paula's and the old man's faces Ben could see they did not like the present situation, as a lot other do not like the present situation, in fact most of the decent people in town are against what is happening to their town.

After having a great meal, his thirst could only be satisfied by a cool beer so made his way to, The Gold Nugget Saloon, pushing through the batwings Ben immediately spotted Grant and the Mexican sat at a table in the far corner of the room, it was the first time the Mexican had been in a position to be seen and assessed, the Mexican had a gaunt face with a large black straggly moustache, wearing an orange shirt, a fancy vest, the gun was high on a leather belt butt forward on his left hand side, the gun could only be drawn by reaching across his body which makes it easier to draw and shoot while sitting down, (the cross draw) the man looked sneaky not a man to be trusted.

Finding a place at the end of the bar a large man with dark hair and streaks of grey over the temples approached from behind the bar.

"Beer please barman"

"Sure" came the reply.

"Quiet night"

"Yeh! Still two days to payday, we won't get any ranch hands in tonight"

"I'm Ben will be here for a couple of days"

"Hi! I'm Sam I own this joint"

"Happy to meet you" Ben said.

Spending an hour or so, at the bar talking to Sam over a quiet glass of ale, just as Ben thought of going up to bed it happened, a man of around forty years old burst through the batwings approached the table where Grant and his Mexican friend sat, the man faced the Mexican.

"You filthy pig stay away from my daughter, she told me what you said and what you done, stay away from her and keep your dirty hands to yourself" the man ordered.

"What is wrong senor, your daughter has beautiful beeeg tits" the Mexican leered at the man obviously trying to provoke the man.

Worst luck his jibs succeeded the insult to his daughter made the man very angry, without thinking the man rushed at the Mexican with his fists up diving at his tormenter with the intention of hitting him, not thinking the man attacked his opponent going at him to fast out of control the momentum making it too hard to stop his forward propulsion the Mexican stood up, stepped to the side, drew a large hunting knife, swung the knife at the man's throat, because of his speed the man could not stop his forward movement, the large blade cut deep going through the windpipe almost taking the man's head off, blood sprayed everywhere, with a gasp the man died.

Ben had been about to intervene when Sam took charge taking any action out of his hand, immediately sending a man to get the sheriff while pointing a sawed of shotgun at the Mexican murderer keeping him covered.

"You hold it right there" Sam ordered.

Ben wanted to see the sheriff's reaction and did not want to be seen so backed into a dark corner where it was possible to observe and listen.

The sheriff arrived, looked at the body, there was no need for a close examination or to feel for a pulse with the head lay on its side the neck almost severed clean through the big knife did a lot of damage.

"OK what happened here" the sheriff asked looking at Sam.

Listening intently at what Sam had to say, Ben nodded as Sam told his story and it was word for word of what had happened exactly, going round the small crowd asking the same questions, the sheriff received the same answer that Sam had given him, if Ben had been the sheriff as a lawman he would arrest the Mexican to find out why the dead man had become angry in the saloon, if the sheriff had asked they would have told him the man was protecting his daughter, In the west a man looks after the women in their family, because females were scarce in the west so every decent men look after them, men caught doing things against women were in trouble.

The sheriff did not ask these vital questions, instead the sheriff turned to the Mexican and asked him for his story, the killer did not say anything about the man's daughter or a reason for the trouble.

"I sat at this table peacefully drinking with my friend Paul, this man came through the batwings rushed at me, I pulled my knife to defend myself, the man ran to fast to stop and ran into my knife I could not stop him" the Mexican told him.

The fact that the way the dead man's head was could only be that way with the slash of a knife, this was not taken into consideration, if the man had run onto the knife it would more than likely penetrate the body. The sheriff turned to the people in the bar.

"All right disperse it is obvious self-defense the dead man attacked this gentleman" the sheriff said.

The persons in the bar raised their voices in protest, the sheriff put his hand up and yelled for silence turned to Grant and asked him what happened, Grant of course came out on the Mexicans side. Ben now knew the sheriff is being paid by Grant and the Mexican, they are definitely criminals, but the sheriff took there side instead of jailing the Mexican, starting an investigation and putting the man on trial.

Ben came to a decision, it is now important to find out what the sheriff is up to, going back to his room lay on the bed, when going to the hotel Ben spotted a man tailing him, this meant he had to convince the man to go away he must look like he had retired for the night making the tail go back to the sheriff and report that Ben was asleep, Ben made his bed up to look like he was asleep in bed, then dressed all in black put moccasins on his feet then slipped out of the hotel window.

As it was Ben could not have timed it better, hidden in a dark alley across the street to the sheriff's office, a few minutes after settling in to his position , the door of the sheriff's office opened the sheriff stepped out locked the door strolled down Main Street keeping to the shadows using as much cover as possible, Ben followed the Sheriff to a small hotel in Shanty town where Grant and the Mexican had a room, going straight to the room Knocked on the door by wrapping two times waiting a second tapped once, the door opened the sheriff slipped in.

Ben thought the sheriff had actually made his way to the hotel to tell the Mexican of and tell them it would be impossible to protect them if they kept on acting the way they are but instead they shook hands and were happy to see each other, finding the window to the room Ben inched nearer to the cracked open window (everyone had to crack open there windows because of the heat this time of the year), the sheriff actually had visited them to tell them his intentions.

The overheard conversation Ben found very interesting, so the sheriff was leaving town soon but the part about how they intended to do it was the most interesting part, melting back into the shadows Ben tailed the sheriff back to the better end of town where on entry to a saloon and collecting a beer at the bar the sheriff made his way to a table at the rear of the saloon near the rear door. Ben nipped quickly around to the rear of the saloon, just inside the rear door was an area of deep shadow standing in this area and by straining his ears what Ben heard in the talk between the stranger and the sheriff was very enlightening.

A look of anger came to his face as what the conversation revealed but controlled his anger and smiled as his escapade had paid off retracing his steps as silent as possible, he returned to the hotel to sleep the remainder of the night.

WHAT A DAY

The day started in the usual way by washing, shaving and checking his weapons, leaving the hotel Ben made his way to the café where after a substantial breakfast went to the livery stable to attend to his horse Shad, while at the livery stable Tim the holster informed Ben that it was certain someone had been prowling around but found no reason why, it was suspicious but with nothing stolen there was little to be done and just told Tim to keep his eyes open, next stop was a visit to the doctors where a certain person was not happy with him.

"Why haven't you been to see me" Jane demanded.

"Sorry Jane I have been busy"

"Oh! Yes, doing what" she enquired.

"I have a couple of things I want to tell you, but I want the doc. here as well" Ben told her.

"It's OK I was only joking you don't have to visit me" Jane said

"I will visit you as much as I can, but I cannot promise when that will be, you will never be forgotten"

"Oh! Yes", Jane said sarcastically.

"Oohhhh! Yes, I'll never forget my teacher" Ben said in a low subjective voice a mischievous smile on his face.

"Ben" she squealed blushing. The doctor entered the room.

"Hi Ben" doc greeted.

"Doc it is important we talk, could you organize three cups of coffee I need your assistance"

The doc went to get the coffee while Ben checked the windows were shut and the catch on plus checking there was no one outside when the doc returned Ben made sure the door was shut.

"Right close in, now I know there is no one eavesdropping, I want to make sure no one will be able to hear us"

"OK Ben what's up" Jane asked.

"Jane, Doc, tonight there will be an attempt on Jane's life, this man is a professional the man concerned normally kills with a knife, entering by the window, the idea is to slip through the open window stab you disappear back through the open window again, but if disturbed his orders are to shoot you get out of there fast" Ben explained.

"H H How H How do you know" the doc stuttered.

"I have not visited Jane for no reason I have been busy, I followed the sheriff last night on entering the saloon the sheriff sat down beside Jane's assassin I maneuvered myself into a position, so I could hear them talking, this man was looking for Jane and the sheriff told him where you are Jane" Ben informed them.

For the first time Jane was speechless, she sat with an amazed look on her face, she knew there was contract out for her to die, for the first time it hit her as reality came to her.

"There is a lot more the sheriff is preparing to move on"

"That's good we will all welcome that, the man is a bad man the sooner the better I say" Doc said jubilantly

"With the banks money"

"Damn no" the doc spluttered.

"How do you know all this Ben" Jane asked.

"The reason I have not been in to see you before now, is because of the people of the town requiring my assistance, a lady in town asked for help, this bunch of folk saw me come to town with you, so they asked me if I was a lawman , I told them yes, they sighed with relief the lady saying we need someone to rely on, what we said has not to leave this room, this bunch of town folk told me about this town and about the sheriff, I said I will look into it, that is the reason I have not been to see you earlier, I have been looking into the towns affaires".

"You still haven't answered my question" Jane told Ben.

"Jane, I have wondered why Grant and the Mexican have stayed, the reason is the sheriff wants them to rob the bank together the sheriff needs there help"

"Look Jane, Doc lets first cover the attempt on Jane's life, I do not want you to shoot the first man through the window, because it will be me, I don't want them to know I am here so I must also sneak in, I want you to leave the window open like you would normally do, I will sneak in we will hide in the shadows of the dark room until the man climb's in, if possible I want him alive because I want information, if I have to shoot him I will" Ben told them.

"I am not comfortable being in this nightdress and my other clothes are still covered in dried blood" Jane said.

"I'll get some clothes for you and drop them off"

"Why do you want him alive Ben" Doc asked.

"A bounty has been put on Jane's head, Why? If it is because she loved the wrong man then the bounty would become illegal as it gives someone permission to kill, if on the other hand they are after Jane because they think she killed him, I know that to be untrue because I was there and saw it"

"You are saying if you can get the information you want from this man you could maybe get the bounty on Jane's head lifted" the doc asked.

"Oh! Your fantastic" Jane said as she grabbed and kissed him.

"Now doc I would like some advice from you" Ben said.

"OK what would you like to know" doc asked.

"Two young men work as deputies, my plan was to cause trouble between them to put them out of the picture, but I am starting to have second thoughts about this idea, now my question is do you know these young men, if you do how do you think I should approach the problem can you think of another way" Ben asked.

"Yes I know these young men in fact I have been there family doctor for years, they are basically good young men who are influenced by the sheriff, if you could get them away from the sheriff get them by themselves, talk to them explain who you are, show them what they should know you could win them over, there is a little bit of leverage you could use, the man who was murdered in the saloon the other night was the father of the blonde girl the two young men are interested in, You get my drift" the doc explained.

"OK doc I understand, the sheriff does not know what I know about him, I have made some calls to the office each day, so I think it would be best to carry on doing so"

"Make sure you get back here with some clothes" Jane ordered.

Giving Jane a kiss and cuddle Ben walked to the door, then without her seeing scooped her old clothes up before leaving, making his way to the sheriff's office the two young deputies were lounging around outside bored stiff kicking stones.

Whistling a happy tune, showing a cheerful face Ben entered the sheriff's office, with a smile on his face greeted the sheriff. "Hi sheriff how's things"

"OK Ben, I haven't any time for chit chat today its busy" the sheriff said but Ben knew this was a lie.

"As you are busy, is there anything I can help you with"

"No not at the moment we will cope" came the reply.

As Ben was about to leave, a worried lady came into the office you could see she was very worried by the look on her face.

"Well what can I do for you" the sheriff asked abruptly.

"My son is missing" she said a tear in her eyes,

"Oh! the boy is old enough to look after himself, the boy will turn up"

"But, he has been missing all night" the lady cried.

"He's a boy Mrs. Taylor, don't worry the boy can look after himself" the sheriff dismissed the lady.

"My boy has never been out all night before and would tell us if there was a reason for doing so" Mrs. Taylor replied.

"What doe's you boy do, out of town" Ben asked.

"Shoots rabbits"

"Do you know which area he's more likely to go to"

"Normally to the southeast of here" Mrs. Taylor said.

"Sheriff I know you are busy today, if your two young deputies are free, maybe they could give me a hand that way there will be three of us, so we can cover more territory when looking for the boy, of course that is if you don't need them" Ben suggested. After a moment's thought the sheriff turned to Ben.

"OK you do that" came the reply.

"Thanks sheriff what's the names of the deputies"

"Phil and Fred" the sheriff replied.

"OK Marm we will look for your boy" Ben told Mrs. Taylor then took his badge from his pocket and pinned it on his vest, Mrs. Taylor looked at the badge Ben's face who winked at her, she didn't say anything just turned and walked out of the door much relieved and a spring in her step.

"Phil, Fred get your horses we are going for a ride" Ben said.

"Who said" they asked.

"The sheriff asks him"

"Right Mister" the deputies chorused.

"My name is Ben"

"OK Ben" Fred said

"Sure Ben" Phil said.

"Mrs. Taylor before you go could you answer a few questions, this is Phil and Fred they are going to help me find your son, we know your son is southeast of town but is there any other information you could give us" Ben asked.

"I don't know if it is significant but when leaving it seemed like for some reason, was more excited than usual" she explained.

"Does your son ride a horse or pony, what colour is it. Is there anything else you can tell me; do you know what type of gun doe's your son carry" Ben enquired.

"A few days ago, his father had Sam shoed, as my son told him the horse needed a new shoe" she replied.

"Do you know if your son has a pistol"

"No just a rifle" she said.

"Well we had better get underway, the sheriff was right in one way the boy seems to know what to do in the wilds so it's more than likely your son will be OK, I'll find him for you"

"Thank you by the badge you are a Ranger is that right" Mrs. Taylor asked.

"Yes, I am"

"Good" she smiled and walked off.

"Let's go boys" they went to the livery stable where Ben picked up Shad.

"That's a great horse" Fred said.

"I agree" echoed Phil.

"Whatever you do stay away from him, Shad's a one-man horse and does not let anyone touch him unless I say so"

About a mile out of town, Ben looked at his two companions then asked them.

"Did you two takes in what Mrs. Taylor told us"

"No, you received the info, (information) so we reckoned it was not necessary to listen" Phil said.

"RIGHT, STOP NOW" Ben said loudly.

"What" Fred said surprised

"You two think NOW, do you want to be lawmen or not, are you enjoying the job, if you answer those two questions correctly, you will have to buck up, now what's your answer" Ben asked.

"I wanted to be a lawman, but I am not enjoying it we spend most of the time sitting in the office, the sheriff said we have to do what he ordered" Phil explained.

"Same for me" Fred admitted.

"I want to have a serious talk with you two, but it will wait we have a job to do first, now as long as you are out with me you will learn, take interest I will be asking questions you understand" Ben told them.

"OK" they both said.

After a short distance looking at the trail suddenly brought the three of them to a halt, looking at what had taken his attention told the deputies to dismount.

"What have you seen as you rode up here" Ben asked.

"Nothing" Phil replied.

"What do you want us to look for" Fred asked.

"Both of you told me earlier you wanted to be lawmen, what are we out here for and what should you be looking for" Ben asked.

"We are looking for a boy" they said together.

"OK it looks like I am going to have to start from scratch, to find the boy we must follow what sign we can, we know the boy from town to this place was by himself and is riding a brown horse"

"How can you tell that" Phil enquired.

"The boy is light, so the prints are not too deep plus Mrs. Taylor in town told us the horse has a new shoe, if you look here you can see a sharper print this is the mark of a new shoe, as the boy rode close to the brush the horse left some brown hairs on the brush" Ben explained.

Fred and Phil looked at each other in amazement.

"Have you got that, now come here look at the trail and tell me what you see" the deputies studied the sign.

"There are two sets of tracks" Fred said Phil still looked at the tracks.

"The tracks joined together over there, the second pony has worn shoes and the rear left shoe has a nick in it" Phil pointed out.

"There is white hair on this bush, so the pony is white" Fred said.

"You see you are learning" Ben said.

As they rode along Ben showed the two deputies where a horse's shoe had hit rocks and left marks in shale, how they could know the direction of travel due to the pressed grass, pointed out broken twigs and branches, you could tell by the looks on their faces the two young men were impressed Ben also told them how to tell signs from horse droppings.

Fred was on the verge of asking Ben a question when they heard two shots ring out, Ben nudged Shad the big horse took of leaving the two deputies standing with open mouth, but they quickly followed, coming over a small mound Ben saw the boy a hundred yards ahead, on reaching him Ben dismounted on the run.

"Hi boy" as passing the boy to get to the prone figure of a girl beside a large rock her eyes were open, but she winced with pain.

"Hello miss let's have a look at you, where does it hurt"

"Head, neck leg arm and chest" she replied through gritted teeth.

Ben checked the wounds.

"OK miss you have a split head, your neck is probably just bruised I cannot see anything, I'm afraid your leg is broken, your arm is black and blue and has a couple of scratches, as for your chest you have hit something sharp there is a small hole there, it looks bad because it has bled, I'll do the best for your wounds, make a drag bed and get you to the doctors" (Ben noticed the tears in her eyes) "Shhh, chin up".

"Mister a rattler scared her pony, she was thrown into the rocks, she was unconscious for a few moments I carried her to this flat rock, I had nothing to fix her wounds, but I did wash them, I built a fire to keep any wild animals at bay" the boy explained,

"You did well son" Ben said.

"OK boy this is what we have to do, the first thing we must do is to look after your young lady and make her as comfortable as possible, we stop and have a coffee and short rest, make a travelling bed set of to town slowly so let's get started"

"Fred, Phil" Ben called.

"Yer! Ben" they answered.

"I see a small wooded area about a quarter of a mile down the track ride down there find two twelve-foot-long saplings or poles three or four six-foot-long staves bring them back here" Ben said.

"OK Ben" they rode off.

"Right son let's look after your young lady"

"My name is Timmy, and this is Sarah" Timmy said.

"I'm Ben, now the first injury to look at is Sarah's chest wound, I have a first aid kit in my saddle bags if in the future you have a problem like this either rip the sleeve of Sarah's or your shirt separated into two pieces, one piece you fold into a pad to go on the wound the second one you use to wash her wounds, right the first wound is just above her right breast you do not need to remove any clothing, we wash the wound and the pad we put over the hole, Sarah's bra strap will hold it in place, the next one is the split head just wash it and wrap it, we look at her arm normally I would use a bandana as a sling but as Sarah has a bad neck we will have to fix her arm to her body to keep it immobile, we will wrap her neck to keep it warm, now the biggest job Sarah has a broken leg get two pieces of wood, we put one each side of the leg and lash it, now make her comfortable, can you understand Timmy what has been done" Ben asked.

"Yes, Ben thank you" Timmy remarked.

Ben built a fire put a pot of water on it to boil to make coffee at this time the deputies arrived back with the items he asked them to get.

"Right it's time we take a rest"

"That's OK by us" Fred said

"Timmy that was a good and brave thing you did staying with Sarah to protect her overnight"

"Thanks" Timmy replied.

"Now what are you two smiling for" Ben asked the deputies.

"We have been talking and figured out we have learnt more in the last two hours from you than in the three months we have been with the sheriff" Fred explained.

"Phil, Fred I would like you to trust me listen to what I say, give up your job as deputies, I have my reasons, I want you to trust me" Ben advised.

"We were thinking of packing the job in anyway, we have been talking about it for a few days now, we would both like to be lawmen but we believe we are not learning anything in our present position" Phil told Ben.

"There is another subject I would like to tell you about, I understand you are interested in a certain young lady called Sally, I had a word with the young lady in question, she told me she liked you both, she is flattered by your attentions, but she has no interest in anyone who works with the sheriff" Ben explained.

"Thanks for telling us" Fred said.

"There is one more thing I think you should take into consideration, I don't know if you know about the killing that took place in the saloon last night, the man who was murdered (yes murdered) was Sally's father, the sheriff said it was self-defense and let the man off, even though a few people told him murder had been committed, if you go near her with those badges on you will not only be ignored but also disliked or maybe even hated"

"Thanks for telling us" Fred said, Phil nodded.

"There is more her father went to the killer to tell him to stay away from Sally, not only did the man make dirty suggestive remarks about her, admitted grabbing Sally's tits, this man has been defended by the sheriff" Ben informed them.

"Who was this man I will kill him" Fred said, and Phil agreed.

"Fred, Phil if you went up against this man you would die, this man is better than you, I can tell by the way you wear your guns you would both be dead before you get your guns out of your holsters, don't even think about it" Ben told them.

"What do you mean by that remark" Phil asked.

"Fred give me your gun".

Fred handed over his gun, Ben extracted all the bullets pointed the pistol in the air and pressed the trigger, gave Fred the bullets ("Put them in your pocket ",) calling Phil Ben repeated the procedure.

"OK holster your guns "the deputies watched as Ben took the bullets from his own gun. "now stand facing me, when you are ready go for your guns" Ben ordered them.

Meanwhile Timmy and Sarah had become interested spectators, Sarah admitted afterword's she became so engrossed in what was taken place, she felt no pain as her mind had been taken of her condition.

Fred and Phil concentrated all their effort into their draw, the two young men's hands grabbed the butts of their pistols, looking at the deputies his assessment was that Fred would be the most dangerous, Fred had his gun almost out, Phil only half way out of their holsters as they heard the double click coming from Bens levelled pistol the two deputies looked at the level gun in amazement.

"I beat you both and I am only average there is a lot of men out there faster than me, OK boys reload your guns, the way you holster your guns give you away and you have little chance of beating someone who knows, as a sheriff it is his job to pick you up and instruct you how to get the best out of your draw, if you were my deputies I would have taught you these things along time ago, we have had our break it is now time to get this young lady to the doctors" Ben ordered them.

"Fred, Phil and you as well Timmy we are going to build a trellis type drag bed just like the Indian do" Ben showed them how to do it, as Sarah already lay on a blanket with Ben's instructions, taken a corner the blanket each they lifted her onto the drag bed attached it to Sarah's pony, then cavalcade set out slowly.

"We are now on the main trail into town, Phil, Fred, Timmy I want you to go slow and don't bounce Sarah about as it could make her injuries worse, Timmy ride at the rear and keep an eye on Sarah, Fred, Phil stay in front make sure that you do not go over any bumps, keep your eyes open, I don't think you will have any problems, I am going ahead but will be back before you get into town." Ben told them.

Ben nudged Shad, they rushed to town.

"Phil, I don't think Ben would lie to us, I am resigning after this job" Fred informed him.

"I agree, Ben has opened my eyes" Phil agreed.

Ben rode at a fast pace into town, made a quick visit to the general store headed immediately to the doctors.

"Doc we have a young lady, coming in with a few injuries she was thrown by her horse, Ben gave him a list, Jane you can help the doc and you will need these" gave her the bundle of clothes, behind the screen she dressed they fitted perfectly.

"How did you know my size" Jane enquired.

"Oh! I should know your size by now" Jane blushed, Ben smiled.

The doc looked at them and smiled, then with a mischief smile on his face told Jane.

"Ben took your old clothes"

"Ohh! You" she yelled picking up an empty bottle threw it in his direction the last thing they heard was his laugher, leaving the house. Jane smiled which the doc noticed.

"It's funny how everyone who meets him feels better afterwards" the doc commented.

"Yes, he's fantastic" she murmured in a quiet voice.

"Jane, you can help me with this girl, another female will make a difference, but when they bring her in, I want you to lie down until the helpers leave, got that" the doc stated.

Ben met the cavalcade a mile from town informed Sarah the doctor is waiting for her

"Right boys we will go straight to the doctor's house."

It being a small-town people knew everything and a cavalcade on the street took a lot of attention as they plainly walked down the main street in the center of town to the doctors house, four persons picked up and transported Sarah into the doc's house, the doctor cleared the place, the doctor and Jane went to check the wounds.

"Looks like someone did a good job attending to your wounds" the doc remarked.

"Ben done it" Sarah said.

"This is Jane she is Ben's friend" Doc explained.

"Ben" her face lit up at the sound of his name.

"This is Ben's work, just like when seeing to my shoulder he doe's good first aid" Jane told them.

Meanwhile outside the doctors the man in question, organized things out in the street.

"Phil, Fred could you get rid of the trestle, thank you boys for your help you did well today"

"Thanks Ben we wish you were sheriff, we would stay on if you would have us" Phil said

"Look boys turn in your badges, I believe this sheriff will not last very much longer, so when a new sheriff is appointed apply for a deputy's job and if you want to you can quote my name" Ben told them.

"Thanks again, that's a good idea" Fred replied.

"Timmy, I have a final job for you, I want you to take care of yours and Sarah's horses and Timmy it would be a good idea to visit Sarah when you can".

"Oh! No" Timmy cursed.

Ben looked in the direction that Timmy looked, walking towards him was his mother plus another couple, the man with an angry look on his face obviously Sarah's parents, But Timmy showed his plucky side by remaining calm.

"Hi mam" he greeted his mother.

"What have you done to my daughter you little sod" the man yelled.

"She is injured and with the doctor at the moment" Timmy said.

"What!" Sarah's mother exclaimed hurried into the doctors.

"What did you do to her you brat" Sarah's father demanded.

"How dare you talk to my son like that" Mrs. Taylor protested.

"Hold it both of you" Ben ordered.

"You can stay ou" then stopped when seeing Ben's badge.

"Why should I hold back, I defend my boy against this foul mouth fat gorilla" Mrs. Taylor asked.

"YOU TWO WILL HEAR ME OUT" Ben ordered in a raised demanding voice.

"Your daughter met Timmy a couple of miles out of town, they went for a ride together enjoying each other's company, when a rattlesnake spooked Sarah's pony which threw Sarah into some rocks which injured her and knocked her unconscious, Timmy picked her up and lay her on a blanket in a flat area and made her comfortable, with a piece of cloth cleaned her wounds and stopped the bleeding, when it became dark Timmy built a fire to keep any animals away with his rifle across his knee's from first light every fifteen minutes firing two shots in the air as you know this is the range SOS, Timmy looked after your daughter all night, she is a lucky girl if Timmy had not been there I hate to think what your daughter would have went through if she was all alone" Ben told them.

"Ah! Ma" Timmy protested as his mother hugged and kissed him.

Sarah's Dad just turned and walked away without a word.

"Mrs. Taylor, Timmy will be home soon, I have given him a job to do. Get on with it son" Ben said

"Yer! OK Ben" Timmy returned.

"OK son I will see you when you get home, I am proud of you I'll get your dinner ready so don't be too long" Mrs. Taylor turned to Ben.

"Thank you" she said.

"OK Marm"

Going to the Sheriff's office Ben made out his report passed it to the Sheriff, putting his badge in his pocket, his next destination was the doctors.

"Hi doc how is the invalids"

"This one is better and a pain in the neck" doc said indicating Jane.

Jane put her tongue out at the doctor.

"OK what you been up to" Ben asked Jane.

"I'm bored and want to get out of here" Jane told him.

"How is the girl doc".

"She will be OK, her neck is just bruised, her leg is the worst problem she may be left with a limp, but we won't know for certain until she is fit again" Doc explained.

"What about tonight, with the young lady here it could be a problem when the attempt on Jane's life occurs".

"My wife will look after Sarah in another room" doc said.

"Are you ready for tonight" Ben asked Jane.

"Oh! Yes, I am OK for tonight, there is nothing wrong with the doc's company, but I want to get out of here" Jane replied irritably.

"Your shoulder cannot be healed yet, even though it is getting better" Ben pointed out.

"You didn't hang about when you were shot" Jane told him.

"Yer! I am a ranger and had a job to do, you know that Jane" Ben reminder.

"You did need attention" Jane told him.

"I admit you helped me, and if you had not been there to clean, massage and dress my wound, I would not have gotten as far as I have, but wounded or not I would have carried on with my job Jane you are safer here with the doc for the time being"

"I would rather spend some time with you, instead of being coped up here" Jane pleaded with Ben.

"Wait until after tonight"

"I'm fed up Ben, I want to get out of here"

"Jane" the words were lost as two pair of hungry lips came together.

"Everything is being done to keep you safe, it's for your protection, when the danger is over the doc will be happy to get rid of you and I will be happy to have you back with me, now trouble do as you are told" Ben told her.

"I'll leave you two and check on Sarah" doc excused himself.

"If she is awake, I will visit her before I go"

"Go" Jane exclaimed.

"I have to go to get ready and some sleep before tonight"

"I would love to sleep with you" Jane whispered.

"So, would I but I do not think I would get much sleep".

After laughing, Jane through her arms around his neck, a pair of hot lips met his, they had a long, lingering, passionate kiss.

"Oh! Ben, I miss you, I wish we could do more, I mean go further" Jane said in a low husky voice.

"It would be great if I could make love to you, at this moment it is not possible, if my teacher is dead how could I"

"Oh! You," she paused" I know you are right Ben, but I'm frustrated, I cannot wait to get out of here" Jane said quietly.

Ben held out his arms, Jane went to him, they again kissed passionately, holding her in his arms, Ben realized Jane had no underwear on under the shirt, his hand slid into her shirt and they both sighed as Ben held the beautiful naked breast in his hand his thumb brushed the nipple, smoothly Ben withdrew his hand as the doc approached.

"Is Sarah awake doc" Ben asked.

"Yes Ben" came the reply.

"Jane let's go visit before I leave"

"Oh! OK" she replied reluctantly

"Hello Sarah" Ben greeted.

"Hi Ben, Jane" Sarah said. Jane took Sarah's hand.

"Doc has patched you up, you will recover".

"Thanks to Ben I will be OK" Sarah said.

"Sarah the person you must thank most of all is Timmy, the boy built that fire to keep wild animals away and stay with you all night, he looked after you, the boy has character, he did what was possible for to help you, that makes him a very special friend" Ben told her.

"Your right Ben" Sarah said softly.

"Sarah, Ben is right, if you have a good friend you should hang on to him and I think Timmy has already proved how much of a friend he is don't you think" Jane advised.

"Yes, you are both right, Timmy is a friend" Sarah admitted.

Ben and Jane took that as their que to leave, allowing a tired girl to get some rest, retiring back to Jane's room they said their good byes by kissing once more they parted.

CHAPTER SEVEN

I LIKE THAT GREETING

Ben woke up an hour before sundown as planned, giving him time to do some things that needed done before darkness fell, going through his normal routines, after pulling on his trousers and slinging the gunbelt around his waist Ben retrieved his revolver from under his pillow put it into the holster.

Washing, shaving, then dressing all in black Ben proceeded to the hotel dining room and ordered a today special, while eating his eyes glanced around the room and fell on the stranger the sheriff had talked to about, (Jane's assassination) of course this man did not know that Ben knew what his intensions are, on completion of his meal, leaving the hotel his next destination was the livery stable, seeing young Timmy there.

"Hi Timmy, you're out late"

"Just checking my horse sir" Timmy answered

"That is good son, always look after your horse, you look after him and you will get him looking after you. Timmy if I had a sick friend, I would visit her tomorrow don't you think" Ben advised Timmy.

"Thank you for the advice" Timmy replied.

SUDDENLY, they both heard the high pitch scream of an angry horse plus the voice they recognized as Sam the holster.

"Leave him alone"

"Piss off you little bastard" came the angry reply.

Ben ran to the stable, where the deputy had put a rope on Shad, as the deputy tried to lead him out Shad had first pulled back with a scream charged at the deputy, the angry man grabbed a whip pushed the young holster aside, as the deputy raised the whip Shad once again charged the deputy knocking him off his feet, not liking it and becoming more angry the deputy grabbed his revolver, drawing it the deputy levelled the gun at the big horses head it was obvious the man intended to shoot Shad, a spurt of flame and the bark of a gun being fired came from Ben's right hip, the deputy screamed as the bullet shattered the deputies wrist, the bone stuck out and blood pumped from the wrist.

"Why you trying to steal my horse" Ben accused him.

"I wasn't" the deputy said.

"You liar yes you were" the young holster yelled back at him.

"I believe you were also" Ben told him.

"No, I wasn't" the deputy said through gritted teeth.

"Don't tell lies you were trying to steal him, like the other horse you stole in fact I am certain you have stolen a few horses" Ben said.

"How would you know that" the deputy said.

"I am a lawman, a trained investigator you are a thief"

"Even if I did you could not prove it" the deputy said.

"I can because I have found a witness" Ben explained.

"Who"

"That is my business, you will see when you get to court, you will be tried for horse stealing, you are under arrest" Ben told him.

A moment later the sheriff burst on the scene, who had heard the shot so rushed to the livery stable.

"Right what is going on here" the sheriff demanded.

"Sheriff your deputy tried to steal my horse, I also have information on other times when this man concerned stole horses in the past, I have a witness, for that reason I have arrested him, the charge being a horse thief" Ben informed the sheriff.

"OK Ben I'll take him in" the sheriff said.

"Thanks sheriff" Ben said, as he went straight to Shad.

Talking soothingly and patting the big horses neck calming him down, in return Shad snuffled Ben's shirt as the big horse slowly calmed down, Ben did not mind the sheriff taking the deputy into the jail, even though Ben expected the deputy to be left so he could escape or shot while trying to escape, the important of this outcome is that the sheriff is now alone, the two trainee deputies have resigned the other deputy arrested for horse stealing a hanging offence, the sheriff is now on his own.

The sheriff was not really worried about the situation because the plan was to rob the bank and ride out within 24 to 48 hours then disappear, if any jobs came in during this period, by informing people of the shortness of staff will get him through.

While Ben ate in the café the sun disappeared from the sky, darkness settled in, so when leaving the café turning right into the dark alley, and left along the rear of the buildings to the rear of the doctors house, in the dark Ben moved slowly and carefully making sure no one heard him and getting there well ahead of the assassin, wearing moccasins allowed him to feel his way more easily in the dark ,as his clothes were all black it enabled him to blend into the darkness becoming vertically unseen.

Finding the window of Jane's room tapping on it twice the signal they had agreed upon, slowly he pushed the window open Ben climbed into the room a hand reached out of the darkness pulling him to the left where a pair of hungry lips met his, responding they kissed passionately.

"Hi" Jane said breathlessly.

"What a greeting I like that"

"I thought you might" she replied.

"I like it but don't get carried away, remember why I am here"

"Oh! Alright" she said sullenly.

"Let's get set up for the business, move over to the other side of the bed, I'm happy we are both wearing black it helps us to hide in the shadows" Ben pronounced.

"Well my double is in the bed" Jane whispered.

"That can't be your double"

"Why not" Jane demanded.

"It's got no tits"

"Oh! You" she said and swung an arm at him.

Ben grabbed her arm pulled her to him and planted his lips on to hers enjoying a long lingering kiss, they remained in there quiet embrace kissing, cuddling and a little cheeky caressing each other's bodies but Ben never forgot why they were there, his straining ears heard a slight sound outside, stopping the kissing Ben placed a finger over Janes lips then drew his pistol (Jane admitted later she did not hear anything) "Shhh" was all she heard.

A shadow fell over the open window, the silhouette could be seen silently pushing up the window, the assassin making almost no sound slipped through the window, this man might be a criminal but was good, Ben had to admit without prior knowledge this man would have succeeded in killing Jane, (the man was well trained and could slip into a sleeping camp kill everyone and disappear). The invading assassin new exactly where to go to kill Jane, his knife slid silently from the obvious lubricated sheath plunged into the dummy on the bed.

If Ben had not been fore warned about this man, it's now certain Jane would now be dead.

"Hold it right there you are under arrest this is the law" Ben called.

Give the man his due his reactions were fast as the assassin dived for the window, Ben aimed low pulled the trigger the bullet hit the man in the left knee making him collapse the body moving forward at such a speed made it seem to dive, his head hit the window frame hard which knocked him unconscious, moving quickly Ben called out.

"Jane light the lamp" checking the man was unarmed,

"Jane get the doc for me"

"OK Ben" then left the room.

Ben pounced on the killer searched the man to make sure the man had no hidden weapons then tied his hands behind his back before the killer came too, slowly the killer came around mourning about his shattered leg.

"Mister you are a hired killer, you were going to murder a good friend of mine, so I want answers otherwise you will be in more pain I will make sure of that, first question you came to kill Jane (WHY)?" Ben asked him.

"Mrs. Macdonald of the Big Mac Ranch hired me to kill this woman who killed her husband Lance Macdonald" the assassin told Ben.

"I was there when Lance Macdonald died who was shot by a man called Paul Grant, which means you were going to commit murder on an innocent woman" Ben accused the killer.

"How do you know the man was Grant" the man asked.

"Paul Grant killed Senator Stevens and his family, being a ranger, I was given the job of catching or killing him I had tracked him for a week, I almost caught him but after shooting Lance Macdonald as I was busy stopping his friends Grant turned and shot me, so I know" Ben explained.

"Can I see the doc now" the assassin requested through gritted teeth.

"I Haven't finished with you yet"

"Alright what do you want to know" the hired man inquired.

"Now we come to the question that decides your fate, it all depends on your answer" Ben told him.

"Shoot" the hired killer meaning what's your question.

"Now you know Jane did not kill Lance Macdonald what is your next move,"

"After the doc fixes me up, I will have to contact Mrs. Macdonald to inform her of the situation" the assassin told them.

"I will have to give it some thought, there is no way I can trust you, doc see what you can do about his leg".

"OK Ben, I ll see what can be done" the doc replied.

"Come on Jane let's talk".

"Why discuss this with her" the assassins called out loudly.

"Since you were sent to kill me, I think I should have a say" she spun the gun on her finger holstered it.

"I see you can handle a gun" the assassin commented.

"Yer! I had to learn because of people like you" Jane replied.

"Who taught you" the hired man asked.

"The man in front of you" the hired man looked at Ben.

"Who the hell are you"

"Ben Brooks Texas Ranger" the killer watched as Ben pinned his badge to his vest.

The assassin looked from Ben to Jane's straight faces but did not say anything.

Ben drew Jane aside steered her through the door, where they talked to each other for 10 to15 minutes, re-entered the room, went to the doc.

"How is our friend doc" Ben asked.

"I'm afraid our friend will not walk properly again" the doc told him.

"What do you mean I will not walk properly again" the killer asked.

"Ben knew you were coming because you and the sheriff talked about the subject, and Ben overheard your conversation, also Ben told Jane and myself not to kill you that is why we were told to shoot low and why you were shot in the leg, unfortunately his bullet hit you in the knee, shattering your knee joint, it is impossible to repair a knee joint meaning you will have a disability for the rest of your life" the doc explained.

"Doc how long does our friend have to stay here" Ben asked.

"Guessing I'd say a week; its possible crutches may be needed" the doc announced.

"Good that will give us a chance to mull this over, if his injuries are as you say there is no threat from him"

"Well that is my assessment" doc said.

"Mr. Williams there is no dodger out for you, of course you did attempt to commit murder I will inform the sheriff and leave your weapons there, you can see the sheriff about them"

"OK "Williams sullenly replied.

"Let's get some fresh air" going out the back of the house onto the veranda with seats on it where they discussed the situation in-between kisses.

"I know you have something on your mind so what is it" Jane asked.

"I'm thinking of Williams, If someone crippled me, and I know the person could have killed me I would count myself lucky, but this man is a trained assassin, takes money to kill people so I think this man will want revenge his anger will keep his hate alive, dedicated as a hired killer and as we know this man has been paid to carry out his task, for that reason we cannot trust him, if he is given a chance this man will try to kill you, now, if the doc can keep him here for a week, we could finish the job and leave" Ben explained.

"What now Ben" Jane asked.

"I'm hoping I can clear my problems tomorrow night, if successful we can leave the following day, there is one outstanding problem we do not know how many men has been sent after you" Ben told her.

"What now Ben"

"I have a job to do tomorrow night"

"Then let's leave it at that" Jane said.

"Not quite" Ben said in a stern voice.

"What do you mean by that" Jane enquired.

"That trick you pulled, swinging your gun on your finger before holstering it could have backfired, you could have gotten into a lot of trouble so don't do it again" Ben emphasized the last faze looking at her sternly.

She took a step back and looked at him in amazement, saw the serious look on his face, she did not understand she had not practiced spinning the gun it had come naturally.

"I want you to be serious about handling a gun, I don't want you to start learning tricks, tricks do impress people if done right, but tricks do not keep you alive"

"Ben, I have not learnt to do tricks the only practicing I have done is to draw and shoot like you taught me, I cannot understand or explain what happened tonight" Jane told him.

"Are you telling me you have not done that before"

"I swear I have not done that before it was an automatic reaction you do it frequently maybe I have picked it up from you" she said.

"I have always done it" Ben admitted.

"Ben, you must believe me" Jane pleaded.

"We have been together long enough for me to know if you lied to me, I believe you Jane, I trust you"

"Thank you, Ben," she replied.

"Right Jane stand facing relax let your arm hang loose, when I call draw, I want you put everything into your draw but don't shoot OK"

Jane took her stance, Ben waited a short time, called draw, Jane's hand lashed down to her gun, there was a double click as Jane's gun clicked a fraction of a second behind Ben's gun.

"Well teacher how did I do" Jane asked teasing him.

"Jane, I cannot teach you anymore, that draw was the best you have ever done, I have to say your draw would beat most men you are now that good"

Ben held out his hand, putting her hand into his, Ben drew her close his arm going around her waist, their lips coming together.

"Jane, I can teach you no more, it is up to you now keep practicing you are good Jane"

"Thanks Ben I'd love to find out If I could teach you more" looking at him Jane smiled a twinkle in her eyes.

At this time, the doctor came out onto the veranda, looking tired after spending quite a bit time trying to do the best for Williams plus it is now after three am in the morning.

"Hi doc how is the patient" Ben asked.

"I have reconstructed his leg the best I could and gave him Laundram, I have splinted his leg to keep it straight also I have knocked him out for the night" doc explained.

"Is Jane fit doc"

"Yes, she has been fit and nothing but trouble for a day or so" the doc told him with a mischievous smile on his face.

"You told me you have knocked Williams out, but supposing the man did come out of this induced sleep as a paid hired assassin his first thought would be to complete his task, (kill Jane) she would be in danger, as a ranger I must protect Jane, so she will come with me to the hotel" Ben told the doc.

Jane's face beamed with delight.

"Yippee! I've been discharged, doc I'll get Ben to tend to my shoulder it will soon get better, it now only aches a little, I can put up with it" Jane said.

"Come on you it's three in the morning and I need some sleep I have another big job tomorrow night" Ben ordered.

Putting his arm around her, they walked towards the Hotel, the doc with a knowing smile on his face watched them leave. Back at the hotel in their room the door was kicked shut the bolt put on, then two pairs of hot lips searched for each other's.

"Jane I've missed you" Ben said breathlessly.

"We have only been apart for a couple of days, Oh! Ben, you don't know how I have wanted to be with you, I have missed you" she replied.

They both reacted in the same way by reaching out for each other coming together in an embrace the two pairs of lips joining in a passionate kiss, Ben's hand automatically squeezing her breast, the next few moments while still kissing were spent undressing each other hurriedly, as his hand felt the naked breast he found her breasts were swollen the nipples proud, Jane felt his erection touching her stomach the juices of love oozed from her crotch, Ben's erection probed into her wanting body, as they wanted each other lust took over, their bodies vibrated and sounds of love came from both pairs of lips, Ben's deeply penetrating erection, going faster, until his body shuddered as the seed left his body, the two sweat covered bodies relaxed Ben kissed Jane.

Satisfying there lust they lay entwined together, snuggling close together as they whispered words of love, Ben kissed Jane tenderly on the lips, to her throat, neck, nibbling her ears as his fingers travelled up and down her spine, touching the sensitive parts of her back she giggled as her back tingled with Ben's magic touch.

The kissing continued when Ben's hand enveloped her swollen breast rubbing the proud hard nipple using his thumb, (Arrr! Yes, yes) Jane murmured as Ben's mouth covered the nipple on her left breast his tongue flicking the nipple, the intake of breath and her muffled words of love showed the pleasure this action gave her.

As his hand moved slowly down Jane's back, the tingling sensation made her push her body into his body his hand moved across the silky−smooth skin of her lovely rounded cheeks of her arse, his other hand delved between Jane's legs (Ohhhhh! Arrrr! Moorreee) came the exciting noises from her lips as his finger brushed the lips of her crotch the private entrance to her body the noises of pleasure increased (Oohhh! Oooooo yes Arrrrr!) as

Ben's finger probed deeply into her body swirling his finger and brushing the clitoris.

Jane grabbed at Ben's erection, her body arched as her arse left the bed her body pushed up as if asking for more as the fingers continues to probe deeply the action caused her to cry out more as the probing kept on touching the clitoris, the juices of love began to flow, she once more grabbed the rampant throbbing erection pleading to Ben (Ohhh! Arr! Now Ben now Arr! Now) Ben delayed until it became impossible to hold back any longer so pushed his erection into the waiting crotch she gasped as the erection pushed deeply into her demanding body.

The sounds of love omitted from both their mouths as they left the world behind the erection probed deeper and faster the pleasure of making love, Jane new she had an orgasm when his body shuddered she felt the ultimate sensation, Ben's body jerked hard when his seed passed into Jane's body causing him to also experience an organism.

"Oh! Ben" she whispered trying to get her breath back.

"Jane"

Lying side by side out of breath covered in sweat Ben reached over pulled Jane to him and kissed her.

"Thank you, Jane that was fantastic, it gets better and better every time we make love" Ben whispered in her ear.

"Thank you" she murmured in a low husky voice, their lips met once more they kissed then fell asleep the two bodies clinging together.

For the first time, as far as he could recall the next morning was the only time his eyes opened after dawn, it was not like him to sleep so long, looking at Jane it was wonderful to see her beautiful face, kissing her, his hand slipped between her legs, she woke gently moaning with a smile on her face, her hand went around the erection nudging her tummy.

"Oh! Yes Ben" they made love again.

Today there was no need to rush things, they lay relaxed talking of what would be a good idea for them to do today, the decision made Ben kissed Jane tenderly before rising, Jane followed and using half the water each, they washed the sweat from their bodies, after massaging Jane's shoulder, rubbing oil into it, they completed dressing, there first decision, is to have a hearty breakfast at Paula's café, the second task was to see to the horses.

Leaving the hotel, the two hand in hand walked out into a beautiful sunny morning, it was a lovely time for a walk, strolling along window shopping arm in arm laughing and joking, quite a few women of the town stared at Jane as she wore jeans with a gunbelt, holster and colt .45 nestling on her hip, reaching the café Ben introduced Jane to Paula and her daughter.

"Hi Paula, could we have two breakfasts and coffee please" Ben ordered.

"Coming right up Ben" she confirmed the order.

"What now Ben" Jane asked.

"First I am going to enjoy this breakfast and relish the coffee"

"You and your coffee" Jane said.

"Jane there is nothing better than a coffee in the morning except a lesson from my teacher"

"Ben Shhh!" the shocked, blushing Jane whispered. Ben laughed.

"Next thing on my list is to look after the horses go for a ride give them a bit of exercise take the kinks out of them"

"That's a good idea" Jane agreed.

"Look you know I have something to do tonight, after our ride I have to Check my weapons and plan what I intend doing tonight"

"OK Ben"

"Jane, we can enjoy today together but I must have a clear head tonight" Ben explained.

"I take the hint no sex tonight" Jane said.

"After last night, I would love to go to bed with you and not get up ever, but you know I am a lawman who has a job to do, now Jane It is possible there is another man looking for you, keep your eyes open and your gun handy" Ben explained.

Jane and Paula hit it off and managed to have a good time having girl talk together, Jane enjoyed it as she had not talked to a friendly female for a while, the meal turned out to be fantastic well cooked and tasted great.

As they approached the livery stable, Ben uttered a sharp whistle then smiled as the sound of a horses call, then the sound of a running horse, Shad came to Ben and snuffled his shirt, Jane could not help smiling as she saw the love between the man and horse, Jane had seen Ben and Shad play games together before, Collecting her horse they saddled up and rode out of town, for the first mile the two horses were kept to a walk, Ben kicked his heels into Shads sides Jane had never seen such a reaction from a horse before Shad changed from a walk to a gallop in a split second, after a mile Ben brought Shad to a halt jumped from the saddle patted the big horses neck (Good boy) slipped him a cube of sugar, by the time Jane caught up to him Ben sat by the side of the trail.

"Jane what kept you so long did you go for a swim"

"Why you! Ben, I have never seen a horse react like Shad did" Jane said.

"Yes, Shad is well trained, climb down let your horse blow" Ben instructed her.

Sitting on the side of the road they spoke in a low voice in between kisses and cuddles, fifteen minutes later they mounted up turning their horses, heading for town, Ben reached over lifted Jane from her saddle to sit across his knee, they kissed and cuddled as they rode back to town.

Back in town with Jane following him, Ben brought Shad to a halt in front of the general store helped Jane to dismount, putting his arm around Jane they entered.

"Jane have a look at the dresses and choose the one you would like" Jane picked a pale blue dress.

Arriving back in the hotel room, Jane could not contain her excitement and immediately began to strip, when you say strip she certainly did as in seconds she was naked, slipping into the dress, Ben turned around, even though there was numerous times Ben had seen her naked before the vision in front of him made the air push through his lips, the dress clung to the curves of the fantastic body showing her beauty like never before, she showed her thanks in her usual way, she slung her arms around his neck pushed her body into his her hungry lips met his, feeling the almost naked body and thought (the little minx I know now what she is up to), gently unwrapping her arms Ben pushed her to arm's length.

"Now trouble get out of that dress" seeing the gleam in her eyes.

"Yes" Jane said excitedly.

"Not for that reason, you have picked a beautiful dress and you look great in it, now I want you to put it away for the time being, I want you to keep it until the threat on your life has ended we will celebrate"

"Ohh! OK, couldn't we just"

"No, we cannot, Jane I must concentrate on a job that has to be done tonight, keep your gun handy" Ben told her.

Ben looked at his weapons, which needed checking but his main reason being, Jane removed her dress stood naked, he needed a distraction, picking up his gunbelt taking it to the bed, Jane by this time had on her underwear in the act of putting on her shirt, Ben took out the gun cleaning kit the next thing was to take his revolver apart, removing the bullets from the barrel, taking out the barrel leaving the way clear to use the brush and clean the spout, with the small brush each tube of the barrel, looking up the now fully dressed Jane had her gun out and followed Bens moves cleaning her gun, wiping each bullet with a dry clean cloth Ben loaded the pistol lowered the hammer onto an empty shell placing it on the bed, picking up the belt after rubbing it to make sure it was clean then filled every loop on the belt, putting it around his waist he dropped the revolver into his holster, made a couple of practice draws, flipped the loop over the hammer.

Doubting the need for a knife but Ben still checked his knife for sharpness and cleanliness, looking at the fully dressed Jane and smiled as she twirled the gun on her finger, sliding it into her holster. Ben had no intension of carrying a rifle but decided to check it out as the other weapons were checked out.

"Come on Jane let's eat"

"OK Ben" Jane returned.

After having their supper, they retired back to the room, Ben and Jane did have a little kiss and cuddles but because of the job Ben had early in the morning they went to sleep, Ben slept for a few hours rose went to the water bowl and splashed water in his face to wake him up wiping the water from his eyes, Jane was at the bowl washing the sleep out of her eyes.

"Now what the hell are you up to" Ben asked.

"I am your backup, Shh!" Jane said the last word to prevent Ben cutting in.

"Don't say a word Ben, it's not right you doing the job on your own, I will stay in the shadows ready to shoot if You need help" Jane told him.

Looking at Jane's determinate face, Ben stopped and thought deeply, even though there was no backup Ben was reluctant to have Jane there, If Jane died, (God how could I live with myself) was his thoughts.

"Jane If I agree I would never be able to live with myself if anything happened to you" Ben expressed his fears.

Jane came in close to him put her arms around him and kissed him.

"We have never talked of love, even though we have made love I have never been happier, when we make love I have never been as happy before and don't want you to stop, I am certain I love you, I do not want to die, If you die when I could have helped you I would rather die myself, Now I AM going with you I will obey your orders" Jane told him. Ben sat silently deep in thought for a moment.

"Thank you. Jane please don't expose yourself"

"You taught me all I need to know to protect myself, I can use this knowledge to protect the one I love" Jane told him.

"All right Jane let's think about the job"

"OK Ben what do we do"

"I can think of possible three ways to rob a bank, which comes down to, two if you wish to do it silently and make an escape, the first way is to break in but you would have to make some noise plus most banks have alarm system it's obvious they will discard this method, the second way would be for the sheriff to be able to duplicate the keys to the bank, I would think this way is unlikely as most managers would not let the keys out of there sight for a second. Jane, I am certain they will go for the third method, as the sheriff I would go to the managers home, I would tell the bank manager I think I can hear someone moving around inside the bank so could the bank be opened to investigate I bet the manager will agree" Ben explained.

"That sounds logistical to me" Jane agreed.

"We know there will be three of them, the sheriff, Grant and his Mexican friend, one of them will hold the horses and act as lookout the third man will slip in behind the sheriff and manager"

"So, what is the routine Ben" Jane asked.

"When the robbers come out of the bank, I do not want to challenge them immediately as they could go back into the bank I want them to be in the open"

"I understand" Jane told him.

Just after midnight Ben and Jane made their move, they were all dressed in black which helped them to melt into the shadows, also they wore moccasins enabling them to advance silently, as the pair of them approached the bank, Ben knew of his mistake as Grant and his partner were already there, this is a surprise as he thought the robbery would be later, the two men were in an alley obviously waiting for the sheriff to arrive.

From there place of concealment Ben and Jane observed the two men, when the sheriff and manager arrived the Mexican followed them into the bank while Grant tended the horses ten minutes later the sheriff and the Mexican emerged from the bank with bags in hand, half way between the bank and horses Ben called out.

"Hands in the air, this is the law" Ben's voice was loud in the night air.

Not surprising the sheriff and the Mexican dropped the bags there hands diving for their guns, Ben fired first the bullet hit the sheriff in the chest missing the heart as the sheriff continued to raise his weapon while going to his knees, Ben fired again at a now downward angle his bullet entered at the top of the nose right between his eyes carried on to hit the top of his spine breaking his neck, causing the severed head to roll forward, changing his aim Ben snapped a shot at Grant which grazed his arm, Meanwhile Jane's first shot hit the Mexican in the leg causing him to stagger his gun firing harmlessly in the air, Jane took her time taking aim she fired two rapid shots both close together ploughed into the Mexicans body, when she saw the body go limp she also took a quick shot at Grant but missed him, Grant not being a fool new that two people had shot at him, grabbing the saddle horn yelling, "Yeh" loudly, as the horse smartly move forward Grant bounced into the saddle lying low along the horses neck rode fast out of town.,

"Damn! Damn! The bugger has done it again" Ben swore.

"This man has all the luck in the world" Jane omitted.

Because of the commotion the people of the town came running to find out what had taken place, looking at his badge a couple of people asked him what had taken place here, Ben spotted the doctor and called him over.

"Doc the sheriff is over there dead, and the Mexican is over there dead so don't bother with them yet, could you check the manager in the bank to see if he is alive"

"OK Ben" doc said.

"You are mister Jordon "Ben said pointing at a man in the crowd.

"Yes, I am Jordon assistant bank manager" came the reply.

"Take these bags and lock them away that's the money from the attempted bank robbery."

"OK Thanks Ranger" Mister Jordon replied.

"Is there any members of the town council here" Ben asked.

"Yes, I am" a small man in a derby hat called out.

"Mister there has just been an attempt to rob the bank one of the robbers who is dead was your sheriff, so you will have to get someone to replace him, can I leave that to you, in the morning I will give you a statement, I must get after Grant."

"Ranger do you need any help" one of the citizens asked. "Yes, could you get some men together and remove those two bodies down to the undertakers' Ben instructed. Turning to the man in the derby hat.

"Are you going to be able to get a lawman"

"We will be OK as we do have a man who will do it on a tempory basis" the councilor said.

"If the man you have in mind needs help there is two young men who would love to train as deputies."

"Mister you have your town back, we have to get some sleep as we have to get onto Grants tail at dawn as soon as it is light enough to track him" Ben explained

"Jane how is your shoulder" Doc asked.

"It's OK Doc" she answered.

"If you wish to you can stay in town OK" Doc said.

"NO WAY, Where Ben goes' I go the fresh air will do me good" was her reply.

"Sorry Doc Jane must come with me as long as the assassin is still in town" Ben pointed out.

"Doc, Ben's right, I feel fine fit enough to carry on with Ben, as long as the wound is washed, massaged, and bandaged I also have killers tracking me, so I am safer with Ben" Jane explained.

"Doc how is your patient" Ben asked.

"He won't go anyway for about a week" Doc replied.

"Thank you, doc,".

"Jane we will sleep I want to get after Grant as early as we can" Ben ordered Jane.

"OK I am knackered anyway" she yawned.

CHAPTER EIGHT

I LOVE YOU JANE

Ben and Jane had been up well before dawn, washed, dressed and packed ready to move, Ben knew Grants routine by now.

When Grant gets tired, the first thing on his mind would be sleep but because of the shoot out and attempt robbery if true to form Grant would use the main trail while it is dark, then follow any back trails when possible, after making as much distance as possible the next day finding a reasonable spot to camp, he would sleep.

Ben knew because the light was needed to track Grant, they could not proceed until dawn this will give Grant a chance to get some distance ahead of them, Ben's estimation that due to the delay, by camping as late as possible and rising early each morning they could catch him around two to three days.

So they would be able to ride at daybreak they rose early to carry out their normal tasks that had to be done before the pair could carry on, putting a clean change of clothing into their bedrolls, rolled them up and tied with straps, there second job was to load there saddle bags with Billy cans (pans) coffee pot and cups, first aid kit, a spare pistol each after checking it, any spare food they have like beans and jerky meat, topping up two large canteens, most important items of all checking their weapons.

Leaving the hotel, hand in hand they strolled down to the livery stable, as they approached Ben let out a shrill whistle, he received in answer a loud (neigh) from Shad the big horse snuffled Ben's shirt in recognition, Jane and Ben made sure the horses had food and water and looked fit to go, on leaving the stable they went to the café which had just opened where they had a hearty breakfast and a bag of food to go with them, after their breakfast they retraced there steps to the livery stable saddled the waiting horses, as the sky started to get light after loading their gear on the horses and when Ben was satisfied they had not forgotten anything they rode out of town.

When most people go in or out of town they walked their horses, but when a horse gallops out of town like Grant did the horses hoofs are closer together and the prints deeper and as far as Ben knew Grant has been the only person who left town early in the morning, following the tracks for about one and a half miles they came across sliding marks as Grant had brought his horse to a halt and changed direction, Jane noticed the frown on Ben's face.

"What's wrong Ben" she asked.

"Grant has left the main trail to early".

"How do you mean why" Jane queried.

"Leaving the trail in the middle of the night would slow him down, unless there was an important reason to do so, maybe Grant had a reason to change direction or destination" Ben explained.

"I love the way you assess things" Jane said and smiled.

"You know some of Grants habits as I have showed you, we have been trailing this man for quite a while and during this time we have learnt a lot about this man, we know most of the time avoiding the main trail is his habit, if you were running away from trouble the main trail would give him the chance to make some distance, but leaving the main trail would slow him down, Grant is a murderer, thief and rapist also his criminal activities have held us up a few times but a fool no Grant has managed to escape from us a few times, no the change in the dark from his usual routine, is not right, there has to be a reason for this change" Ben explained to her.

"So, what now Ben" she asked.

"We must follow the sign"

"OK Ben" Jane said.

"Look Jane if Grant has a destination in mind and keeps going it's certain the distance between us will increase, now it depends on when he gets tired, if Grant camps early and we bed down as late as possible we will slowly gain on him" Ben told her.

"Right Ben" Jane acknowledged.

Following the traces, of sign Grant left behind they travelled for around four miles, coming across a clearing hidden by trees all around it, they spotted straight away the cold remains of a fire, Ben told Jane to stop and stay while, dismounting Ben started a though search of the area going from one side to the other, where the horse stood checking the droppings they were not quite cold, the marks on the ground showed Grant had pulled something from a pit under the trees, in the pit left behind Ben saw something shinning, picking up the medal, there is a picture of a horse on one side and the name of Senator Stevens on the other side.

"So that's what it is all about" Ben said Jane dismounted and joined Ben.

"What you found Ben" Jane asked.

"Grant had stolen a lot of loot from Senator Stevens house, it would not look right carrying a bulky bag into town, Grant came here to retrieve the loot that was buried before going into town but when picking up the loot the medal was left behind this is where he relieved himself –of the engraved items" Ben explained.

"Is that good"

"Finding the medal proves Grant has the loot, but best of all if it took him a time to retrieve the loot it could mean it would slow him down giving us a better chance of catching up with him"

"Ben are we staying here long" Jane asked.

"We will let the horses blow a little while, we can have a quick snack and something to drink, then get going"

"Do we have time for you to massage my shoulder it's getting stiff I need some oil rubbed into it"

"Oh! Jane, I am sorry I have not thought about your shoulder, damn I am sorry Jane"

"It won't take long"

"Of course, we will make time to do your shoulder" Ben kissed her.

Jane slipped of her shirt to allow Ben to rub the oil into her injured shoulder the oil felt cool and Bens hands were soft, they remained there for about twenty minutes before moving on, following the sign left by Grant, with a few short stops the pair carried on through the day until just before dark as they came across a fertile bowl with a running stream nearby.

"Right Jane let's set up camp, make a fire and get water on for coffee"

"OK Ben" Jane replied in a tired voice.

For the next half, an hour they made camp, the horses were happy as they were relieved of their burdens, the scabbard and rifle, the bedrolls, the saddle bags and saddle, then left to Roam free. With the coffee and the food, they purchased at Paula's place it was time to relax after a busy day.

"Come on Jane how about a swim before bed"

"That sounds good" she replied as her clothes dropped onto the bedroll.

After a refreshing swim and a bit of loving they returned to the camp, Ben rubbed oil onto Jane's shoulder, putting the fire out they turned in for the night after a brief kiss and cuddle.

Just before dawn Ben's eyes opened, lying still his ears listened for the dawn chorus produced by the waking birds, after listening to the normal sounds of dawn, (the horses munching the grass, the rabbits scurrying around, the birds started singing) as the red ribbon of dawn showed on the horizon heralding the coming day, rising Ben made the fire, put on water to boil for coffee, by this time it was light enough to see the sleeping Jane, stripping Ben went for an early swim.

The cool water soon took the sleep out of his eyes, swimming back and forward across the pool, a smile came to his face as a beautiful naked body started to swim alongside him. Ben's intension was to have a swim while Jane slept after breakfast mount up and carry on, if you are a man and a beautiful naked body comes to you throws her arms around your neck kisses you pressing her body into yours, it is normal for you to get turned on and Jane knew this as her hand closed around his erection, she giggled which changed to moans as Ben's finger entered her crotch and rubbed her clitious , opening her legs the throbbing erection entered her now tingling crotch, giving into their wanting for each other there vigorous movement of the act of love disturbed the water so much it looked like the pool was boiling.

Holding each other's hands they walked back to the camp, Ben rubbed oil into Jane's shoulder, massaging it to relieve the stiffness half way through dressing Jane turned and kissed him.

"I love you Ben" Jane said seriously.

Ben hesitated looking at the beautiful angel in front of him with a solemn face, putting his arm around her drawing her close to him kissing her softly.

"I love you Jane" Ben told her.

Jane squealed with delight threw her arms around him her mouth searching for his lips, they kissed passionately.

"Oh! Ben, I have waited for you to say that, I didn't think you loved me and was just using me" Jane told him.

"I fell in love with you the first time I saw you standing naked in the pond, but Jane it troubles me, that is why I have not said so earlier and I am not certain whether I should have told you now" Ben ended.

"Why Ben"

"Sit have a coffee"

"OK" was all she could say puzzled by his remarks.

With them sitting on a rock a coffee in his hand Ben explained.

"Jane we have rode together for a while now and think it would be obvious , I am a lawman and believe I am a good one because I feel good and love my job even though it can be dangerous at times, I am sometimes away for long periods, I would have to leave my wife behind and I believe that is not right, During our time together I have thought a lot about this, I do love you and would like to ask you to marry me, (Jane caught her breath) but I don't think it is the right thing to do, you could end up a widow, I have never met anyone like you, who makes me feel great, and when we make love I do not want it to stop, but I feel guilty and uncertain again" Ben explained.

Jane sat patiently listening, waiting for Ben to stop talking by this time they were fully dressed holding a cup of coffee in their hands which Jane had poured out, she ordered Ben to sit and be quiet.

"Now it is my turn, you have had your say, first I love you, and the answer is yes, I will marry you, Shh! " she said the last word to stop Ben cutting in on her, "Second I would not think of you not being a lawman, I have spent the happiest time of my life with you over the last couple of weeks, It has been fascinating watching you carry out your job I do not think anyone could have done better even when wounded, you pressed on determined to carry on with your job, third as for being left a widow, that has already happened to me twice, It has I admit been a horrible, hurting, depressing feeling in my life, making me feel ill each time it happened. Ben with you I will take the chance anytime and go through it all over again, the more time we spend together the more my love grows for you, I learn something new about you every day, I love you" putting down her cup she threw her arms around him their lips met.

"With all you have seen during the period together, are you sure you want to marry me, knowing the job I do" Ben said.

"Oh! Ben even though we have been together a while you still do not know about women, If a woman loves a man it does not matter what his occupation is she will do anything for that man, Yes I have seen what you do and no way does it put me off, (I am going to marry you)" Jane emphasized the last sentence.

"I tell you what I'll complete this job, we will talk, if you have not changed your mind I would be honored if you would become my wife, if you do marry me I will be making some changes in my life, I'll tell you about that later",

"Ben, I will not change my mind, I love you" Jane told him.

Making sure they broke up the camp properly by burning any rubbish, extinguishing the fire, filling the hole, leaving the area as tidy as possible, mounting up they carried on following Grants sign.

Paul Grant must be sure of himself as the sign left behind was easy to read, Grant had never been good at hiding his tracks normally, but by the occasional bits of sign kept Ben on the right tracks which means that they can move faster and therefore giving them the chance of catching up to Grant.

Grant himself felt comfortable about the way life was at this time, he had managing to escape from some tricky situations, as far as Grant knows it is possible that no one has recognized him and thinks he is in the clear, based on this summery his next idea is to ride on until reaching the next town, where his intention is to rest for a couple of days, rob the general store, then head for the border as his thinking is that he is home free, but did not know how near Ben was to him.

Meanwhile working things out by the sign Grant left behind, Ben made an estimate that they were less than a day behind Grant and if they travelled tomorrow at the same pace by sunset tomorrow evening there is a good chance, they would close the gap and be approximately four hours behind him. By cutting the time as much as they can and with a bit of luck it could be all over the next night, they must camp as late as possible, rise early before dawn.

"I estimate we are less than a day behind Grant, we must ride as long as possible tonight, get up as early as we can, in the morning that could put us only four hours behind him" Ben told Jane.

"OK Ben I guess we will not be making love tonight, I ll probably be to knackered anyway so as much sleep as we can is on the cards after you have massaged my shoulder we sleep" Jane said.

"Of course, I will"

Travelling all day, Ben and Jane pushed themselves to the limit, Ben found a reasonable camp site late in the evening just before sundown the site had no stream, but they had full canteens.

"Jane, we will camp here for the night we will have a cold camp sleep, proceed early" Ben explained.

No answer came from Jane, she yawned loudly and nodded her head, there meal consisted of the remainder of the sandwiches and cool water, after massaging Jane's shoulder she fell asleep while Ben checked the horses, lay down listened to the sounds of the night turned over and fell asleep.

As a red streak of light appeared on the horizon Bens eyes opened the light heralded the coming dawn, lying still Ben listened to the sound of the dawn chorus satisfied everything was as it should be rising and building a fire to heat water for coffee, a moment later the musical tones of Jane's voice was clear in the crisp morning air.

"Ah! Coffee".

"Morning" Ben said as handing Jane a cup of coffee.

"Thank you"

"We will eat, I will see to your shoulder, before we break camp, darling we will have to get on"

"You don't have to; my shoulder is OK this morning the stiffness has gone" Jane informed him.

"Good after breakfast we will ride".

After eating, Ben put the remains of the coffee onto the fire to extinguish it, packed the horses, put his arms around Jane and kissed her long and passionately.

"Come on we had better ride Jane"

"OK Ben" she said in a husky voice.

Carrying on Ben picked up Grants sign knowing the man's habits it was easy to see the way to go, going by Grants actions and behavior which Ben had picked up made the tracking easier, four hours later they found the remains of Grants last camp, dismounting, feeling the remains of the fire, they were still hot, Ben now knew Grant could not be far ahead, the hot ashes of the fire and the fact that Grant would normally rise late told Ben he was no more than a few miles ahead.

"Jane, I estimate Grant can be no more than two hours ahead of us"

"That's good Ben"

Letting the horses blow for a few moments the pair of them chewed on jerky meat and drank water from there canteens.

As they proceeded through the day following Grants sign, they eventually after about four and a half hours they saw the trail became more worn, a mile further on a sign post had been erected.

1 MILE AHEAD DUKES HOLLOW POPULATION 263.

A typical small western town where everyone knew everyone, the good thing about this is that the man at the livery stable would have the information about arrivals in town.

"Jane, it looks like we will sleep in a bed tonight"

"Oh! Yes, that sounds great" Jane returned.

Riding down the high street Ben spotted the sign, (HOTEL) directing Jane to the hitch rail, dismounting slinging their saddlebags over their shoulder they walked into the hotel, stopping at reception.

"Evening sir madam how can I help you" the receptionist asked.

"A room for two please" Ben asked.

"Of course, sir No 20 on the first floor to the left at the rear of the building sir" then handed Ben the key.

"Jane, I ll leave you to unpack, I will see to the horses and will be back soon, we will have dinner that bed looks good" putting his arm around her waist drew her to him, they kissed.

"Oh! Ben that was lovely. I will unpack take your time I need to wash my body to get rid of the dust we have collected, see you soon"

"I ll be back soon" Ben told her.

The first place Ben visited to the horse's delight was the livery stable there was really two main reasons for this stop one to get the horses a place for the night and two it is the best source of information.

"Hello son" as the livery stable attendant arrived.

"Sir my name is Sammy can I help you".

"Two stalls please Sammy and I am Ben".

"Nice horse you have sir"

"As I said my name is Ben, yes Shad is a good horse, but Sammy don't try to touch him Shads a one-man horse you can put out feed and water out for him, this is my pal and doesn't like any strangers touching him".

"OK Ben I'll see to him for you".

"I see you are busy you are nearly full up" Ben said looking around.

"Yes sir, this little town hasn't had a stranger here for a while, but today we have five, two men came in early this morning, then one man just after lunch now your two horses" Sammy explained.

"It is nice to have the extra work it means a few more dollars in your pocket don't it"

"Your right their Ben"

"Sammy what is the town sheriff like, I have to visit him and would like to know what the man is like"

"Ben, Jeb is a good sheriff and has been here for quite a while, also liked by everyone plus I have never heard a bad word said about him"

"Thanks Sammy have a good night"

"Bye Ben see you tomorrow"

Ben's next stop is the telegraph office to send a wire to Ranger HQ the message read.

To;   Lone Star Ranch.

    Texas.

    DAD have arrived Dukes hollow   stop
    Will carry on tomorrow   stop

    Ben

"Sir I am about to shut the office for the night could your message wait until morning" the telephonist told him.

"Please send this small message of for me I will pay you double" Ben said to him.

The agent looked at Ben's smiling face

"OK Sir" Ben stayed and watched the man send the message of just to make sure it had been dispatched.

The two main parts of the message were one the Lone Star Ranch which is a real ranch, but it is also the Headquarters of the

Texas Rangers, the second bit of the message is the word DAD in capital letters means Commander so the message has been sent to the head of the Texas Rangers.

Ben's last call was to the sheriff's office, walking through the door first a look of amazement came to his face to be replaced by a broad smile, walking briskly to the desk with his hand out.

"Jeb how are you" Ben greeted his old friend.

"By god I don't believe it, Ben it's great to see you"

"Sammy at the livery stable told me the sheriff is called Jeb, no way did I expected it would be you"

"It's good to see you, is this call business or pleasure" Jeb asked.

"It's definitely a pleasure but Jeb I'm sorry but it is Business"

"By that statement you are still a ranger"

"Yes, did you hear about the death of Senator Stevens and his family" Ben asked.

"Yes, it went through Texas like a wild fire"

"The man who carried out that crime is in your town".

"I understand the crime had been carried out by three men".

"That's true, now only one left".

"Yeh!" nodding his head in understanding.

"Who is this man Ben".

"His name is Paul Grant"

"So, what's the problem".

"The problem is all the evidence even though I have no doubt Grant is the killer is circumstantial, I know by tracking him and seeing the crimes committed by him, this man is evil and kills without remorse, if I arrest him and take him to court the first question the defense will ask is, (Who saw this man commit this crime) and apart from a sleepy young boy and a reviving drunk, no one else " Ben explained. "Look Jeb I have seen what this man is capable of (Ben told Jeb about the crimes Grant had done) once again I can tell you about his crimes, but I did not see him do them" Ben ended.

"You have a plan, that's why you have come to me, why don't you come home to dinner we can discuss the problem, there is always enough food, Diana always cooks more food because of the kids"

"Jeb, I have a lady with me" Ben stated.

"Bring her along I am certain Diana would love some female company".

"OK how about an hour, where do you live"

"An hour will be great." Jeb told Ben his address.

Ben headed immediately back to the hotel on entering the room Jane was ready in Jeans and shirt.

"Get those clothes off"

"What before supper Ben" Jane said with a twinkle in her eyes

"Come here you"

Ben took Jane into his arms, they kissed passionately, getting his breath back.

"Jane, I have met a friend, we have been invited to dinner, I want you to put your dress on".

"OK Ben" Jane replied.

"Jane my friend is the sheriff, we have been friends for years, rode together as Rangers, but we lost touch, I walked into the sheriff's office and was surprised to see him sitting at the desk, I did not know of his move up here"

Ben pulled out his clean clothes as Jane stripped to her underwear slipped into her dress, the blue dress Ben had bought for her, the dress fitted like a glove and seemed to emphasize her lovely curves, (she is beautiful) after a wash and shave, wiping the dust from his belts and boots looking reasonably smart, Jane put her arm through his arm as they walked to Jeb's house, Ben knocked.

"Hi Ben, come in" Jeb said enthusiastically.

"Jeb this is Jane" Ben introduced her.

"Howdy Marm come in welcome" Jeb said.

"Jeb, Ben said my name is Jane"

"OK Jane I'd like you to meet my wife Diana, and these two trouble makers are John and Patsy" Jeb said.

"Oh! I don't believe that" Jane said as she looked at a boy about five years old and a girl about four, she smiled.

"Hello, I'm Jane" the two kids smiled as they took in her mild manner to their heart, they became fascinated by this lovely warm young woman.

Everyone settled down to a lovely dinner cooked by Diana it was a pleasant evening talking together and Jane played with the children before they went to bed, while Ben and Jeb talked Jane and Diana washed the dishes together entered the lounge with beers in their hands.

"Ben be serious for a moment, I want you to fill me in about the problems" Jeb inquired.

Starting from the beginning when giving the Senator Stevens job Ben told Jeb everything that had occurred, the story of the tracking of Grant and the crimes committed by him, the story up to the present, both Jeb and Diana's eye brows lifted at the mention of the price on Jane's head.

"Grant can get out of anything I have told you because there is no proof, it's my word against him, if I get the chance I could shoot him but as you know carrying a badge has a few restrictions you cannot take the law in your own hands unless Grant starts something, but I know him, I know I can get him" Ben told them.

"How" Jeb asked.

"I am sorry it has to happen in your town Jeb, Grant will rob your general store, before riding out it will be about seven thirty to eight o clock tomorrow night, I bet Grant will survey the store this evening after a night's sleep that is his normal routine, he will rob your store, they skip town, ride hard till dark, camp for the night light out before dawn, but will get complacent, but I don't want him to get that far I want to catch him when leaving the store, once in the open I should be able to take him" Ben explained.

"As this crime is about to take place in my town, we will take him".

"OK Jeb you're the boss" Ben agreed.

"I'll get the coffee" Diana told them.

"I'll help you" Jane volunteered.

"Jeb how come your sheriff of this town" Ben asked.

"Love Ben"

"Love"

"Yes, I enjoyed my job as a Ranger, but the day has to come when you think of the future, I had a little help, I met Diana and fell in love with her but I was on a job which I had to complete, on completion of the job I came across this town who needed a sheriff I sent a message to Diana told her about the sheriff's job and would she marry me, she said Yes so here I am" Jeb explained.

"I see"

"It looks like you're in the same position Ben"

"Yes, I love Jane, and I guess I am in the same position as you were Jane and I have already talked about it, we do love each other".

"Ben finish this job, then see if you can find a town that needs a sheriff, check the town out if you like it apply for the job, with your ranger connections you have a good chance of getting the job" Jeb advised Ben.

"Don't you miss being a ranger".

"The one good thing about being a sheriff, is the diversity of the job as a ranger we were mostly sent out to help other officers, but as the sheriff you have to solve all sorts of problems, getting cats out of trees to robbery and murder and town security I am never bored".

"It sounds good" Ben said.

"I find the job very interesting, I have a young man training as deputy so on a Sunday I take Diana and the kids for a picnic and swim most Wednesdays I go hunting stay out overnight, Diana used to come along with me before the kids came along, she knows I must have a little time to myself and so does the town" Jeb explained.

Next door in the kitchen Jane and Diana talked about the same subject, Diana started by asking Jane if she and Ben were in love.

"Yes, but Ben is a Ranger and wants to remain a lawman."

"Jane! Jeb used to be a ranger, one day I met him in my home town, we fell in love, it broke my heart when Jeb rode out of town, we had a very short time together, Oh! But Jane we made love and at the time I was a virgin it was wonderful, a few days later I received a wire from him, I was elated as it meant his thoughts were of me, over a short period of time I received letters from him, then I received a letter with some money in it and a two way ticket to Dukes Hollow, I followed his instruction and on my arrival Jeb was there to meet me I flew into his arms after a moment Jeb explained" Diana said.

"Diana, I have applied for the job of sheriff in this town, because of my ranger experience they have said yes, I told them I would only take the job if my girl liked the place and says she will marry me, so what do you think" Jeb asked.

"Jane, I jumped into his arms saying yes over and over again my heart was pumping so fast, I laughed and cried and even though we were not yet married we slept together that night it was fantastic" Diana recalled excitedly.

Jane asked Diana the same questions that Ben asked Jeb, about freedom, the sheriff's job and what it's like being a sheriff's wife, then all the questions one woman would ask each other. The rest of the evening pleasantly went over they enjoyed each other's company. Diana and Jeb looked at each other they understood Jeb winked at her with smiles on both their faces.

Leaving their hosts house Ben and Jane walked silently but hand in hand back to the hotel, getting back into there room there first act was to embrace and kiss passionately.

"Darling I must complete this job, seeing Jeb, Diana and the kids being so happy has got me thinking, do you think you would be happy as a sheriff's wife, I could finish this job, look for a sheriff's job then we could marry is that a good idea" Ben asked. A body crashed into him two arms clamped his body and a pair of hot lips searched for his, the two pairs of lips met as they took part in the biggest passionate kiss they have ever had. Getting her breath back Jane omitted though an excited husky voice.

"Oh Ben, Yes, Yes, Yes. Talking to Diana and seeing the children has made me envious, Ben I want us to be happy together and have a family like Diana and Jeb I will do anything you say, I will stay with you and marry you when you think it is time, I love you".

"I love you also and we will do it as soon as possible".

"Ben, I have no roots or anything to hold me back, so we will stay together and marry when we can".

Ben pulled her to him their lips met again as Ben's hand slipped into her shirt and gently squeezed her breast.

"Yes, bed" seconds later two naked bodies came together in the bed.

The two bodies became entwined as their lips met a second later Jane omitted a muffled squeal as she felt cool fingers travel down her spine from her neck to the gripping the lovely soft cheeks of her arse.

As her spine bent pushing her body into Ben he whispered, "I love you" his lips kissed her slender neck and nibbled her ear lobes, "Ohh! Ben" came from her lips as Ben kissed her lips, her neck, her throat nibbling her ears and shoulders.

While the kissing continued Ben hand caressed her lower back and the cheeks of her beautiful smooth rounded arse, Jane's body pushed into his body causing her to omit a low "Oh" as she felt Ben's growing arousal touch her belly.

Jane placed her hand onto Bens arse pulling him into her as Ben's hand moved from her arse to cup her breast his hand moved lovingly feeling, gently caressing her breast as his thumb rubbed her nipple, Ben continued kissing her, his hand and thumb caused Jane's head to go back as moans of love came from her lips, "Arr! yes Ben" her moans became louder and more precise as Jane's breasts began to swell her nipples becoming prouder.

The kissing changed as Ben's mouth moved to Jane's right breast his tongue flicking the nipple his hand still feeling her left breast, "Ohhhh! Arr! Yes, yes." his right hand continued to enjoy the feeling of the soft smooth ball of flesh in his hand.

"Oh! Jane, you are beautiful I love you" Ben whispered in her ear.

Kissing Jane's mouth passionately then moving back to her breast the renewal of this action causing passion.

With an intake of breath and the tightness of her body as it pushed up in anticipation when Ben's hand left her cleverage moved over her rib cage and swirled around her belly button over the smooth tummy between her legs to rub the lips of her crotch, with another sharp intake of breath which changed to sounds of love, Ohhhh! Oh! Ahh! Arrrr! Yes more.

"Oh! My beautiful darling" Ben whispered.

Jane's legs opened, and she gasped as the probing finger probed into her private entrance to her body Ben moved his finger in and out deeply as possible when swirling the finger, the finger brushed Jane's clitiuos sending a new level of pleasure through her body, Ahhrrr! Yes, Ben Ben Ohhh! More, her hand grabbing his erection.

As Ben's fingers pushed deeply and vigorously rubbing her clitious causing her back to bend her arse lifted from the bed as she pushed up asking for more also pulling his erection harder, Jane's crotch became moist with the juices of love lubricating the lips of her wonderful crotch (Ohhhh! yes Ben Ahhh Arr) sounds of love came from her sweet lips as the invasion to her body continued and she held the fully erected, vibrating, rampant penis.

"Ohhhh! Ben now, now Ben Ahhrrr!" she pleaded.

Ben thrust his erection through the wet waiting lips wiggling the erection around inside, began to withdraw again, Jane's hands grabbed his arse pulling him hard into her, moving his erection slowly in and out she gasped with the movement she became lost to the world as love took over as the deep thrusting erection probed deeper and faster, sounds of love could not be prevented as they both made them disappearing into a world of their own his seed transferring into her body as Ben's body shuddered giving them the ultimate pleasure an organism, the pleasure could also be seen as the two sweat covered bodies relaxed, they looked into each other's eyes and smiled Ben kissed her struggling for breath.

"Thank you darling I love you that was fantastic" Ben said his body started moving the erection still in her body in and out again.

"AArrr yes Ben" she said to the motions of love, Jane and Ben in fact made love for half the night.

With the pleasant evening, they had enjoyed with the thoughts of their talk and decisions that had been raised their arousal level in a big way the thoughts of marriage loving, and children turned Jane on in particular. After satisfying there wanting to make love Ben withdrew their arms still entwined as they relaxed once more smiles were on their faces.

"Thank you Jane I love you".

"No thank you darling" Jane said in a husky voice.

Two knacked contented bodies cuddled for a few moments as they fell asleep.

CHAPTER NINE

HE'S NOT GETTING AWAY THIS TIME

The first crack of light on the horizon heralded the new dawn, Ben woke like normal at this time in the morning, Jane lay in his arms looking at her the long eyelashes fluttered two beautiful blue eyes opened looked at him.

"Good morning darling" Ben whispered, their lips met.

"Good morning" a husky breathless voice replied.

"Jane, we were wonderful last night, I must congratulate my teacher"

"Last night my pupil taught me, Oh! Yes Ben" the last three words she said as she felt the hand between her legs, they made love.

"I love you Jane"

"Oh! Ben, I like it when you say that, I love you also"

"I hope I can make you happy"

"Darling you already make me happy, when we make love, I think it is fantastic, when we do marry, I know we will be happy" Jane whispered. Ben pulled her to him and kissed her again.

"Jane, I am going to get up now, you can lie a bit longer, I am going to take care of the horses, when I return, we will go to breakfast."

Rising Ben walked to the dresser, pouring half the water in the jug washed and shaved with a hand towel dipped it in the water and washed his body all over, Jane lying on her side looking at Ben and sighed at the naked Ben, she had seen naked men before and could not help admiring Ben's torso, the broad shoulders tapering down to a narrow waist, the rounded cheeks of his arse, muscular arms and legs, she smiled.

Ben dressed into a clean set of clothing, swung his gunbelt around his waist, picking up his pistol after checking the load spun the gun on his finger, dropping it into his holster putting the loop on the hammer, kissing Jane tenderly, telling Jane to be in the lobby in an hours' time, leaving the hotel Ben walked to the stables.

"Hello Sammy" Ben greeted.

"Hi Ben" the young man replied.

"You still busy boy" Ben enquired.

"Surly no one has left yet" Sammy told him.

"It keeps you busy, also means a few more dollars to spend don't it" Ben said slipping fifty cents into the young man's hand.

"Gee, thanks Ben, I think your horse has heard your voice" Sammy said, they both turned and looked in the direction of Shads Stall Shad stood looking at him.

"Thanks Sammy" Ben said then walked towards Shad, Sammy smiled at the big horse pretended to bite Ben suppressed a laugh as man and horse played games.

"Hi! Boy" Ben said to the big horse then patted his neck.

Talking all the time to Shad while filling a nose bag and putting it on the horses neck, filled the trough with fresh water, moving into the next stall Ben did the same for Jane's horse, during the time the horses ate Ben picked up two hand brushes and briskly brushed Shad's sleek coat, when the two horses showed they had completed their breakfast, Letting the two horses out into the empty corral so they could run, jump to take the kinks out of their bodies.

"Sammy could you muck out the two stalls for me" Ben asked.

"Sure Ben" Ben gave him another dollar.

Now satisfied everything had been done for the horses Ben made his way back to the hotel, Jane was dressed in jeans and shirt and in the progress of putting on her gunbelt, looking at Jane she belted up tied the throng around her leg picked up the colt checked it swirled it on her finger holstered it.

"Where we eating" Jane asked.

"I thought we would try the town café I've been told its good and is called, (SALLY'S SHACK) Sammy at the livery stable said it is a good place to eat"

"Sounds good let's go"

"I want to stop at the telegraph office on the way" Ben said.

"OK"

As they walked together through the town Jane found it fascinating stopping to look into every shop window, stopping at one window there was on an aisle with a picture of a solid wood double bed, (Ben that would be great for us when we marry,) Jane commented, Jane next stopped at the Millenary shop to ogle the large picture of a model dressed in a wedding dress, (Oh! Ben its lovely) she said, they were happy window shopping being together, seeing things they would like to have helped their dream, the town was not big meaning everything was just moments away, but because of their window shopping it took half an hour to reach the Telegraph office.

"Hello, have you an answer to my wire" Ben asked.

"Sir your timing is perfect, I have just received it"

"Good thank you"

"Here it is sir" the Telegrapher said.

Opening the telegram, after a glance at the message passed it to Jane but she admitted she could not understand it, steering Jane outside Ben explained the coded message the message read.

Ben Brooks   stop.

Dukes Hollow   stop

Contract cancelled   stop

Two pairs and a joker sent   stop

Keep well son   stop

Dad   stop.

"What does it mean Ben" Jane asked.

"The first part of the actual message says contract cancelled this means the rangers have been to see the family and the contract on your head has been lifted, "

"Yippee! Yippee! I'm free". Jane said.

"Whoa! Whoa! Not too fast"

"Why Ben"

"You have not heard the second part of the message, it says, Two pairs and a joker, sent, this means five gunmen have been sent after you two pairs and a single man, we know we beat two men when you were wounded, and Williams the assassin with the knife would be the joker, that means there are a pair still looking for you" Ben explained.

"Oh! No" Jane looked deflated.

"The third part of the message said, Keep Well son, it only means keep your eyes open, don't worry as the message says we will just have to keep our eyes open" Ben assured her.

"What do we do next Ben"

"We carry on to breakfast"

"BEN be serious"

"I am there is nothing we can do, we just have to wait and keep our eyes open, now wait a minute I think these men are in town, Sammy at the livery stable told me that two men and one man had arrived in town before we arrived I think the two men could be the men after you"

"What do we do now Ben"

"Nothing until they make their move"

"But"

"But nothing Jane we have nothing on these guys, as far as the law is concerned, if they have done nothing, we cannot touch them as far as anyone knows the two men have committed no crime"

"Alright breakfast"

"Now that's my girl, we will see the rest of this town before breakfast"

"If I had of been by myself, I would probably panic but with my teacher with me I will take his lead" Jane smiled,

"There is nothing we can do at this time and worrying about it will just make you ill, if we have to face them keep calm and clear your head and concentrate" Ben told her.

"OK where to next"

"General store"

"Right",

The general store in a small town, sold almost anything, it is sometimes a bank, it's often a meeting place, Ben wanted to see the manager, Jane started looking at the clothes while Ben talked to the manage who went out the back of the store then returned to Ben with something covered in his hand.

"Jane would you come here".

Jane walked over, the manager uncovered the tray of rings in his hand, Janes eyes lit up as Ben said.

"Would you like to pick an engagement ring".

"Oh! Ben" she murmured excitedly.

"If you don't like any of them, we will have to have a look at the catalogue and wait a while"

Jane picked up the tray and for a moment, looking at each ring Jane picked a gold ring with one small diamond set into it.

"I like this one darling"

Ben paid for the ring, asked Jane for her finger, slipped it on her finger it fitted OK without adjustment quite a few people had by this time come into the store, the people cheered as Jane jumped into his arms and kissed him, Ben blushed, and Jane laughed.

"I love you Ben"

"I love you also" he whispered.

Ben and Jane left the store, Jane was chattering away as she was happy, one or two of the elder women of the town always looked down their noses because Jane wore jeans and a gunbelt. They were on their way to the café around about half way there, Jeb, Diana and the children were coming towards them, Diana was on the verge of calling to Jane when Jeb grabbed her and the kids stopping them from going any further as a loud man's voice rang out.

"Jane Collins" a thick set bearded man called and stepped into the street, she looked at Ben who nodded.

"Yes, that's me" she called back, Ben stepped into the street, Jane followed in the Centre of the street they turned and faced the two gunmen.

"Mister we only want her" the big man said.

"Jane is my fiancé, if you want her you have to go through me"

"You will have to take both of us" Jane said stepping forward to stand at Ben's side.

Almost everyone in the street could see Ben's mouth moving, but could not hear what was being said, keeping his voice low and most of the people thought Ben was telling her of, Ben knew it would be impossible, so made the decision to tell her what to do. Jeb understood and started repeating Ben's words. (Jane the man in front of you is wearing a swivel holster on his right hip, when they go for their guns, as you draw your gun grip it in both hands move four or five paces to your right point the gun and keep shooting until the gun is empty).

"Mister the contract for Jane's death has been lifted" Ben told the men.

"We have not been told this and we have been paid to do the job"

"If you have been paid you can walk away"

"That's not in the contract and you could be lying"

"Jane slowly lower your hand and take the loop of the hammer move your hand away from the gun" Ben advised, "OK Ben"

"Mister there is no need for this" Ben said giving it one more try to prevent the shootout.

"When you take a man's money, you do the job" the gunman said.

"When you're ready" Ben called the play.

Time seemed to stand still as the whole town stood silent watching the scene in the street, after a pause the two gunmen as one made their move, hands going swiftly for their guns.

Jane carried out Ben's instructions lifting her gun she moved to her right the young man facing her was fast his first shot tore the sleeve of Jane's shirt the bullet creased her arm if she had not moved to the right as Ben instructed she would have been dead, Jane fired the first bullet missed the man but the second and third hit him in the chest causing his pale blue shirt changed to crimson, there was a look of amazement showed on his face, blood pumped from his wounds as his body crashed to the dusty street, convulsed for a moment then lay still.

During the pause before them going for their guns Ben read the man's stance, the man facing him was going to do a straight draw is hand almost touching his gun, Ben thought (this man is fast) as the man drew his gun Ben as drawing dived to the street the gun bucking in his hand as his shots went upwards his second shot entered under the man's chin going up through his skull to blow the top of his head sending his Stetson high in the air, the man's head exploded sending a spray of blood and brains into the air the lifeless body crashing to the street.

Ben's first thought was for Jane who stood a little dazed, her colt in its holster, her right arm across her body holding her bleeding left arm, Ben held her to him for a second or two then looking at the wound it was not to deep. Taking of his bandana Ben wrapped the wound.

Jeb arrived at their side followed by Diana and two wide open-eyed children as they surveyed the bloody scene in front of them.

"Hi Ben, you OK" Jeb asked.

"Yeh! Jane has a crease on her arm, I'll take her to the doctors, Jeb could you do me a favour" Ben said.

"Sure Ben"

"Could you get someone to clean up the street, if there is any money on their heads put it to the town development fund" "OK Ben".

"Well you did give them the chance to back down, I take it they were after Jane" Jeb commented.

"Here Jeb" Ben handed the wire to him.

Jeb read the wire being an exranger understood it straight away.

"It says two pair and a joker" Jeb enquired.

"Yeh! We took care of the others earlier" Ben informed him.

"What a day this is turning out to be" Jane said.

"What do you mean" Diana asked

"Ben asked me to marry him officially, bought me an engagement ring, I end up in a shootout all before breakfast I hope there is no more surprises today" Jane said and showed Diana the ring.

"Congratulations" Diana said and hugged Jane.

"Thank you" Jane replied.

"Jane, I didn't know you could draw and shoot the way you did I have been taught by Jeb to shoot but not from the hip".

"Ben showed me how to do it for my own protection before we fell in love and I am glad" Jane told Diana. Ben put his arm around Jane.

"Right you doctors"

"OK darling"

"We will go with you" Diana said.

"After you see the doc, we will go to the café for breakfast, I haven't eaten today, and I am starving" Ben said.

"Oh! A typical man thinking of his belly and not of my injured arm, Diana, Jeb would you like to join us for breakfast" Jane said.

"Yes, we will, I for one want to hear about the proposal and what your plans are for the future" Diana told Jane.

The remainder of the day turned out to be successful, they had breakfast together after eating stayed together for the rest of the day, in the park area of the town they played football with the kids and all enjoyed themselves, the gunfight was the only thing that put a shadow on the day, but it was soon put out of Jane's mind as she played with the kids.

As the day went on Jane and Diana spent quite a bit of time talking their conversation covered most female subjects, love, marriage and children, Diana and Jane told each other there secrets of their love lives each one of them knew all about each other's love lives like the first time there made love, special incidents in their love lives, the one thing they both agreed to was how they were both lucky and happy to find men who loved them.

Finding love in the west was sometime not easy, at this time in the west there was a shortage of females so love did not always come to you as you would wish it, many men when deciding to settle down and needed a wife to share his life, therefore lonely men married saloon girls, prostitutes or even sent away for a mail order bride, you can now see how Jane and Diana are lucky to have met men they loved and are loved, which makes a marriage very special, celebrated by everyone often in a small town everyone gets to know and celebrate with you, Jane smiled during the conversation,   Diana looked quizzically at Jane.

"Sorry Diana I just thought how lucky I am to have Ben".

"I know I think the same way about Jeb"

"Diana, I have always wanted kids I want a family but until I met Ben my love life has not been good, I look forward to the day I have kids of my own "

"Jane, it gives you a lot of work, but I love my kids and it is rewarding I can tell, you will be a great mom by the way you get along with my kids" Diana told her.

"What's it like being a sheriff's wife" Jane asked.

"Most of the time life is just normal, once a week I have a morning when I entertain the ladies of the town where we discuss town social events maybe discuss having a dance, Jeb might need me to search a female prisoner , not very often I admit, most of my time is taken at home with the children and the gardens, I also practice shooting on our range out back, I can shoot ,most of the time I hit what I shoot at, but I cannot draw and shoot like you" Diana explained.

Meanwhile Jeb and Ben talked together about old times they experienced in the Rangers, also caught up with old times, about old colleges, and what the future holds for them, eventually they came back to the present.

"What about this guy Grant" Jeb asked.

"Grant if you saw him in the street you could walk right by him, but we have seen the evil crimes this man is capable of , he has no scruples and will kill anyone who gets in his way including women and kids even a baby in its cot, Jane and I have seen his crimes first hand, but we have also learnt a lot about him, the one thing that is positive every place, this man stops in a crime is committed by him, unfortunately this time it is your town, as this is a small town ,the most richest place is the General store, since the store closes at seven pm in the evening and it is not dark until ten so I estimate Grant will rob the store at six thirty which will give him about four hours to escape, of course Grant does not know I know this and I will be ready this time I will be waiting at the store" Ben said.

"This is my town we will do it together Ben"

"I suppose it will be best to be ready by six pm to make sure, the café is almost opposite the general store, I think it would be an ideal time to have a cup of coffee, that way I will see him enter the store" Ben announced.

"Right Ben I will be a little south of the store, to stop him running to the border" Jeb told Ben.

The remainder of the day went over pleasantly, as the friends sat and talked for a time, after having the time to talk Ben and Jane left their friends to give Ben a little time to prepare, at five pm Ben took Jane in his arms and kissed her.

"Jane stay here, I'm going for a walk, get some fresh air"

"I'll come with you"

"No stay here, Grant could shoot you"

Going straight to the livery stable, Ben went straight to Shadow's stall, he saddling up, took him out of the stall tied the reins back, around his neck leaving him to move free in the corral.

"Sammy don't touch him OK"

"OK Ben"

At around five thirty Ben arrived at the café, luckily enough the table by the window was free, his back against the wall he ordered a coffee, sat watching the front of the store.

Jane came into the café picked up a cup of coffee and sat at Ben's table.

"What are you doing here I told you to stay in the room"

"Having a cup of coffee"

"Jane, I said you should stay at the hotel"

"Ben, I tried that, I couldn't do that, you being here, look darling I will stay in the café when you go out to get him"

"Alright, I don't want you to take any part in this episode"

"I'm not going to do anything, but I will be here in case you need me" Jane told him.

"Darling you and I know more about this man than anyone, we have seen the result of his handy work, you also know how evil this man is, if you are a woman or child you get in his way and you can bet your dead, stay in the café" Ben said.

As time slowly went by six thirty came and went Ben started to think, (had his assessment of Grant been wrong,) the store shuts at seven pm looking at the clock it was a couple of minutes after quarter to seven when out of the corner of his eyes Grant came into view riding towards the store, stopping outside the store Grant was being very careful, before dismounting he scanned the street, dismounting his deliberate slow steps plus pausing on the boardwalk, he once more check his surroundings, before he entered the store.

Ben rose from the seat, patted Jane's shoulder walked past her towards the door, strolling slowly from the café, finding a place of concealment opposite the store Ben pinned on his badge and waited, when Ben and Jeb were talking they expected Grant to rob the store and pistol whip the manager get away without making a sound jump on his horse and get out of town, but the unexpected happened three shots were heard coming from the store Grant ran out of the store carrying a bag, this is when Grant ran into luck and Ben fell out of luck.

As Grant left the store, by chance a young couple were walking past Grant crashed his pistol on the young man's head, his arm going around the young lady's throat pulled her tight towards him, levelling his pistol at the ladies' head pulled and held back the hammer.

"Lower your gun you are under arrest" Jeb called out.

"Sheriff you shoot me, and the hammer will drop" Grant answered.

Grant held the pistol in a half cocked position if he let go of the hammer the lady will be died.

"You can't get away, you will be hunted by every lawman in the west" Ben called out.

"I'll take my chances" Grant called back with a smile.

The barrel prodding her, she did what Grant ordered and backed up to his horse, taking the reins Grant walked to where the boardwalk stood a couple of feet high allowing him to climb into the saddle, keeping hold of his captive after climbing into the saddle, threw the lady over his saddle horn his pistol pushed into the middle of her back, nudged his horse forward.

The street was deserted as Grant rode out of town nudging his horse into a canter. Ben stood still Jane came out of the café as Grant rode out of sight, Jane looked amazed looking at Ben, it was not like Ben to stand and watch she knows Ben is a man of action, and was on the verge of asking him why, when Ben walked into the Centre of the street and uttered a shrill high pitched whistle, the noise of a racing horse could be heard before Shad came into sight, Shad stopped, Ben grabbed the saddle horn and leaped into the saddle, Jeb and Jane looked at Ben amazed, caught by surprise as Ben yelled.

"He is not getting away this time" as he rode out of town.

"Damn trust him to think of that" Jeb said as he ran for the livery stable, Jane followed a smile on her face nodding her head, as usual Ben had thought ahead of them, why should she be surprised, Jeb and Jane saddled up as quick as possible followed Ben out of town.

As Ben rode, his thoughts were of what Grant would do, putting himself in Grants position, having a captive and a sheriff chasing him make it a bit different to the times Ben has chased him before but being logical Grant cannot afford to stop so the woman should be safe.

Grant thought the posse would be about half an hour behind him so raping the girl was out of the question, stopping for any reason would be stupid Grant was not stupid, so cannot stop to tie her up, what Grant did not know Ben had taken a chance and took what was a short cut therefore at this time Ben was in a position to shoot him with a rifle but could not take the chance as there was the chance of hitting the horse or the young lady all Ben could do is pace Grant and hope there is a chance he will get a break.

Meanwhile Grant still had a problem how to get rid of his Burdon, his estimate was that the distance travelled would be approximately five miles, getting rid of the girl would allow him to travel faster, looking ahead a smile came to his face, gripping the back of the ladies' dress on reaching the Centre of the stream pulled hard on the dress the lady screamed as she flew through the air and submerged under two foot of water Grant laughed, nudged his mount to go faster.

Standing in the middle of the stream drenched dripping water from head to toe as Ben rode through the stream yelling to the lady.

"The sheriff is behind me wait there" the lady waved to him.

The young lady now realized she was free and being told to stay where she was, giving her the chance to take in the beautiful countryside around her, she sat on a rock and waited until Jeb and Jane rode up.

"Jane stay here with the lady" Jeb told her.

"Hi! I'm Jane"

"Hello, Jane, I am May" the lady said.

"How about you getting up behind me and we will ride back to town" Jane suggested.

"Jane could we ride a little upstream and while my clothes dry I could we go for a swim" May asked.

"Sure, why not I'll join you" Jane said.

Jane knew that the two best men were after Grant and that she would not be necessary, so why not go for a swim it being a nice evening.

While the ladies enjoyed themselves, Ben was close on the trail of Grant, keeping a safe distance from Grant, Ben could have shot his horse a couple of times but the last thing in his mind was to shoot the horse but it was in his mind that as a last resort shooting the horse maybe the only way of stopping him, if it was possible to get a little closer it might be possible to take the shot.

Grant still kept his horse at a canter, this of course is understandable obviously wanting to keep the horse from tiring early and leaving something in case it was necessary to run, Ben did not worry about that as Shad if given his head could out run Grants horse if required, but for the same reason that Grant did not run, was the reason Ben held back it was not necessary to tire Shad.

For over an hour they travelled through a wide valley, through a rocky gorge, a thick tree area, Grant kept moving in the same direction, and had only one thought in his head to carry on until the border was in sight and because of that reason did not want or think of hiding his tracks, it came to Ben that Grant already thinks if his horse is kept at the same pace and keep ahead of the posse therefore making the border before they could catch up but did not know Ben was close.

After a few miles luck came Ben's way because Grant had to stop for a call of nature (he needed to go to the loo) Grant dismounted walked into some bush's, on seeing this Ben also dismounted unsheathing his rifle and levelled it ready, as Grant started to go towards his horse Ben fired the bullet hit Grant in the arm so made him jump back into the brush his horse shied away, this is good with Grant wounded and his horse out of reach, Actually Grant was lucky Ben had shot to kill as it was important to stop this man, but Grant turned at the last minute the bullet hitting him in the arm.

"Grant give yourself up you cannot get away" Ben called.

"I'm willing to take my chances" Grant returned snapping of a shot in Ben's direction.

Nothing needs to be said it is now a job of stealth because the area they are in is a dense wooded place, the thick bushes made it hard to see each other, there is spaces where it is possible to see the other person but for Ben it is mainly by sound, the thick brush was more like a maze. Ben stopped and stood still and remained quiet everything was silent, because of their presence the birds have stopped singing and the animals were all silent because of the intrusion of their spaces, Ben needed to know Grants position, picking up a stone Ben threw it in Grants direction, Grant did not shoot but Ben who was listening intently did hear a rustle of leaves and knew Grant had moved, on hearing this sound Ben moved a few paces in that direction but paused again, everything went quiet once more, Ben dropped to his knee his ears strained to hear any sound after hearing a slight sound to his right, lowering himself as low as possible to put his left ear to the ground to detect any vibrations, by doing so Ben could see Grants foot under the bush, estimating where Grant's trunk would be Ben instinctively shot through the bush Grant stood behind, Ben heard a surprising cry, a thud like a falling body hitting the ground, moving quickly forward, Grant lay on the ground his hand holding his stomach blood pouring between his fingers as his other hand raised a revolver, Ben's rifle spurted flame, the bullet went through Grants neck almost separating the head from the body, it was not necessary to check the lifeless form.

Hearing a noise behind him Ben spun round rifle ready to shoot but relaxed as Jeb rode down to where Ben stood, uttering a whistle Shad came to him.

"Hi! Ben" Jeb greeted.

"Howdy Jeb" Ben returned.

"I see you got him" Jeb said.

"Sure, I made sure this time" Ben told him.

"I'd do the same"

"Jeb would you get Grants horse, we will wrap the body in his bedroll and tarp"

"OK Ben" Jeb said.

By the time Ben and Jeb rode into town it was dark, going straight to the undertakers, turning Grants body over to the undertaker they next called into the sheriff's office, Jeb put the stores money into the safe, filled in the log, next stop was the livery stable where Ben received a nice surprise.

"Hello darling" came the magical tones of Janes voice

"Hi! Sweetheart" Ben smiled then dismounted.

"You finished the job" she asked.

"Yeh! Grant is no more" Ben replied.

"You killed him".

"Yes, I gave him the chance to give himself up, but like the Grant we know his answer was a bullet, so the fight was on and I won"

"Knowing Grant, I expected him to fight than to face Justice" Jane said.

"Well that's one job I'm happy is over" Ben replied and kissed Jane.

"And what did you get up to" Ben asked.

"Oh, the young lady May's clothes were wet so while they dried we had a swim" Jane told him.

"I see while we are working you enjoy yourself "Ben teased.

"I enjoyed it, but it would have been better if you were there" Jane teased back.

All this time Ben and Jeb looked after their horses at the livery stable, then on the way to the hotel the three of them together, Jane asked Jeb.

"Jeb the hotel has bar meals, we are going to eat would you like to join us"

"No, If I don't report home, I will have Diana looking for my scalp she will get worried if I am too late" Jeb told her.

"Give our love to Diana and the kids, see you Jeb" Jane said.

"Jeb thanks for your help and support in getting Grant it's been a hell of a job, I'm glad it is over" Ben thanked Jeb with a man hug.

"Anytime Ben, I didn't do much, but you can always count on my help Ben" Jeb returned.

"See you Jeb"

"See you Ben ". Jeb strolled of down the street.

"Jane it's a bit late, we will have supper and a quiet night tomorrow we will stay over for another day, I will have to send a wire to the headquarters confirming the job was complete, we will then enjoy ourselves for the day. The next day we can start heading back to report, I am happy the job is over but I don't feel like celebrating tonight, we will do so tomorrow instead" Ben explained.

"I understand darling" Jane said.

"Tomorrow we will take the time to enjoy ourselves and the present environment, the following day we will start back to HQ and report and tell the boss I will be leaving the Rangers" Ben told her.

"That sounds good to me" Jane replied.

CHAPTER TEN

A SWIM EVERY NIGHT

The next morning, As the job is now over Ben and Jane could relax so woke up a little later, the sun was just peeping over the horizon. Ben lay back against the pillow, Jane snuggled in his arms.

"Oh! Ben this is wonderful just being together"

"Yes, Jane it is" they kissed.

Ben kissed Jane, pulled her body to him and cuddled looking at and feeling the body beside him, and the feeling of the start of an arousal between his legs could only mean one thing, as Ben put his hand between her legs, she giggled.

"Yes please" she murmured they made love.

A little while later the two heavy breathing bodies lay together the two smiling faces look into each other's faces.

"My beautiful darling that was fantastic, I love you" Ben whispered.

"Ben last night you said you did not feel like celebrating, but by Christ you could not have started the day better I loved every minute of making love this morning, I love you" Jane's low sexy, husky voice said.

Ben pulled Jane to him their lips came together.

"Thank you darling, I love you, now let's get up the extra wonderful activity has made me hungry I'm starving "she pretended to hit him.

"Trust you to think of food" she told him but did not tell him she was hungry herself and secretly admitted it is a good idea.

Rising each one of them used half the water to wash their bodies and in Ben's case water to shave. They dressed then proceeded to Sally's Shack for breakfast, breakfast over hand in hand they strolled to the telegraph office where Ben sent the acknowledgement of the completion of the job, carrying on they arrived at the livery stable, sitting on a bale of hay watching the feeding horses.

"Jane what would you like to do today" Ben asked.

"Now the job is over, and we do not have to think of Grant's actions, and we are free to do what we want, I know we are going to visit Diana and Jeb this evening, I want us to be by ourselves in a place where it is just the two of us". Jane said softly.

"OK while the horses blow, we will leave, you go to the café and get some food, I will get us a couple of beers, we will then ride have a picnic and spend a quiet time together" Ben suggested.

"Oh! Darling I think that is a great idea" they kissed.

The two separated to acquire the items that they wanted Ben added a blanket to his items, twenty minutes later the pair came together once more at the stable, saddling up they rode out, after a couple of miles Ben and Jane kicked the horses into a gallop and rode for a mile to give them some exercise, slowing the horses to a walk Jane climbed out of her saddle to sit on Ben's lap, spending a pleasant time kissing, cuddling and talking as they ambled along.

Ben and Jane did find a spot to stop and have their picnic, the place was not ideal but they decided to remain there together in each other's arms after eating, it did at least give them a place where they could talk and plan for the future, time went by as the two of them enjoyed the time together, three hours later mounting up and headed for town.

"We should get back in time to change before we go visiting Diana and Jeb" Ben commented.

"And the kids" Jane said.

"Alright the kids as well, you like the kids don't you Jane"

"Yes, I do, but I'm looking forward to us having some children of our own and be able to settle down as a family, it will be fantastic" Jane replied her face beamed her voice husky and smoldering eyes.

"As soon as we are in a secure position, I think we should have a couple of kids" Ben told her.

"What!!! Only a couple" Jane said in a raised voice a smile on her face.

"OK we will have as many as you want"

"That's better" she put her arms around him and kissed him.

Now back in there room Jane and Ben started cuddling their kisses were deeply passionate, changing clothes took a little longer than they expected but at five pm in the afternoon Jane in her blue dress and Ben in smart clean clothes stood on the porch of Jeb and Diana's house they were greeted by all the family including the kids.

Jane gave the kids some candy she bought from the store earlier and took no time to play with the kids which did not go unnotested.

"Ben, she loves kids" Diana said.

"Yes, she does" Ben replied.

"Have you any idea's when you are intending to get married" Diana asked.

"When I get a sheriff's job we can then settle down" Ben told her.

"You should get married as soon as possible" Jeb told Ben.

"I'd love to" Jane's voice could be heard.

"Jebs right Ben, you know you will have a better chance of getting the job you want if you have a wife" Diana explained.

"What do you think Jeb" Ben asked.

"I'd listen to Diana she is right if you are married you are more staple and if you had kids it would be even better, they would know you are happier and would want to settle down" Jeb explained.

Jane playing with the kids had her ears tuned into the conversation she did not say anything, she looked at Ben their eyes met Ben and Jane had already expressed their desire to get married but Ben had always thought it would be best he should finish the job and report back to HQ before doing so.

"I thought it would be best to complete the job at Ranger HQ"

"You can marry anytime you want to, it's not necessary for you to delay, you can send a wire to complete the job, If Jane agrees to marry you that is all you need so there is no reason for you not to get married is there" Diana asked.

"You don't have a priest here" Jane pointed out.

"We will have tomorrow" Jeb assured them.

"Of course, you will have to stay a little longer" Diana told him.

"If I was you first thing in the morning, I would send a wire to HQ, tending your resignation, informing the old man you are getting married, I am certain the boss will understand" Jeb advised.

"Are you sure the priest will be here tomorrow" Ben asked.

"Look Ben father Conway comes to town every month on the same day and time, you can set your watch by him," Diana assured him.

"Now then are you two staying on" Jeb asked.

Ben looked at Jane and gazed at his beautiful fiancé who looked back at him waiting for his answer and knew there could only be one answer.

"At this time, the only thing I want to make my life complete is to marry Jane and make her happy, we will stay and get married if she wants to" Ben stated.

Jane yelled with delight her body hit his, two lips met his they kissed, Jeb, Diana and the children smiled then congratulated them the kids were laughing also but did not understand.

"Yes, I want you, I love you" Jane told him.

"I love you" Ben said.

"Oh my god, I cannot marry, I have nothing to wear this blue dress is the only one I have" Jane exclaimed.

"Don't worry we will sort something out" Diana stated.

"OK listen you lot, Jane you will stay the night we will work out what we need to do dress etc. Ben, you will have to sort out what you are going to wear you don't have to do anything about food or drink Jeb and I will supply that" Diana took charge.

After taking the kids to bed, Diana and Jane joined the men for a snack their conversation was mainly about the wedding, and who they could invite in such short notice.

"OK Ben you will have to go now, you may require something from the general store for the wedding and you have little time to do so, Jeb you go about your job as sheriff and don't come back until after your night rounds, it is now time for girl talk before we turn in" Diana once again taking charge.

"Yes Marm" Ben joked and saluted with a smile on his face.

"Sure, darling Jeb said.

"You come here" Ben looked at Jane, coming together they kissed

"How does Mrs. Brookes sound to you Jane" Ben asked.

"Music to my ears darling" she replied.

"Right you two go now Ben Jeb is the boss in town but in this house, I am the boss get it" she looked sternly at him.

"Yes Marm" gave a mock salute ducked his head and then ran for the door, Jane and Diana could not help laughing, as Ben ribbed them because that's all it was, Ben knew what Diana had said is the truth.

"I have a few things to do but I will be at your office at ten to do rounds with you" Ben told Jeb.

Ben took a quick trip to the general store to check if he had forgotten anything, seeing a new pressed white shirt and visualizing the shirt in the hotel, buying it was not an option also buying a string tie to go with the shirt then made his way back to the hotel, Putting his moccasins on gave him the chance to clean his black leather boots, his trouser belt, after washing his black leather vest was now satisfied everything was now ready for his wedding.

True to his word Ben arrived at the sheriff's office around nine forty-five this meant there was time for a cup of coffee before doing the rounds of the town.

"Hi! Jeb" Ben greeted

"Hiya! Ben you ready for tomorrow".

"Yes, I have things in hand"

"OK Let's do rounds" Jeb said.

"Let's go".

Rounds in a small town did not amount to much, but every dedicated lawman carries out there jobs, his actions mean a lot to the people of the town who hire you, it is important that the people feel secure in the knowledge that someone is looking after them, most of the job is walking around making sure everyone is happy, the other part of the purpose of making rounds is to check the security of various premises in town like the general store all shops in town including the café. If any saloons that are closed are checked, but most saloons would stay open until the last customer left. Most times the rounds are done while a saloon is still open, like tonight they checked with the bartenders to make sure everything was OK, the last building in town is the brothel the house with the red light outside it. There is one place left to check on and that is the livery stable Where Ben checked on Shad before they both returned to the office Jeb filled in the log.

"Ben, I had better get home hopefully the girls have finished talking, see you in the morning Ben"

"See you Jeb" Ben replied.

Back in the room Ben felt lonely tonight, thinking of the many nights of being on a job by himself miles away not even bothering him, that is before Jane came along, tonight for the first time Ben felt loneliness, Jane is not only a beautiful woman, she is always happy, the type of person who brightened up everybody's day and it was effective, Ben smiled as his thoughts of how during the time together they have had very few bad words. (I love you and miss you) Ben said thinking of Jane before drifting off to sleep, Ben had no real problem getting to sleep as over the years has trained himself to sleep through any situation.

Jane on the other hand had difficulty in getting to sleep due to the thoughts of what tomorrow will bring, Ever since meeting

Ben she had thought of marriage again and now it is going to happen she was elated her heart thumped (I love you) she said thinking of Ben.

Before retiring for the night, Diana with Jane's help made decisions about the food and drink, looking through Diana's clothes there was a white dress it looked OK, but Jane told Diana she was going to the general store first thing in the morning, Diana agreed, it soon became easy to make a list of guests

The manager of the general store was surprised to see two ladies waiting for him to open the store Diana and Jane had camped for an hour, the only thing on their minds were to find a dress so headed straight to the clothes section of the store, the sooner they could get the dress the better in case any modification needed to be made. At first the ladies were disappointed as they did not immediately see any white dresses, completely by chance Jane saw a piece of light blue material, she tugged the cloth to find it to be the sleeve of a white dress with light blue trim around the sleeves neck and helm, Jane was about to discard the dress but Diana persuaded her to try it on, to her surprise the dress fitted perfectly, Jane's figure seemed to bring the dress to life, Diana sighed.

"Its beautiful Jane, you will knock Ben of his feet"

"It does fit nicely and feels good" Jane said excitedly.

"Jane, it is fantastic"

"It does not need any adjustments do you think"

"No Jane" Diana said watching Jane look into the mirror.

"It is a lovely dress, I like it, but it is to plain and since it already has a little blue on it, I think it would be better if it had a little bluer on it like a belt" Jane told Diana.

Looking through the store they were disappointed not finding what they wanted but up on a shelf there was a roll of cloth the colour Jane required, calling the manager over Diana asked him to get the material down.

"Jane, it would not take long to make a sash"

"OK Diana let's get back and do it".

Before leaving the store, Jane bought some candy for the kids headed back to the house to make arrangements, as the preacher does not normally arrive in town until ten am, Jeb reckons the wedding would have to be 1300 at least.

Meanwhile Ben as usual woke up early his first thought was of Jane, knowing it was not necessary to get up early Ben tried to go back to sleep or have a lie in but found it impossible, as was his nature, the only thing to do was to get up and dressed which is the action Ben took leaving the hotel his objective to visit Sandy's shack for breakfast on completion of eating a substantial breakfast washed down by a lovely fresh mug of coffee, the first coffee of the day which he relished.

Ben new there was plenty time before the wedding on his way to the livery stable called into the telegraph office and sent a wire to HQ

Lone Star Ranch	stop
Texas	stop
uncle	stop
I resign	stop
Getting married	stop
Town sheriff job	stop
Ben	stop

Ben put in the last entry after a bit of thought knowing at HQ, they will read between the lines it might help, it would definitely do no harm, on his arrival at the livery stable a welcoming neigh came from Shad.

"Hi Boy" Ben made a fuss of Shad patting his neck

"Hello Ben" Sammy greeted.

"Morning Sam had a quiet night"

"Yes, Ben word has gone around you are getting married today"

"Yes, I am".

"Congratulations Jane is a wonderful person".

"She is thank you Sam"

"Right Ben I'll take care of Jane's horse for you

"Thanks"

Ben spent a bit time in the stables, by mucking out Shad's stall giving him fresh water and a nosebag of oats, then before leaving gave the big horse a brisk brushing.

On his arrival, back at the hotel Ben realized there was still a bit time left, this period of time gave him time to clean and check his weapons before going to the barber shop where they had a bath and shower room, Ben had a shower dressed sat in the dining room and waited for his best man Jeb, checking in his vest pocket to make sure the wedding rings were still there.

"Hi Ben, I see your ready been here long" Jeb greeted.

"I have not been here long do you want a coffee"

"No let's go"

"OK" Ben said.

"If we stroll along to the town meeting house, we should get there in a reasonable time" Jeb informed him.

The women of small towns on hearing there is someone getting married go and attend the wedding service, so Ben was caught by surprise as people congratulated him.

As Jane and Ben had only been in town for a short period of time, they expected their wedding to be very small,

At one pm precisely Jane arrived with Diana as bridesmaid the kids trailing behind, Ben took in a sharp breath at the first site of Jane, the white dress Jane bought is beautiful plus a perfect fit it does nothing to hide any parts of her body, it has a low neckline which showed a generase amount of cleaverage hugging her body the dress showed her narrow waist and rounded hips the blue sash did set the dress of she looked like an angel. (Phew! Beautiful) Ben sighed.

Ben knew how beautiful Jane is, by the number of times they had seen each other naked you would think there was no way Ben could be surprised but the way Jane was made up and dressed the way she was, Ben had to admit Jane was so beautiful more beautiful than she had ever looked before. At normal times Jane dresses in shirt and Jeans, a couple of times she has worn the blue dress and on all occasions, she has looked beautiful, but this time Diana has taken charge and dressed Jane for her wedding, Ben admitted never in his life had there been such beauty.

At one thirty-five Jane and Ben were married there was nothing special about the wedding, everyone in the hall yelled and clapped when Ben kissed Jane at the end of the ceremony, even though they had only a short distance to go, a buggy and two horses had been laid on, a bag of rice had been split open so everyone who wanted to could grab a handful and throw it over the happy couple.

It was a short ride to Diana and Jeb's house but Ben bursting with pride put his arm around her and kissed her.

"I love you, darling you are beautiful"

"Thank you darling" Jane glowed with happiness.

"Mrs. Brookes" Ben looked at her.

"Yes, Mr. Brookes" they kissed again.

On arrival at the house they were overwhelmed by the laid-out tables the drinks it was a good party, Jane and Ben really enjoyed themselves of course after Jane threw her bouquet Ben was once more left alone for the next hour as she decided to play games with the kids for just over an hour until they were put to bed. Ben said thank you for him and his wife to everyone left leaving Ben, Jane, Diana and Jeb alone.

Sitting around the table Diana poured out a last drink for each of them, for the next hour the four of them sat and talked, just before the newlyweds left, they thanked Diana and Jeb for making their wedding day special.

Walking arm in arm Ben and Jane strolled to the hotel, slowly climbing the stairs to the room, opening the door Jane was about to enter when Ben put his arm around her waist swept her of his feet lifting her into his arms walked into the room, slammed the door with his boot two sets of hot lips met, lowering Jane's feet to the floor, instantly they came together in a embrace, lips once more coming together in a long passionate kiss.

"Oh! Jane, I love you" Ben whispered in her ear as his hand made patterns on her back.

"Bed" Jane returned.

They both undressed then slipped into the bed Ben looked into the beautiful face in front of him before drawing her body to him their lips met, they lovingly kissed,

"You are beautiful"

"Ben when you put your arms around me and hold the way you are doing now, I feel wonderful, secure and loved."

"I do love you, Jane" he said tenderly.

Ben's fingers ran down her spine she sighed her body pushing into his it felt great as the tantalizing hand smoothly ran over her body gently gripping the cheeks of her arse the smoothness of her skin felt great, as the fingers caused a tingling sensation as they moved back up her spine to the sensitive spot on her shoulder.

"Oh! Ben, I love you" she murmured.

His answer once again was to kiss her lips, her neck, nibble her ears in between pausing to whisper in her ear, "My beautiful darling" Jane gave out a sharp (Oh) as Ben gently smacked her backside, Jane's hungry lips searched for his as her passion rose a bit more.

"Jane, my darling, Jane darling" was only shut off by another bout of passionate kissing, lips, neck, ears and shoulders, (Oh! Ben that's nice) Jane said in a low voice.

"I love you Mrs. Brookes"

"Mrs. Brookes that sounds good I love you" Jane replied.

Kissing once again, this time Jane caught her breath as she felt his hand gently caress her breast (Ohhh! Yes, yes) as it felt good. Ben could not help loving the beautiful soft ball of flesh, feeling caressing and kissing it with care his thumb flicking the nipple, Oh! Jane your fantastic I love you as their lips met again, Jane's body once again crushed into Ben as she giggled because of Ben's hand on her back.

As the hand left her back to hold her right breast the thumb brushing the nipple, his lips leaving her mouth kissed down her neck on to her shoulder then his mouth covered and sucked the nipple of her left breast (Ohhhhhh!) a long lingering sound came from her lips as her breasts began to swell, the swelling breast and proud Harding nipples Jane could not contain the sounds of pleasure as it made her tits more sensitive, she omitted sounds of love from her lips (Ohhhh B Benn).

As Bens thumb flicked Jane's right nipple, and his tongue vibrated the nipple on her left breast caused more pleasure plus she felt Ben's erection pushing against her stomach Arr, Ohhh Yes, she uttered.

"Oh! Ben oooo"

"I love you Jane"

Grabbing Bens arse she pulled his body into hers the erection pushed firmer into her tummy (Oh! Ben) her hand automatically held his Erection.

Jane's body stiffened in anticipation as she felt the hand travel down her body from the valley between her breasts over the rib cage, around her belly buttons across the smooth skin of her lovely soft tummy as she sucked in, she tensed as the fingers neared the private entrance to her body, a light triangle of dark pubic hair emphasized her crouch, the fingers rubbing the lips of her crouch causing another rise of pleasure her body pushed up the beautiful rounded arse leaving the bed as her back arched. The noises of love became longer and louder as she experienced more pleasure of her arousal her head thrown back, (Ohhhhh! Arrrr), Jane's legs opened, as her hand wrapped around Ben's erection.

Jane's body tensed she gasped as a probing finger invaded through the private entrance of her body, this intrusion gave her more pleasure causing her to open her legs more the finger thrust deeply swirling around inside her crouch brushing the clitious (Ohhhh! Ohh! Ahhrr) as his finger withdrew she pulled on his erection demanding more, re-entering her body the probing, thrusting, swirling invader once more rubbing the clitious causing her to cry out showing her enjoyment as she came to full arousal her juices of love soaked her crotch lubricating the lips of the crotch her arse left the bed once more pushing up wanting more, (now Ohh! Now Ben).

Pushing the throbbing rampant erection through the wet lubricated lips of her crotch, with deliberation Ben pushed slowly in and out as she gasped omitting cries for more, grabbing his arse pulling him to her, Ben being in full control resisted her move and continued his slow in and out motion deeply thrusting into her body, bit by bit Ben increased the speed of his thrusting probing erection as the two bodies moved fast pulsating in union, in the movement of their love took over, everything in the world disappeared, forgotten as their actions took them into a world of their own, neither Jane or Ben could suppress the sounds of love they omitted.

Ben's body jerked violently as the seed transfer caused Jane to shudder calling out her eyes open with the pleasure, as she experienced an organism making her feel fantastic as her body felt as if it had been taken lovingly apart and gently put back together again. As their actions came to an end the two sweat covered bodies clung together Ben's erection still in Jane's body their lips came together in a lingering kiss, Ben's body once more began to move his erection thrusting slowly in and out (Oh! Yes, do it again) Jane whispered.

The two lovers made love most of the night until completely knackered, so knackered they fell asleep, cuddled together.

A pair of beautiful blue eyes fluttered open and looked straight into the face of the man she loved, two pairs of smoldering eyes met then two pairs of searching lips came together in a passionate kiss, feeling the hand between her legs rubbing the lips of her crotch, her hand felt the erection, (yes) was all she said as they once more made love expressing their love for each other.

"I love you Jane" she heard him whisper

The love birds continued satisfying their desires for each other, Jane rose from the bed went over to the basin and jug, poured some water into the basin she splashed her face, two hands came around her body holding her breasts, oh! she said loudly as she felt the erection rubbing the lips of her crotch, opening her legs she allowed the erection to probe deeply into her, Ben had taken her by surprised again and she loved it as his seed once again passed into her body.

"Thank you, Jane, I love you" Ben whispered.

"I love you I hope you have made me pregnant" her husky voice replied.

"You are fantastic Mrs. Brookes" Ben said in a soft voice.

"I love you darling"

"I love you also" taking the naked body to him, they kissed.

Each taking a hand towel they washed their bodies, Jane dried herself then started to dress, after Ben put his trousers on and his gunbelt around his waist he started to shave, looking at Jane as she started to put on her white dress.

"You know how to pick dresses Jane, when I saw you in the blue dress I think it suits you and fits you and you look fantastic in it but I must admit this new dress is even better, you knocked me of my feet when I saw you in the hall where we married, you are beautiful my darling and I love you" Ben complimented her.

"Thank you darling I love you" (Jane felt wonderful at her husband's compliments) "Ben its Diana you must thank for how I looked, if I had of done things myself, I would have thrown the dress on and combed my hair, but Diana said (as a bride you must look the best person in the room) so she made me up, thank her" Jane explained.

"My beautiful darling, I Know who was the most beautiful person in that room, she did not need to be made up, you"

"Thank you darling" she blushed

"Now come on let's go to lunch, what do you think the café or hotel" Ben asked.

"The café, what about breakfast" she smiled with a cheeky look on her face, Ben looked at her they both burst into laughter. Needless to say, with their extra activity this morning it was too late for breakfast.

Leaving the hotel, they walked arm in arm through the town, Ben and Jane thought the wedding had went over with only a few people knowing about it, so was surprised that they were continuously congratulated by citizens of the town, being a small town news of the wedding was known by most of the residents, arriving at the café the newlyweds spotted Jeb sitting at the table by himself with a cup of coffee in his hand.

"Ben, Jane pull up a chair".

"Where is Diana and the kids" Jane asked.

"I am waiting for them, young Jeb fell when playing around this morning, Diana has taken him to the doctors to get him checked over" Jeb explained.

"Ben have a coffee until I return" Jane said then walked out the door.

Twenty minutes later, Jane, Diana and the kids, the boy had a small bandage on his arm.

"It is OK Jeb just grazed his arm nothing broken" Diana told him.

"That's good, you OK son" Jeb asked.

"Jane bought me a lolly dad" little Jeb said.

"And me, and me daddy" his little sister said.

"Yes, she is good to you" Jeb said.

"Yes daddy" they said together.

"Let's all have our lunch now" Diana suggested.

"Young Jeb is OK Diana" Ben asked.

"Oh! Sure, after Jane made a fuss of him, started playing just as normal, Ben she loves kids and gets on with them" Diana hinted.

"Sally over here please" Jeb called.

"OK Jeb there in a moment" Sally returned

Sally owned the café she has named it (Sally's shack) which is known for the good service, cleanliness, presentable, full plates of well-cooked food, Sally walked over to the table, spotting Ben and Jane straight away.

"Ahh! The newlyweds, your lunches are on me as a wedding present" Sally said.

"Thanks Sally"

"Yes thanks" Jane followed.

The meals arrived, the conversation around the table was general as you might expect.

"Ben now the Job is over what do you intend to do, any plans" Jeb asked.

"Well getting married and all that I haven't put much thought to it or discussed it with Jane yet, If Jane agrees we will spend a couple of days here in town with you Diana and the kids, then we will ride out spend a few nights alone like a honeymoon. What do you think Jane, we will look at the map take a direction and ride" Ben asked?

"That sounds good to me" Jane replied.

"We will leave on Saturday morning" Ben told them.

"Where are you going" Diana asked.

"Nowhere in particular we will ride, camp and swim every night" Ben looked at Jane and winked.

Diana did not miss the looks between Jane and Ben, nodded as she understood what they meant.

"Well you two have a good time, remember our door is always open for you" Diana told them.

"When we settle, I will write to you giving you our new address so if you wish you can visit or write when you want to" Jane said.

"That will be great" Jeb said.

"We will visit you when we can" Diana told them.

The now newly married lovers spent the next two days with Diana and Jeb. Jane spent quite a bit of her time with Diana and the children while Ben shadowed Jeb getting the feeling of a town sheriff by doing most of the chaos plus carrying out morning and evening rounds, Ben of course knew how to do the job of sheriff but it does no harm getting a bit of experience, at night they made love as after a talk they came to the conclusion it was time to think of starting a family.

Saturday soon arrived but even though they came awake at seven but did not get to breakfast until ten am, after their breakfast the next stop was the livery stable, when getting there they found Sammy had fed and watered their horses.

"Sammy, you have done a great job, here is the payment for our horses, and this is a little tip for you" Ben said.

"Thank you, Ben, congratulations Mr. and Mrs. Brookes I am sorry you are leaving but good luck where ever you go" Sammy said.

"Thanks Sammy we will be back in an hour to pick the horses up".

"Thank you, Sammy," Jane said, his face went red as Jane kissed him on the cheek.

As time was nearing one pm Ben and Jane with horses loaded ready to go stood saying goodbye, tears trickled out of the corner of Jane's eyes as she said goodbye to the children they were on the verge of mounting up when the telegraph operator ran to Ben.

"Ben, Ben Brookes hold it" the operator called.

The operator handed Ben a wire, after reading the wire turned to Jane.

"Darling I'm a ranger for another week and have one last job to do" Ben explained.

The Wire.

From uncle   stop
To son   stop

1.   Accepted a week from today   stop
2.   Congratulations   stop
3.   Steve Spencer sheriff   stop
4.   Carters Cross   stop

Thanks, stop.

"Jeb do you have a territorial map" Ben asked.

"Yes, in the office" Jeb replied.

"OK let's go" taking up the reins of the horses they walked a few doors down to the sheriff's office.

"Jeb what do you know of this sheriff Steve Spencer" Ben asked. "Ben, you will like him, I have met him, Steve must be getting on now, a nice old man who has been a lawman all his life" Jeb told him.

"Right let's see that map, have you a compass also Jeb"

"OK Ben".

Ben laid the map on the table and with a rule and pencil drew a straight from line town to Carters Cross, checking where streams and waterhole were nearest to the route, marked a route from water to water marking it with the pen and pencil, writing it down in a notebook.

"Jane go to Sally's and get a bag of food, I'll top up the canteens I also need ammunition, we will go by the quickest route"

"You could go a little faster".

"I want to take my route and take it easy as I want me and Jane to have as much time together, this means having a swim every night before we get there" Ben told him.

Jane who sat listening with a serious long face, suddenly stood up smiled walked over to Ben and kissed him, Jeb noticed the look between Diana and Jane again.

Jeb later took Diana aside and asked her.

"Diana, I saw that look between you and Jane, what are you up to".

"Oh! Jeb, Ben said they would swim every night"

"So" Jeb enquired.

"Not very long ago we used to go for a swim didn't we"

"Yes, we did" Jeb admitted.

"What did we do after a swim" Diana asked.

"We made love"

"That is what Ben has just told her, she is happy about that because she wants to be a mom and will be a good one" Diana explained.

"I understand, I have missed those swims we used to have as soon as I can train a deputy and the kids are at school would you like to go for a swim" Jeb asked her.

"I'd love to darling, but if its sex you want there is a bed next door" Diana suggested.

"I love you" Jeb assured her.

CHAPTER ELEVEN

NOT HIM AGAIN

"**J**ane if we get there on the Thursday morning we will have five days and five nights together" Ben informed her.

"Oh! That will be great, just the two of us" Jane smiled back"

"OK darling, we will move out in an hour"

"Right I'm of to the café, I'll see you back here in half an hour" Jane told Ben.

They met back at the sheriff's office almost on the hour, once again they said their goodbye's, mounting up Ben and Jane rode out of town a few people who saw them waved to them.

About two miles out of town Jane moved from her saddle to sit on Ben's lap they travelled like that for most of the first day, two hours before sundown Ben brought them to a halt at the first camping site that Ben had planned and marked on the map, as the two of them had travelled many times before the camp was made up in record time.

With the sun shining all day it has made the water in the bowl warm plus the sun has not gone down yet so it was a beautiful evening Ben drew Jane to him and kissed her, Jane was excited as Ben said in her ear.

"Let's go for a swim".

"Yes"

They went for the swim as they planned to do, which meant making love, that night they used one bedroll after making love most of the night until too tired so fell asleep, the next morning the two lovers woke up as the sky became light, Ben kissed Jane starting a new session of making love again.

"That was fantastic, darling I love you" Ben whispered.

"Oh! Ben it's wonderful, just the two of us, I love you darling".

An hour later the pair of them rode out, Ben carried on following the route intended, avoiding all other populated areas with frequent short breaks for the horse's to blow, Ben being a lawman kept alert and still spent most of the time in close together, the fact that being alone all of the time made the journey extra special.

The next few days were a repeat of the first day, but on the Wednesday evening this being the last night together, as they are due to arrive at the destination tomorrow, so Ben made the stop early.

"Are we going to bed early" Jane speculated. Ben smiled.

"We might do just that darling, but at this time I first have to be serious for a while we need to do some checks of our equipment and weapons, tomorrow about midday we get into town, we have to be ready to do the job I have been sent to do, we must talk and be ready for any situation" Ben explained.

"OK darling, I understand" Jane told him they kissed.

The two of them spent the next two hours planning for the coming event and talked about what the task could be, taking their time the next job was to check their weapons leaving nothing to chance, on completion they had supper.

Standing up Ben held out his hand.

"Come on darling I promised you a swim every night before turning in so come on let's go" Ben invited her.

Taking his hand, she stood up went straight into his arm's two pair of hot lips came together, two piles of clothes dropped to the ground, the two naked figures held hands then jumped into the water, for a short period they swam and played together, but eventually coming together the two naked bodies joined to kiss the start of their passion.

Ben deemed himself very lucky, apart from the fact that Jane is beautiful she will make a wonderful wife because she wants to start a family. Standing facing each other their bodies pressed against each other, could only have one effect, as his hands felt her body, his erection started to grow.

"Oh! Jane, I love you" his hand pressing into her back forcing her body into his kissing passionately.

Jane is so lovely she can turn Ben on at any time, kissing and caressing Jane was something that was much cherished by Ben just holding her naked body close to him with his hands exploring her beautiful curves, a second later Ben and Jane made the same (Ohhh!) sound as Jane wrapped her hand around his erection, Jane gasped and omitted a loud (Arrr!) when Ben's hand stroked the lips of her crouch and a probing finger invaded her crouch brushing her clitious.

Jane's head went back her legs opened, the erection probed deeply into her waiting expecting body the loud grasp sounded even louder in the night air as the quickness of his movements took her by surprise, Ben was so aroused it was impossible for him to hold back any longer, Jane did not complain as she herself was also aroused wanting him to enter her body, the water around them looked like it was boiling at the action of the pulsating bodies, Ben had taken her by surprise and oh how she loved it, Ben always found some way to surprised her, during the time together there craving for each other had grown more and more, then his seed transferred to her body.

"Oh, Jane you never cease to amaze me you are fantastic I love you thank you" Ben whispered in her ear

"Darling I enjoyed every moment as usual, I love you"

Both of them submerged for a second to cool off after hitting the surface Ben picked up Jane in his arms and walked out of the water getting towels they dried each other as Ben dried the curves of her beautiful stature his erection grew again, Jane returning the procedure could not help noticing his penis erecting.

"I think we should get to bed Mr. Brookes" Jane advised

"I agree Mrs. Brookes" Ben returned.

Lying side by side they kissed passionately, caressed and cuddled and making noise as the pair of them spoke words of love, since the both of them were already sexually aroused there was little foreplay required his hands did stroke the firm breasts flicking the proud nipples as Ben's hand went between the open legs Jane grabbed and pulled his erection, the passion built up so much there was no way they could wait any longer the vibrating erection once more slid through the lips of her crouch.

The invading erection moved faster and deeper until his body shuddered when his seed passed to Jane, relaxing Ben withdrew the two sweat soaked bodies lay as she snuggled in his arms.

"Thank you darling that was fantastic you are wonderful" Ben said.

"Thank you" she said gruffly smiling at her husband's compliment.

"I love you Jane".

"I love you darling" she replied they kissed before going to sleep.

His eyes opened but he lay still his ears strained listening for any unusual sounds then smiled as he heard the dawn chorus, Ben always checked when waking it is a habit so always did even though knowing that Shad would have alerted him of any disturbance .

Moving slowly making sure not to wake the sleeping beauty, still naked went to the stream and through himself in the cool water when hitting his warm body refreshed him and brought him fully awake, letting Jane sleep Ben dressed, restarted the fire, put water on to make coffee, took time to shave while waiting for the water to boil, putting the skillet over the flame, throwing thick slices of bacon on it, smelling the bacon as it cooked was lovely.

Putting together a thick bacon sandwich and a mug of coffee gently woke up Jane, the beautiful eyes flickered open a lovely smile came to her face.

"Good morning darling" Ben greeted her.

"Good morning what no early morning swim"

"Not this morning darling"

"Ben, we have every day had a morning swim together"

"Not today darling now eat your breakfast"

"Breakfast in bed" Jane whooped

"Jane take your time have your breakfast then get up I'm going to see to the horses"

"I understand Ben I can take a hint I love you" she smiled knowingly.

Leaving their camp area Ben went to see to the horses, Shad was delighted to see him as the big horse trotted over to him neighed and snuffled his shirt, Ben patted Shads neck.

Ben looked after both the horses which took a little time, therefore meaning him missing Jane's morning routine on purpose because today they need to get going and knowing it would be awfully hard not to leave.

After eating her breakfast Jane just stood up, displaying her beautiful naked body to the rising sun, she raised her arms above her head and yawned the sight of this beautiful girl would have turned any man on,

Ben knew this, Jane walked over to the stream and threw herself into the cool water.

When Ben arrived back in camp Jane was dressed buckling the gunbelt on, tied the thong around her leg picking up her revolver, checking it she automatically twirled the gun on her finger then dropped the gun into the holster, Ben could not help smiling at the ease she could settle down to a routine she has copied from him, watching Jane's draw Ben nodded with satisfaction at the smooth way she handled the gun, reflecting back to when she first strapped the gunbelt on, the fun times when she wore the belt in the nude, just her learning to handle a gun gave him some laughable moments but she has learnt to draw and fire better than most men Ben walked over to her and put an arm around her.

"That draw keeps getting better darling" they kissed.

"Thank you darling I had a good teacher" she replied.

Collecting the horses, bringing them into the camp area each of them saddled their own horses, packing all the gear away and loading it on to their mounts, Ben walked around the camp area making sure it was cleaned up and there was nothing left behind, mounting they rode out, keeping the horse to a slow walk, talking about all things in general, how much they loved each other, reflecting on how the wedding went over, but Jane noticed Ben's eyes looked everywhere, she nodded and said to herself (back on the job). Jane spotted how alert Ben was.

After riding for about an hour they travelled on a well-worn piece of land that could not be anything else but a trail into town approximately a mile ahead it was confirmed as they stopped to let the horses blow, right in front of them stood a sign.

CARTERS CREEK   5 MILES   POPULATION 308   last count

Following the trail a short time later they turned a bend in the trail in front of them was the main though fare MAIN STREET of the town called "Carters Creek" as they advanced first thing they noticed was how quiet it was then looking down the street two men faced each other hands hovering over their guns, pulling into a gap between two buildings, where a bunch of the towns citizens stood under cover.

"Howdy mister what's going on" Ben asked.

"That man over there, (pointing at the man concerned) has challenged the sheriff to a shootout so his boss can take over the job" the man explained.

"Who is his boss" Ben enquired.

"That man in the suit three doors up" the man indicated.

"Jane it's an old acquaintance" Ben told her.

"Not him again" she replied.

"Did the man come to town alone" Ben enquired

"No when the big man came to town there was three men with him I have not seen the other two men ". the old man said.

Everyone in the vicinity of Ben saw him suddenly stiffen becoming alert his eyes narrowed then starting to search the street, surveying the town.

"Right you men are you for the sheriff or against him" Ben asked.

"We are on the sheriff's side" the men chorused.

"OK you two men go to the hotel up to the first floor to the room pointing north there is a man with a rifle don't be polite bust in and shoot the man. Now you two men there is a man with a rifle in the hay loft of the livery stable, once again don't give him a chance just shoot him do you understand" Ben ordered.

"Yeh! We understand, why should we take orders from you" a big burly man asked.

Ben reached up to his shirt pocket removed his badge, pinned it on his vest.

"I'm a ranger"

"OK ranger we are with you" they chorused.

"Ben what are we going to do now" Jane asked.

"Well we have two men taking care of the man in the stables, we have two men taking care of the man at the hotel, it looks like the sheriff can take care of himself, that leaves our friend I'll just go to him to make sure there is no funny business" Ben explained.

"We will" Jane said ardently Ben looked at her.

"Oh! Come on then" Ben told her.

Moving slowly Ben and Jane prevented their boots making a loud noise on the boardwalk came up behind the unsuspecting man who did not know of Ben's presence.

"Keep your hands where they are stand still no sudden moves or you will be dead" Ben ordered.

"I'll kill you for this mister" the man growled.

A split second later the sound of two guns rang like bells in the silent street as a body of a man dropped from the first floor of the hotel, after pause two more shots came from the loft of the livery stable where a second body fell into the stable yard.

All the people of the town turned there attention back to the Centre of the street just as the gunman made his move, the killing of the other two men seemed to spur the gunman on as his hand lashed down for his gun, the sheriff being an old hand at this situation was not alarmed and did not look around, being a lawman had taught him to keep his mind on the problem in front of him.

By the looks of it both the sheriff and the gunman drew at the same time and speed, the sheriff dropped to his knees and fired three rapid shots, the gun man had been fast the sheriff felt the bullet pass his head, the gunman jerked from the impact of the bullets a look of amazement came to his face, the blue shirt turned red, the gun fell from a lifeless hand as the gunman fell face first into the dusty street, the sheriff stood up, checked the gunman, turned then walked straight towards Ben, Jane and the boss of the gunmen.

As the sheriff walked towards them Ben and Jane were surprised the sheriff must be in his late sixties with straggly grey hair and moustache therefore must have been a lawman for a long time.

The sheriff walked straight up to them.

"Mister Forbes it seems your henchmen are no longer available to you, I never at any time considered your request to replace me"

"Mister Forbes when we knew him his name was Williams" Ben said.

"That's right" Jane acknowledged.

The man called Forbes body stiffened on hearing the words spoken behind him not recognizing Ben's voice but Jane's voice that was different, as his attempt to assassinate her had failed she would show no remorse. Forbes turned around.

"Brookes, Collins "the assassin Said a little surprised.

"The name is Brookes" Jane told him the sheriff broke into the conversation.

"Forbes, you came to my town to take it over with no thoughts of the citizens of the town, on top of that you had two back shooters ready to cut me down from cover in cold blood" the sheriff accused him.

"I don't know what you mean, I don't know those men" Forbes said.

"I'm going to give you a chance which is more than you were giving me, walk into the street and face me" the sheriff offered him.

"Hold it their sheriff I have the right to face him first, this man tried to assassinate my wife" Ben told him.

"Oh! No, you don't, I have the right first, it's me this man tried to murder" Jane said.

"Jane, you are not a lawman and don't have a badge, the answer is no" Ben ordered her.

"Ben, I know you are trying to protect me thanks, I am in on this so shut up now" she demanded.

"Hold it right there, I am the law around here and I make the decisions do you hear me" the sheriff said loudly.

"Look sheriff we both hear you, but I am faster than you" Ben said.

"And so am I" Jane butted in.

"Forbes, I have been a lawman for a long time, I must be mad as I'm going to make a decision of the type I have never done before" the sheriff stated

"Then why make it" Forbes said.

"You and your kind are a blot on this country and it is my job to get rid of you and people like you"

"Well what's this decision you are going to make" Forbes asked.

"I'm giving you the chance to nominate which one of us you want to face, I must be crazy it's a thing a lawman should never do, you have the choice, make it" the sheriff ordered.

"Brookes, I have seen you draw, and you are too good for me, marm you have a conformance in your ability with a gun, sheriff as you are getting older and slower, I'll face you" Forbes delegated.

Ben turned to the nearest two men.

"Draw your guns point them at him any movement from him shoot him, sheriff I'd like to talk to you"

"Don't worry Ben I hope this idiot does move I would love to shoot him" Jane informed him.

Forbes looked at Jane and could see the determination on her face.

"You will not change my mind" the sheriff informed Ben.

"I still want to talk to you" Ben told him.

"OK it will not do any harm to listen to you, but you will not change my mind" the sheriff stated.

Ben took the sheriff aside, making sure his back was to Forbes and the other, not wanting anyone to see or hear what was said Ben talked to the sheriff for a couple of minutes.

"Sheriff pretend I'm trying to change your mind, shake your head, point at your star but listen to what I have to say".

Talking to the sheriff Ben made it look like he was angry, informed the sheriff of what was on his mind the conversation ended when the sheriff said angrily.

"I've told you I am sheriff here and you will do what I say and that is final." the sheriff called out loudly.

"OK I have tried, I will say no more" Ben ended

"You, Forbes get in the middle of the street, I do not want innocent people shot by accident "the sheriff ordered.

"All right with me" Forbes answered.

The two men moved into the street and stood about twenty feet apart, Forbes called out

"I'll make it easy for you old man" then started walking towards the sheriff Forbes moved about ten feet the sheriff said.

"Hold it right there, that's far enough"

"OK sheriff"

"I've heard you are a coward Forbes"

"Who said that" Forbes said in anger.

"You only go up against persons you know are weak"

"That's a lie"

"Why did you get a gunman to go against me"

"I told you before I did not know that man" Forbes said getting angry. (This is what the sheriff wanted)

"You're a liar"

"I'm facing you sheriff"

"Only because you could not back down, when you're ready"

Lifting his hand away from his side Forbes scratched his nose then his hand started to brush back his hair, the sheriff lifted his gun, stepping to the left his gun barked twice, Forbes hand lashed forward from behind his head the thin throwing knife left the sleeve of his coat the knife went into the sheriff's shoulder as his bullets hit Forbes causing him to fall back with the impact his white shirt turning red.

Ben leaped forward Jane followed, Ben disarmed Forbes who still lived, the sheriff and Jane joined Ben to look at Forbes.

"How! How! Did you know" Forbes struggled to talk.

"Ben told me"

"I knew you were dangerous Brookes" Forbes coughed his back arched, air expelled from his lips the body relaxed as the life went out of him.

"Come on sheriff we will get you to the doctors" Jane advised.

"Thank you marm" the sheriff said.

"The name is Jane, not marm" Jane retorted.

"According to Forbes you are good with a gun, how did you learn to shoot" the sheriff asked.

"My husband taught me, Ben" she pointed at him.

"It's good you learnt to shoot I think everyone should learn to handle a gun" the sheriff said turning to speak to Ben.

"By the way, how did you know about Forbes actions Ben"

"While my wife Jane and Diana Jebs wife played with the kids Jeb and I talked" Ben smiled as Jane poked her tongue out at him.

Jeb and I talked about the job I was presently on, because of him being sheriff I thought it was right to tell him, during the conversation I told him about Williams and the attempt assassination.

"Do you mean Jeb sheriff of Dukes Hollow" the sheriff said through gritted teeth as the doctor removed the blade from his shoulder,

"Sure, Jeb and I have rode together a lot as rangers"

"I know Jeb we have met" the sheriff told him.

"There is something Forbes did which I did not know about, that is his way of closing the gap between you by excusing your age I wasn't told that but Jeb did tell me Forbes favorite way of killing would be with a throwing knife, the sign to look for is when he scratching his nose then push back his hair" Ben explained.

Jane walked over to Ben and kissed him in the street in front of everyone.

"You knew about Forbes, that's why you did not want me to go up against him as I could get killed, I love you" Jane said.

She looked at Ben who looked back and smiled and then winked at her, she loved this man and knew what the wink meant she smiled back at him.

"How come you are here anyway" the sheriff asked.

"The Commander of the rangers sent me, I suppose the job you wanted a hand with has been completed" Ben explained.

"I didn't request help, even though I'm glad you came along I would be dead if you hadn't" the sheriff said,

Ben took the wire received from ranger's HQ from his pocket and passed it to the sheriff, the sheriff took a pair of spectacles from his pocket, read the wire, looking at Ben and Jane a cheeky smile came to his face.

"I take it you two want to settle down, you just being married and all that" the sheriff asked.

"Yes, Ben is going to look for a sheriff's job" Jane explained.

"In my young days, I was a ranger and the Commander of the rangers and I rode together, the Commander is an old friend of mine the last letter I sent to ranger HQ, was to tell him I have to retire and need a relief and would it be possible there may be someone that he knew who could take over from me" the sheriff told them.

Even though Ben and Jane were not slow, it took a second to filter into their brains, they finally realized what it all meant, Ben had not been sent to do a job for the rangers as they believed that was why the commander of the rangers had sent him here for, Ben had actually been sent to replace the sheriff, Jane whooped kissed Ben then kissed the sheriff.

"That's great it looks like a nice town" Ben said.

"Ben, I have been here a long time and the people are great it is a good town" the sheriff acknowledged.

"It's fantastic we can settle down and have a family" Jane burst in.

"When can you start Ben" the sheriff asked.

"Anytime that is best for you" Ben told him.

"OK I have a few things to clear up say three days' time" the sheriff announced.

"Good that will give us time to have a look around" Ben said.

"Will we be staying at the hotel Ben" Jane asked.

"For the time being yes but, in the future,, I would like us to have our own cabin" Ben told her.

"Steve, I would like you to stay on for a while as my deputy, you can show me the town and introduce me to the citizens of the town, when I train a young deputy you can either retire or stay on, what do you think" Ben asked him.

"I would deem it an honor Ben" came the reply.

"Right Jane we had better book into the hotel for the time being" Ben told her.

"What next Ben" Jane asked

"We will have to look for a house to rent until I can have a cabin built for us." was the answer

"See you later sheriff" they said as they made their way to the hotel.

"See you later son" came the reply.

"What now Ben" Jane asked.

"Jane, we have three days, say tomorrow we brows around town checking general store and other stores of interest, the second day we will ride around the outside of the town have a picnic, if we find the right place maybe have a swim, what do you think" Ben asked

"Oh! Ben, you think of everything, yes, yes", she looked happy.

"Of course, there is still one more job to do, and I think we should urgently get on with it" Ben told Jane.

"And what job would that be" she demanded.

Stopping her pulling her close then whispered in her ear.

"Having a baby"

"Oh! Yes please, I love you, I wonder what the hotel bed is like, come on let's find out" she said in a low husky voice.

CHAPTER TWELVE

JANE'S STORY

Ben had now been the sheriff for around six months Jane sat in a rocking chair on the porch of their lovely picturesque cottage, Jane now happily married to Ben and settled down in their own home, looked back on her passed life and said under her breath, (Thank you god).

Jane was quite popular at school, even though she excelled in most things her popularity was due to her looks, to put it mildly Jane was the best-looking girl in the school, Jane has a high school sweetheart by the name of Barry Wilkinson, Barry was a quiet boy and the son of one of the influencel men of the town.

When they went out together Barry would kiss Jane but even though she is a virgin it puzzled her that Barry did not make advances to her like feeling her tits, she put it down to him being a nice person.

A year before leaving school Jane had some sad news her father who was a seaman died on a trip to South America, Jane's mother was good with a needle and thread and made clothes specially for children, this gave her a reasonable income as kids always need clothes they had a comfortable living.

At the age of seventeen and a half Barry and Jane married not until then did Jane find out that Barry new nothing about love, Barry really turned out to be a sadistic bully and things did get worse, living of his father's money Barry drank, (Bored with easy living he drank a lot) this made it worse for Jane as the only real time Barry wanted her was when the drink took over, her introduction to love was basically rape.

The worst thing about this situation is that she is now married to Barry, in America at that time women had no rights once married, when a woman marries she becomes her husband's property just like owning a horse the husband owns her, also all her worldly goods become his the other thing if a woman so much as thinks of divorce she is shunned by men and women alike.

Jane as expected had to be a dutiful wife and do as her husband told her to do and carry on with life, Barry turned out to be a bully, one day Alan Wilmington Barry's father at dinner one day told him.

"Barry my boy I have bought a general store in a place called (Jacks Stop) I want you to go there and take over, it will give you a bit of adventure my boy and will make a man of you son".

"Yes dad" Barry said without any enthusiasm.

Barry was not brave and had been set in a certain life style doing nothing, living of his father's wealth, doing anything this spoilt brat wanted to do like getting drunk, also he did not treat Jane well, after getting drunk of course his idea of making love was to force her which amounted to rape, once again like a dutiful wife she just had to put up with what her husband demanded.

A couple of months later Barry and Jane with a wagon full of goods headed south out of town, Jane had said her tearful good bye to her mother, but they knew they had to part and in this world, they live in it is possible they will never see each other again.

It was now just past Jane's twentieth birthday and Jane has blossomed into a beautiful young lady, her dream had been to marry, settle down have children, but life does not always go the way you wanted it to go, she did not know why she is not pregnant with the number of times Barry had taken her, it had not happened maybe it would get better when Barry is away from his family.

The situation to put it bluntly, neither of them had been out on the range before, (tenderfoots,) being in the west was not easy, you have to learn a completely new way of life, you have to learn to do even the simple things like building a fire, even cooking food became a burden, Barry did not have the ambition to do anything, eventually Jane learned by preservation how to cook meals over a fire plus lots of other things that had to be done, Barry being a lazy sod left her to do what was necessary.

It was almost half way through their journey when they came across a small town, while they rested at this town for a while Jane suggested to Barry that it would be a good idea to have a look at the general store during the time they are there, Barry agreed it will be a good idea this would give them an insight into what they could expect, Barry while in the store noticed the store keeper wore a gun.

This made Barry think about the fact, that as they were going further west it would be a good idea to get some protection in case of attack, with this in mind Barry bought a gunbelt a handgun plus a rifle.

It never occurred to Barry that you need to be taught how to use a gun before being able to use it properly, they spent the night in town then set out the next morning and travelled most of the day but when they stopped Barry left Jane to make camp while strapping on the gunbelt and dropped the gun into the holster, it was easy to tell Barry knew nothing about weapons, the holster was not tied down and the thong was not on the hammer, finding drawing a gun was no easy but after practicing for a while until convincing himself that his draw was not bad little knowing a ten year old boy in the west could do better.

Meanwhile after setting up camp and the water on for coffee, Jane looked at the rifle give Barry his due or maybe it was his father's money because unknown to him the rifle is the latest model Winchester, picking it up Jane did what she had seen men do she put the butt on her shoulder and looked along the barrel, putting her finger on the trigger she found she could not pull it, now Barry might be a bit slow at times, Jane on the other hand was smart and did not give up it was like a puzzle to her but she found the catch that released the trigger, the safety catch obvious it was not loaded but Jane was happy she had figured it out.

"Barry coffee is ready" Jane called.

"Thanks Jane" came the reply.

"Barry bacon and beans" handing him a plate.

"Thanks" they ate and drank as it was still light, Barry went back to his pistol practice Jane washed up.

Jane before this evening knew nothing about guns, Jane's dad had once told her, (If you hold weapon right, point it in the right direction, finger on the trigger and you look like you mean to use it folk will be wary of you and back down)

Jane realized she must learn to shoot, so once more she picked up the Winchester and examined it she saw the slot on the side of the brass chamber of the rifle, (is that where you load it) she thought on examination of the rifle she could not find any other place, she pulled back the trigger, but when she tried to push a bullet in she found it would not fit, for a second she thought of asking Barry but she knew that would not be a good idea

Jane would not give up but decided to take a break and think about it over a coffee, having a slurp of coffee she took a deep breath put a bullet on the slot on the side of the rifle and tried pushing gently. She did not want to break the gun there will be hell to pay if she does, nothing happened, taking another slurp of coffee she examined the rifle again, she could not find any other place to, load except the slot on the brass chamber, (Damn it) she said to herself putting a bullet on the slot again she pushed hard the gate opened and when the bullet was pushed half way in the loading mechanism took over, as she did not know the magazine took thirteen bullets she slipped just three more bullets into the magazine.

"Barry I'm going a few yards from the camp to shoot this gun"
"OK jane"

Jane walked a hundred yards, putting the rifle to her shoulder she pointed to a large tree, pulled the trigger, there was a click as the hammer came down, but it did not fire, sitting on a log she cursed   ((Damn what is wrong) once more looking at the rifle, Jane as I have said is smart and after a short time found out that the rifle had a lever as this lever is the only thing she had not touched Jane pulled the lever she heard the bullet being moved into the firing position from the magazine to the barrel, levelling the rifle again she pulled the trigger the rifle fired, she missed the target by a mile and the recoil of the rifle knocked her of her feet.

The first Winchester rifle is a modification from the Henry rifle but when the Henry Ammunitions company employed Oliver

Winchester in 1859 as an armorer, by keeping the Henry style, Oliver changed the rifle to the Winchester rifle in 1866 by changing to a brass chamber, the main feature was the side loading slot it meant you could load faster a good man with the Winchester could fire 30 rounds a minute.

Jane sat on the grassy bank rubbing her shoulder, but smiled as she knew she had done what she set out to do, that is learning about the rifle by firing it, looking around you could see it is getting darker Jane picked up the rifle dusted it of put on the safety catch on then walked back to the camp.

Because Barry wanted to push on getting to the destination faster Jane did not get very much practice with the rifle, but after a bit of thought she decided the rifle was unimportant as most of the time they will in the store so there would be no need for the long gun but if necessary the knowledge of the rifle may come in handy.

Driving the team and wagon over the brow of a hill they saw JACKS STOP for the first time, both of them were shocked, Barry's father had not looked into this place before buying the store, it was an extrading post the place could only be explained as a hole, a blot on the land, it is a small place consisting of about thirty people all men mainly prospectors, Barry was shocked, it was worse for Jane as she found out she was the only female there.

"God! Barry can we ride through and find another town".

"Don't be silly dad bought this store" Barry said

"Barry"

"Shut it Jane sooner we unload the better" Barry told her.

Glaring at Barry she climbed down from the wagon it was obvious Barry could not understand her position or its possible there was no care for Jane's feelings.

Barry and Jane unloaded the wagon keeping the store closed for twenty-four hours to give them time to stack the shelves, Jane decided to wear loose shirt and jeans in an attempt to hide her figure in a way it did but Jane is a natural beautiful woman so it was very hard to disguise her looks, one thing they did not have to worry about goods JACKS STOP is so small the wagon full of goods will last a long time that means there was no need to worry about stock.

The store did get off to a good start, there was a constant flow of citizens to the store, Jane soon new that some of the men were coming into the store a lot and not buying anything, looking at these men she found it was not the stock they were interested in but her, some of them did not hide the lust and longing in their eyes, ignoring there looks she pretended not to see them but she was scared and told Barry about it.

"Look Jane we will have to give it a go, things may get better, at the present rate goods will last for quite a while, let's see what happens if it does not improve, by the time the goods sell we will leave" Barry explained.

Jane's shoulders slumped she has no choice but to do what Barry wanted to do, Jane knew she was trapped she would just have to do her best.

After a few days one of the men who came into the store frequently asked Barry to come out to the saloon and have a drink, so they can get to know him, Barry agreed but stated only two drinks as it was necessary to open the store tomorrow morning.

Jane became worried but showed a brave face pretended it was OK, Barry had managed to stay of the drink mainly because they had no booze in the wagon, since leaving the city Barry had stayed of everything including sex, why? She thought, Barry never asked, Jane just went along with him.

Two nights later Barry went to the saloon as invited, his new-found friends looked after him, telling him it was great to have a store in town and showered him with drinks. Barry walked home walked in the door.

"Jane get your knickers of or I will take them of" Jane knew it was meant because a while back that had actually happened.

Jane would not mind having sex and making love if Barry did make love to her properly, but Barry only wanted her when drunk Jane's naked form now lay on the bed, Barry dropped his trousers, violated Jane by ramming his erection into her basically raping her, Jane stifled a scream because of the pain his action had caused her.

That one night in the saloon put Barry back to the way of his previous life, getting drunk every night and at first attacked Jane in the same way, but Jane being wise noticed his drinking was getting worse she also found she could avoid him raping her, she found out that when Barry came in really drunk she could delay him a little making him fall asleep, some nights when not drinking a lot she would get him a coffee making him more sober, and would go to sleep normally not even kissing her this of course did not happen all the time, Jane learned by estimating roughly how much Barry drank by his manner.

Of course, it did get worse Jane did not know but Barry had started gambling, she only found out as they were losing money, she asked him about it, for the first time Barry really became angry, and started to beat her repeatedly before raping her.

Whether it was intential or not Barry was drinking and gambling and knew that losing his father's money was wrong but in a cowardly way took his frustration out on Jane.

Jane had a feeling that things were getting out of hand, each day it looked like things were getting worse, she sat down with a cup of coffee and started to think of events leading up to the present time, then started to think what she could do about it and how she could help with the situation, her first thought was to let Barry's father know the facts, she wrote a letter to Alan Wilkinson went to the post office combined telegraph office, she gave the letter to the postman, and also wrote out a wire that had to be sent informing Alan Wilkinson the letter was on the way, what she did not know the postman was crooked and did not send them.

The second task was to load the rifle ready for use, Jane was a strong young lady but as she began to look at the desperate situation, she was in, she almost cried if anything happened to Barry she would be in trouble as far as she can see there is no way she could get out of town by herself.

As it happened Barry and Jane managed to hang on for quite some time a few months, with Jane having to except the situation as it was but to Jane it meant she has managed to exist one more day that is all she is doing as far as she was concerned, every once in a while customers would stop as they passed through town which broke the boredom, Jane of course knew she could ask if she could ride with them but her duty stopped her, she was married to Barry even though it was not much of a marriage she would stand by him, Jane just hung on.

The day she had dreaded finally arrived, it was eight in the evening the store was closed Jane was in there room over the store she sat in a rocking chair reading beside her stood the rifle, Barry has once again went to the saloon, since that first day it had become a regular occurrence for him to go to the saloon each night also drinking a bit too much they played five card stud as the dealer went around the table asking if anyone wanted cards when the choice came back to the dealer who said (I'll take two cards) Barry had been watching and saw the dealer take a card from the top and one from the bottom of the deck.

Whether Barry saw the cheat by accident or the man did it on purpose no one will ever know, If on the other hand Barry had been sober or had not drank as much, chances are caution would have prevailed but with drinking too much his senses dulled, (You are cheating that last card came from the bottom of the deck), which brought a quick response from the accused man, the man kicked back his chair drew his gun and shot Barry his shirt changed to red as his body flew back to lay prone on his back dead eyes staring at the roof, as for Barry his gun was still in the holster the thong still on.

The situation this created would put Jane into an almost impossible position, Jane soon saw her problem as the man who was the town constable came to see her, to inform her of Barry's demise. The man told her of Barry's death then said she would be OK, and that his intention was for him to stay with her and keep her safe, but it was not the fact of what she was told, but the way she was told, the suggestion being instead of I'll look after you, I will sleep with you.

Jane stood with the Winchester in her hands and levered a shell into the chamber.

"Thank you, constable I can look, after myself, is there a man in town who bury's people" Jane asked

"Sure, we do I'll get him to come over" the man said

"Not tonight ask him to come to the store in the morning" Jane told him.

"OK marm" then the constable left.

Jane is a strong and sensible woman there was no tears for Barry she stood by him, as his wife, she never received any support from him when she needed it, but she was still sorry about Barry's death, getting a cup of coffee she sat in the chair and starting to think of her position and what she could do.

She had been in JACKS STOP long enough to understand that every one of them she has seen had not hid their lust and would love to take her knickers of, so she thought of her options.

1) Take food and the rifle, slip out of town during the night, but being a city girl, she would have no chance out in the wilds.

2) She could assess which man in town was the strongest and take up with him, but her assessment of the men of this town was not good she was certain the man she selected would take what he wants from her then sell her onto another man, if a man put her up for auction in a town full of men they would get a good price for her.

3) If that was going to happen, she may as well put a red light outside the door and become the town whore, because of her beauty she would have no problem about customers and get paid for sex.

4) Shoot herself.

5) Hang on for as long as possible and hope a solution to the problem comes up.

Jane sat for a moment and thought of her options, deciding on option number five.

She also decided to open the shop during the day with the gun handy, then at night she would lock herself in, she was brave taking the option she did with hope.

When she opened the next morning, there was a large group of men there some with posies in their hands, Jane stepped back from the counter and addressed the crowd.

QUIET ALL OF YOU, BY THE LOOKS OF IT YOU HAVE ALL HEARD OF THE DEATH OF MY HUSBAND, I AM NOT IN THE MARKET FOR ANOTHER HUSBAND, SO ALL OF YOU WHO HAVE COME FOR THAT REASON OF TRYING TO WIN ME OVER CAN LEAVE THE STORE I AM ONLY OPENING THE STORE FOR CUSTOMERS WHO WANT TO BUY GOODS. PASS THE WORD AROUND.

One man who took no notice of her tried to grab her Jane grabbed the hunting knife for sale on the side, she was angry and did it without thinking drove the knife through the man's hand pinning it to the counter, she once more stepped back, operating the lever on the rifle and pointed it at the crowd, one man separated from the others called out.

"Your bluffing" his hand going for his gun.

The man was only six feet away Jane levelled the rifle gripped it with both hands to steady it, (because of the recoil) pointed at this man and pulled the trigger, the man dropped his gun grabbed his stomach blood seeping through his fingers, staggered through the door.

This action cleared the store except for about five genuine customers. Jane pulled the blade out of the man's hand who quickly left the store. Resting the rifle on the counter she calmed down, addressing the first man to the counter.

"Hello sir, how can I help you" she said calmly.

"Marm I was told to come to see you this morning I am the boot hill grave digger" the man informed her.

"I want you to bury my husband, take everything from his pockets bring them to me then I will pay you understand". Jane ordered.

"YYYYes marm" the man stammered.

"I Know what my husband normally has in his pockets so don't try to steal anything you got it"

"GGGot it "came the reply.

"Next" she called Jane carried on through the remainder of the customers when finished she made a sign and put it on the door and closed the store.

DUE TO A BEAREVMENT IN THE FAMILY THE STORE IS CLOSED

Jane now by herself sat at the table a lot of built up emotion came out she at first could not understand how she shot a man and putting a knife through a man's hand she shuddered at the thought of the blood and almost cried. Suddenly she thought if someone has emptied Barry's pockets they would have found his key's Jane went to the door then smiled as she looked at the other two doors, she almost shouted in joy, the people who had this store before them must have had a similar problem to her own, she found the three doors had places for padlocks but no padlocks but they do keep padlocks in the store.

A week went by. She opened the store each day the men came in saw her hand on the gun, so she had no trouble, they knew she only had to pull the trigger and because of the incident a week ago they were not going to try anything unless they were certain of success.

The men of the town became more wary of her as one night one of the men of the town had not learned the lesson and tried to break in on what they thought was a vulnerable woman all by herself, so the man tried to get into the locked room Jane pointed the rifle at the door and shot twice through the door, this stopped anyone else from trying that again.

Jane was no fool and was being extra careful she knew the longer she stayed there is more of a chance is she will make a mistake.

On the tenth day after Barry's death a group of men rode up to the store Jane recognized the man leading them a rancher who had been in the store before, when he previously passed through.

"Hello sir, how can I help you" Jane asked.

"We are just resting the horses and get some tobacco while we are here" the rancher replied.

Jane knew this is a miracle, this is her way of escaping getting out of here.

"Excuse me sir are you going far" Jane asked

"My ranch is about five days south of here and my name is John McDonald not sir"

"Would you let me ride along with you" Jane asked.

"Where is your husband" John asked

"Dead shot ten days ago" Jane told him.

"Yes, you can come along with us" John said.

"John most of the goods have been sold but there is a few things like tobacco, coffee and other things, as I am going to leave the store as it is, you and your men can have a look around take what you want free of charge I am going to get ready to go I will be ready in twenty minutes" Jane informed John.

"Take your time we will wait" John assured her.

Jane decided to leave the wagon but to use the two horses the first horse she put a saddle on, the second she loaded what she could lots of coffee, beans, eggs a side of bacon a change of clothing the rifle and a few boxes of shells, the bag that had the takings from the store. After loading all she could she dressed in jeans and shirt leaving what was left she mounted up, rode out of town and did not look back.

The ride with John and his men went well, without incident on the evening of the fifth day John McDonald took her to the hotel and made sure she had a room the town being half a day's ride from the ranch, she did have money so has no problems when John left she decided to see if the hotel was still serving meals, finding the dining room still open she had some supper, looking round she smiled at the sight of other women in the room.

Going back to her room, Jane had stayed strong for so long that the sight of the other women and the feeling of safety caused her to breakdown and cry with relief, after a while she composed herself she went to bed deciding to scout the town before making any plans on what to do, she lay awake for a long period before drifting off to sleep.

The next morning Jane ordered from the hotel a bath and water, she felt great stripping naked, lowering her beautiful body into the water, with a bar of soap, her hands ran over her body enjoying the feeling of relief, freedom just being able to relax made her feel great and free, feeling the soft clean underwear and slipping on her dress made her feel even better still.

Before leaving the hotel, Jane wrote two letters one to Alan Wilkinson and the other to her mother.

The letter to Alan Wilkinson sent by Jane explained to him about the conditions in JACKS STOP, told him about Barry's drinking and how his son gambled away the stores money and was shot after calling a man a cheat, she informed him of there being little stock left and how she had to leave it to save her life.

"Taking a leisurely walk through the town. Jane appreciated the chance to walk around the town she talked to a few women in the town, on her walk she saw the town did not have a Millinery shop, now the one thing that Jane did get from her mother was her ability with a needle and thread.

Jane advertised on the board in the general store that she was a seamstress, jobs came in from the women of the town, small jobs like stitching first until they got to know her, before Jane could properly get into her knew life she had to suffer two devastating blows, the first blow was a letter sent to her from a solicitor informing her that her mother had passed away this information hit her hard she loved her mother and she was the only family she had, in fact she had been thinking of either going home to live with her, or if successful bringing her out to the west to live with her, after composing herself she read the rest of the letter to find there was some good news.

Her mother a few years ago contacted the solicitor where she made out a will long before Jane was married her mother of course put Jane down as her sole beneficiary.

Her mother had her own house, she had a business, a good collection of arts and crafts probably brought back by Janes father which was sold so left Jane quite a sum, a sum that could set her up for the rest of her life, she bought a millinery shop and became the town seamstress.

The second letter that came two days later, it dealt her a blow which came out of the blue, she did not expect such a dambing letter but found out Alan Wilkinson was as bad as his son.

On receiving Janes letter Alan Wilkinson also hired a solicitor and the story was the biggest most devastating lie anyone could make up.

The letter from Alan Wilkinson's solicitor read; ---

1) Jane had persuaded Barry to come out west, Mr. Wilkinson did not want his son to go but Jane made him do it.
2) She had cost Mr. Wilkinson a lot of money, as she told Barry to get money from his Dad to set him up in business.
3) She was the cause of Barry's death because she had drove him to drink
4) She had left the general store with lots of goods in it to be ransacked which had cost Mr. Wilkinson a lot of money.

The letter went on with claim after claiming It was all lies, it was obvious the father was as bad as his son a coward and a liar, who would blame anyone but himself getting what it could be possible to get out of the situation.

With the letter came a list of claims and prices with a total at the bottom.

Looking at the total Wilkinson claimed, she could not help thinking how close it came to the sum of the inheritance from her mother if she paid the amount claimed she would be left with two thousand dollars only. Jane wrote a letter immediately to her mother's solicitor asking for his advice, the return letter was not encouraging as the letter said she should pay Wilkinson, giving her a list of reasons;---

1) As her mother died before Barry died, the law states her money belongs to him, so she really has nothing anyway.

2) It would take the rest of her life to prove what she claims Alan Wilkinson has said is lies.

3) She is a woman and as she should know women have little rights by law.

4) Mr. Wilkinson may be all she says he is, but it is her word against him it would be almost impossible to prove her view.

5) I do not like to advise you to do what I must advise you to do, but if you look at it like this it is probably the best advice, I can give you, pay him off and get on with your life.

Jane admitted she was forced into taking his advice, because she was not happy about Alan Wilkinson having her mother's money, this man seemed to know how much she inherited down to the last cent.

She agreed to Alan Wilkinson's terms as long as she is given a document of proof to say that is the end of it and there will be no more claims against her. Wilkinson agreed and all documents were completed through her solicitor.

Jane was now left with her freedom, her shop and two thousand dollars which quarter of it had to be spent on the business buying materials to make her style of clothing but the different type of lady's underwear and niknaks she had to import.

Life after all she had been through settled down as a woman with a dress shop, her life settled into a regular pattern, she became well known by the women in the town a lot of them she could call her friends, the women of the town also new she was a widow, John Macdonald came to town once a month and always called in to have a chat with her, life continued like that for the next two years, because of what had happened to her previously she enjoyed the staple circle of her knew life.

One day on one of his trips to town John Macdonald asked Jane if she would like to go on a picnic with him, Jane knew John was married but also believed she owed this man her life. (If John and his men had not come to JACKS STOP) she shuddered at the thought, she owed this man so agreed and said yes.

"John yes only the once in secret" Jane told him. "OK Jane"

The following Sunday Jane slipped out of town meeting John a little up the trail no one saw or suspected them meeting. John living in this area for a long time knew exactly where to take Jane, It was a beautiful bowl surrounded by bushes with a beautiful bowl of water it was an oasis's in a hidden valley, the two of them sat talking for a while had their food, John moved in closer and kissed her, (Jane said to herself this is not right he is married) but again thought what harm can it do, she had not been kissed for a long time so why not she still felt she owed this man, (I think I will let things take their course it is only once) Jane thought.

John kissed her again and she responded, she did not stop him when John placed his hand on her breast, unfastening her blouse a sigh came from his lips as his hand held the beautiful breast, Johns tender kisses his caresses and his words of love made Jane mellow, the feelings she was feeling she had never felt before the sensations of arousal she felt were fantastic, Jane could not help moaning and making sounds of love, their clothes disappeared, there actions of love continued when Jane felt his erection enter her body without pain and feeling good the pleasure she felt as she learned about love for the first time, it was fantastic everything she did was suggested by him at the end of their love making lying together John got his breath back leaned over and kissed her.

"Thank you, Jane that was wonderful," John said.

"Yes John" she replied. She felt great and her heart swelled with happiness because John thanked her.

Standing up John held his hand out to her, they had a beautiful swim the warm water of the pool swept over their bodies, going back to the bedroll Jane noticed his erection.

"Let's make love again Jane" his words were asking not telling.

"Yes John" she whispered.

At the end of the day together John told her how it would be great if they could do it again.

"John, I would like to, but you are married, and people would become suspicious" Jane said.

"Jane every Sunday I go up to the high range by myself that in fact is where I am now according to the crew at the ranch, what about next Sunday" John asked her.

"Alright John same routine next Sunday" Jane agreed. They kissed then parted.

Jane and John's love grew and talk of leaving his wife came into the conversation time had gone by John and Jane made love every Sunday for three months.

Six months before John and Jane had their picnic John had employed a young man as a ranch hand called Frankie aged eighteen his job was to clean out the stables each day, one Sunday the ranch hands were on the range and John had as usual went to check on the high range, Susan Macdonald who had been watching from a distance as frank worked, this morning she called him to the house on some pretense and seduced him so every Sunday she took her lover to bed with her.

Susan Macdonald had everything going for her, john had a large ranch so was wealthy enough she had no complaints John would give her anything she wanted unknowing to her husband she had a young good looking young man to satisfy her sexual desires when John was not around, just after the ninth week John and Jane met.

Susan from a friend heard that John and Jane had been seen together, Susan did not really care if her husband was making love with another woman in fact she wondered how many saloon girls John had actually bedded.

If John gets killed she also would not worry as his sole beneficiary she would inherit everything and as long as she did not marry again it would all remain hers, but if John divorced her to marry Jane she would lose the lot.

The next Sunday she as usual called for Frankie took him straight into the bedroom through her clothes on the floor.

"Frankie make love to me"

"Sure Sue" came his reply, after making love Frankie was surprised as they normally spent some time together.

"Right get up and get dressed ", she still lay there naked.

"Why" Frankie asked

"Saddle up a horse go to the high range see if you can see my husband if possible don't let him see you, come back and report, have you got that" Susan ordered.

Frankie returned with the information that John was not on the high range, looking at the clock she took Frankie to bed again before John came home.

The next week on the Saturday evening Susan took a stroll down to the corral and gave Frankie some orders.

Sunday morning John and Jane had their normal time together in there now favorite place, talking, laughing making love and swimming really enjoying themselves.

An hour later Frankie rode into the ranch went straight to the house where Susan waited in a flimsy negligee she took him straight to the bedroom it took only seconds to undress lying on the bed Frankie reported.

"Did they make love" she cut in.

"Yes" frank replied.

"Tell me every detail" Susan said,

"OK Sue"

"Tell me how John fucked her every detail and, do to me the same" Susan said.

Susan enjoyed every minute of sex that morning the thought of her husband's actions and the fact it was being repeated to her drove her to the ultimate Hight of passion, this was the first time she had an orgasm with Frankie she screamed in delight.

Lying together after the sex she told Frankie to tell her everything from the time John left the house to his return to the ranch.

"We still have time do it again Frankie" Sue told him.

In a way Susan got her way the following Sunday as John was shot dead as they played in the pool after making love, there place of love and happiness became the battleground between a Ranger and three criminals, one of these bad men called Grant shot John in cold blood as John stood naked in the water.

Susan even though she had no proof put a bounty on Jane's head accusing her of murdering John Macdonald.

As she sat in her rocking chair now pregnant with Ben's baby Jane reflected how lucky she was but also how much stronger she is because of her experiences, how many women are out there being raped every night for the rest of their lives by their husbands and are in an almost impossible situation like she was in with no chance of escape. She shuddered as she looked back at how she could have been the play thing for a town full of men passing her from one to another. How many women had travelled by themselves and just disappeared of the face of the world.

Lots of women were forced into cat houses selling themselves to live, how many brides had been picked out of a catalog for mail order brides ending up with a vicious man who beat her every night, how many women married one man to find out she would be shared with his three brothers.

Yes, Jane did have a terrifying time but now knows there is a lot of women who had gone through similar horrors and got through them, in the environment she is in now she understood she is one of the few as she looks around her she see's lots of happy ladies. The fact that she did go through that part of her life and was fortunate to be rescued makes her appreciate life more, (she stopped for a moment and a tear came to her eyes as she thought of John for a second,) Yes because of what she has been through and what she has learnt makes her love her new life to the full.

When John made love to her she at the time thought this is love and thought it could not get any better because she had never known love as Barry did not make love to her, but third time lucky, meeting Ben a man her own age who had never made love before, she had to stop she was getting turned on just thinking of the night she taught him to make love, she smiled as Ben came to her kissed her.

"Hello darling, I love you" putting his hand on her tummy and kissed her again.

Jane had no thoughts of love in her head when they first met, she asked him for help because of the bounty put on her head, the only thing she could think of was how to save her life. Riding together she became fascinated by the skill and dedication when tracking Grant, once she knew she was away from the town she felt safer so took more interest in what Ben was doing, waking up on the fifth morning she could not explain it, she knew she loved Ben, teaching Ben to make love she thought was fun, and now he finds ways to thrill her every time they make love.

Jane and Ben were now happily married with a baby on the way, Ben is the town sheriff Jane the sheriff's wife which makes her happy thinking about it, still sitting in her rocker she felt her stomach smiled at Ben who stood in front of her with his hands out pulling her gently from the chair straight into his arms they kissed passionately.

"I love you" Ben said breathlessly.

"I love you. Ben" she smiled with a twinkle in her eyes.

THE END

THE PREFACE

As Senator Stevens and his family. His wife, daughter, son and baby started their evening meal, it was a pleasant evening so the door was left open to allow air in, but instead the house was invaded by three criminals lead by a man called Paul Grant a (vicious killer), the three men invaded the house to get the payroll the Senator had in his safe, when they were stopped from getting their way these criminals killed the whole family including the baby.

The massacre was found the next morning, the sheriff was called organized a posse and a tracker and set off to try to catch the three men but lost the sign and therefore had to give up the chase, the sheriff knew these men had to be brought to justice, as a last resort the sheriff rode out to the Lone Star Ranch headquarters of the Texas Rangers, he told his long time friend the commander of the Texas Rangers, who at once dispatched a Ranger to capture or kill these evil men.

THE AUTHOR

My name is J.G. Thompson (Joe) butt I write under the name of J.G. Tee I am seventy-seven years old/young I have been writing about my favorite subject the (Old American West) during my twenty five years at sea, twenty two in the Royal Navy, I read every western I could get my hands on. I also gathered a lot of experience as AA patrolman It has taken a long time to be able to write this book, I enjoy reading my books and I therefore believe other people would love it when they read it also, I am a Loyalist and a Royalist and one of my proudest moments was when I was decorated by Her Majesty the Queen who presented me with the (BEM) the British Empire Medal.

Notes of interest.

When writing its best to write as realistic as possible so the violence and sex parts in this book are as realistic as can be made do not class the sex parts as pornographic I have written about two people who find love and make love, because of this I call my books (Pocket Erotic Westerns)

9 781965 632079